To Alex

Copyright Diane Saxon

Under the Full Blooded Moon by Diane Saxon

Since he lost his father and his childhood at the age of ten to a witch's curse, cynical journalist Stuart Caldwell has searched the world in his quest to find the key to his family's centuries-old curse.

What he finds when he lands on the Scottish island of Breggar is far from what he expects. Instead of a battle to the death with the cruel enchantress he believes resides there, Stuart finds he's the one in the firing line, and the target is his heart.

Dedication/Author Notes/Acknowledgements

With love, as always, to Andy, Laura, and Meghan. Special thanks to my sister, Margaret, for her undying faith and continuing help.

A big thank you to Phil Dawson for allowing me free reign with his wonderful photographs of the moon for promotional purposes.

The Inner Hebrides consist of many small islands, but the one I use in this story is a figment of my own imagination and has no connection with any real island or community.

Prologue

Kilchoan, Mainland Scotland 1672

Swathes of wet hair clung and tangled around her face in a heavy curtain, enough to obscure her view as another spasm seized her. Pain far worse than she'd ever imagined wrenched through her, and clutched deep into her belly to tear at her insides.

Pride refused to allow her to cry out.

As she surfaced, she snatched another lungful of air. The frigid waters chilled her to the bone, sending a fresh rash of shudders through her between each painful contraction.

The villagers crowded closer, faces twisted with fear and rage. People she'd known all her life, people she loved. Women she'd tended in childbirth, and men whose wounds she'd healed.

The sentiment turned vicious as the sun dipped below the horizon and the moon rose in the darkened sky.

After a full day of her tied to the ducking stool, their disgust in her was palpable at not obtaining the confession they sought.

How could she confess to something that wasn't true?

She'd never consorted with the devil.

Hysteria driven, they leaned in closer to scream their blood lust.

"Kill the witch, kill the witch." The terror of the moment was overcome with something far more important.

Another stab of pain seized her body, forcing her to contort once again, but she pried open her eyes and met his frigid, slate-gray gaze across the wide expanse of water.

Tall and regal in his gentleman's finery, there was no trace of the passionate lover she knew so well. His handsome features were carved into a cold mask.

He could say something. In silent entreaty, she begged him to intervene. He could save her.

He chose not to. Instead, he took hold of his pregnant wife's hand and turned away to stare up at the night sky.

Her heart died long before her body.

Tears flowed unheeded down her cheeks to streak through the slime of mud coating her skin as she sucked deep breaths into her lungs, ready for the next duck of the stool into the stinking, fetid depths of the river. She knew it was all in vain.

Death was upon her.

Moya drew on her last ounce of strength and concentrated. Every muscle in her body contracted as she bore down to push, while her power waned. The ducking stool plunged once again, to submerge her into the icy depths and steal her breath away. The burn in her chest spread while she held the air in her lungs for as long as she could, but it was pointless. She closed her eyes and forced her muscles to relax. Her body floated a little above the stool. The ropes stretched in the cold and the wet. Moya raised her hips high, and her attention never wavered as she remained centered on this last, essential feat.

Little effort was required to weave the curse, for any witch knew a curse did not need to be spoken aloud. Instead, she focused the last of her energy to accomplish her final deed.

Eyes wide again, she stared up through the dark murkiness of the water, into the night sky, where blood smothered the full moon and spread its tendrils out to blur beneath the overpowering cast of light.

She recognized her death written in the blood. Death and rebirth. She took cold comfort in the knowledge her curse had worked.

Agony clenched her body. She drew her lips back from her teeth and expelled the final, desperate clutch of air she held in her lungs. In a wild, frenzied scream, distorted by the bubbles, the sound carried to the surface. Ice froze the blood in her veins to numb her mind and dull the pain as she expelled the bairn from her womb in a cloud of thick mucus and crimson blood. It bloomed through the dark waters while her child spewed into the evil world.

The heat of her own blood stroked a tender warmth over her frozen hands in farewell as Moya floated, lifeless, to the surface.

The full moon, obscured by a blood-soaked cloud, transformed the land into a desolation of deep shadows and dark craters while the scarlet waters around Moya turned inky black as it bubbled and steamed in the chill of the Scottish night.

With proof of the witch's existence, their screams pierced the dark as the villagers fled to hide behind closed doors and deny the wrongdoing they'd taken part in that night.

Chapter One

Breggar, Inner Hebrides, Present Day

Thick gray storm clouds rolled in, threatening to obscure the view of the mainland. The promise of yet another miserable spring hung in the air, to make the summer a short sprint toward winter for the third year in a row.

The poor weather had started to take its toll. The islanders were already restless. The younger ones left in droves in search of jobs. While they typically stayed for the summer months on the small island with a bustling, active community, hope had dwindled, and they flocked to the mainland with ideas of a better future. A future she craved for herself but held back for the sake of her grandmother. How could she leave her when life on the island was a constant struggle? One she couldn't imagine leaving her grandmother to deal with alone.

Ruth stared out over the bleak concourse into the white mist.

It had been so long since she'd seen the pale golden days of sunshine, she wondered if she ever would again. The sun attracted the visitors. Visitors they hadn't seen since the previous pitiful summer.

The prospect of the mainlanders coming to spend their money dimmed just as surely as the view.

Damp tendrils of hair clung to her skin. She swiped at them with the back of her hand, just to have the strands spring back again. She parted her lips, breathed in the taste of salt and hopelessness.

Her twenty-sixth year. Her last four months before she turned twenty-seven and time ran out for her. Not just a question of money, but comfort, security and the knowledge that if she left, her grandmother would be fine without her. A big step, a giant step, and her heart was torn. No one waited forever, no matter how valued she was. If things didn't go well during this summer, she ran the risk of losing her future.

She squinted into the distance. No matter how hard she tried, she couldn't conjure up the image of the local ferry transporting passengers to the isle.

Another day without it. Another day without the tourists' money.

Time trickled away.

Black clouds thickened along the horizon and filled her throat with the taste of ozone. A thunderstorm raced in. Worse than she remembered.

Fear swept over her skin with an icy chill and raised goose pimples as a delicate shudder trembled through her. She tried to ignore the threat of something far more ominous than a storm in the air. Sinister. It seared her, bone deep. The sense of unease over the last couple of years had kept her on the island, close to her grandmother in case she was needed. Needed for what, she had no idea, but the disquiet had built until it became so tangible she could almost touch it.

Ruth turned her back on the gloomy sky to scurry ahead of the storm, through the rambling cobblestone streets of the village, back to where she belonged. Back to the old gift shop, *Serenity & Charms*, run by her grandmother.

Icy raindrops splatted onto her head and shoulders, the forerunner of the downpour. The sky grumbled its building annoyance while slashes of bright white illuminated the darkened land.

She tucked her chin deep into the woolen collar of her coat and ran, head down, toward shelter. She mourned the oversight of taking her snood with her. She rarely misjudged the weather, but this storm had come in fast and low without warning.

Eyes downcast, she groped for the door handle and the protection of *Serenity & Charms*, flashing a glance up at the last moment. Her breath strangled in her throat as she hurtled straight into a mountain of a man and smashed her forehead into his black leather-clad chest. An ominous shadow, he formed a solid barrier between herself and safety.

Her head reeled while bright lights flashed before her eyes. The screech she let out should have sent the form running for mercy. Instead, Ruth found herself wrapped in a vise of steel, her arms trapped between her body and the rock hard one in front of her.

She untucked her chin and tipped her head back, farther than she anticipated to stare up into the face of the man whose grip on her never weakened. Her pulse tripped, and her heart gave an unfamiliar hitch.

Laughter spurted from her lips before she could contain it. Perhaps the blow to her head had turned her brain to sludge.

A cowboy.

An honest to goodness cowboy held her in his arms on the doorstep of her grandmother's gift shop on the little island of Breggar. If she didn't know better, she'd have thought she was hallucinating, but the cowboy had such a firm grip, he had to be real.

If he were her fantasy, he'd have a wide grin on his sexy mouth.

His straight, sober lips were the only part of his face visible as she shifted her gaze to take in his black Stetson pulled low over his forehead. It threw the upper part of his face into deep shadow in the pale light. Her laughter stuttered to a halt while she stared transfixed at his chiseled lips and square jaw. Delicious and dangerous enough to send a shudder skittering up her spine and a flicker of heat ignite in her belly.

She licked her lips and choked down another spurt of hysterical laughter as the cool scent of rain mingled with man in a seductive contrast. He made no move to let her go. Nor did she have any desire to release herself, except maybe to give into the temptation to reach up and cup his face in her hands, smooth her fingers over the darkened stubble on his cheeks, and touch the ebony hair that fell straight to his shoulders. Almost delirious, she narrowed her eyes to gauge what was beyond the thick shadows. If his eyes were as beautiful as his mouth, she was in deep trouble.

He'd sucked the breath right out of her, dashed away the chill with the heat of his body. And yet, there was more to see. If she could just tip his hat up a little, she'd have a better view of the rest of his face.

One fat raindrop plopped from the rim of his hat straight onto the top of her nose, trickled down the short length of it and trembled on the end before it dripped off.

Amused, she wrinkled her nose as the next droplet hit her square on the forehead. She opened her mouth, intending to make a light quip, but all that came out was a soundless huff while the pulse in the base of her throat beat out a rapid tattoo.

His lips twitched, but he stayed silent. His eyes remained a shadowed mystery while he dipped his head closer as though he was about to whisper in her ear. Ruth braced against him and pushed back to give herself room to think, grateful when his arms slackened without protest, so her brain stood a chance of kick-starting again.

She swept her wet hair back from her face. He may have addled her brain for a moment, but she needed words to make her focus. "Och, would you believe this weather?" In the absence of any response from him, she tried again. "I dinna see the ferry come in."

His lips parted, and her pulse thundered in rhythm with the pounding rain while an uncanny flutter deep in the pit of her stomach sent a shot of heat to flood her face.

"It didn't."

A man of few words it appeared, but the words he'd uttered were deep and husky, with no trace of Scottish brogue.

She took another step away. Regret curled in her stomach when cold air replaced the warmth of his arms as he let them fall to his sides. She curved her mouth up in a half smile, a gentle encouragement for him to speak. "How did you get here?"

His lips twitched again. This time, impatience showed. He might think she was merely nosey, which she was, but he was the first stranger she'd set eyes on this year. Not only had she felt the pull of instant attraction, but he intrigued her both by his physical appearance and the fact he'd arrived there by all accounts under his own steam.

"Did you swim?"

His hard lips stretched into a straight smile.

"Nope. I came across in a fishing boat."

She widened her eyes and assessed him again. American. Tall and rangy. Quite obviously an idiot.

"Why in God's name would you do something like that? Can't you see there's a gale blowing in?" She flung her arm out to indicate the black storm clouds which coated the sky as unreasonable fear grabbed at her chest. "You could have been lost at sea."

Undeterred by her accusation, the man crossed his arms over his chest, his wide shoulders stretched the leather coat and made her mouth water.

"I managed to get here before the weather set in." No alarm tainted his voice, just a calm rationale which, for some reason, irked her more.

"But you may not have." She had no idea why the thread of panic laced its way through her veins, but it did, and she couldn't help but blurt out her concern.

This time the smile widened to show his white, even teeth, the shadows dipped into the creases of his cheeks. At his dismissive shrug, her heart gave an uneasy hitch. Something about the way the man moved had the desire to step back into the circle of his arms whip through her. The quick zap of pure lust took her by surprise.

"I think the skipper of the boat pretty much knew what to do." He angled his head and made her stomach jitter as she was teased with a promise of the sight of the rest of his face before he raised his hand, tugged the brim of his hat lower and obliterated her hope.

"If you'll excuse me. I have somewhere I need to be." His words were polite enough, but the tension of his lips showed his impatience to be off and signaled she was in his way.

A warm flush bloomed over her cheeks. Evidently, the quick burst of attraction she'd felt in the tall, dark stranger wasn't reciprocated.

Words to detain him hovered on her lips, but he sidestepped her, striding away before she summoned up a thought in her head to keep him there. Ruth narrowed her eyes to watch as his full-length, black leather coat swirled around the ankles of his cowboy boots while he strode away with purpose, only to be swallowed up by the mist, wraithlike and unholy.

Ruth squinted through the torrential downpour for a moment longer. A damned shame she never caught sight of his eyes. Or maybe just as well. If they were as attractive as the rest of him, she might well have expired on the spot.

Weak, she leaned against the door while the strength he'd just melted from her bones to leave her feeble and listless, took its own sweet time coming back.

With a last, regretful glance over her shoulder, Ruth let herself into the gift shop.

"Nana?"

"Aye lassie, I'm here." A quiet voice quavered from the little room beyond the shop as Ruth rushed through, her hackles rising in defense at the sight of Nana, frail body curled over in a spindly wooden chair, while she rested her elbows on her knees.

"Are you okay? What did he do to you?" Fear laced her voice.

Faded green eyes glittered at her, and the thin skin of the old lady's cheeks crinkled as she cracked a broad smile. "Nothing except set my heart on fire. Did you see his eyes?"

"No." Quick to answer, she raked her gaze over her grandmother, taking in the rapid flurry of breaths and heaving of the woman's narrow chest. "No, I did not. He had his hat pulled low, and he was rude. I think he was rude." She sniffed, disturbed by the florid color in her grandmother's cheeks.

"I didn't find him rude. I found him very pleasant."

"Good."

Relieved to hear it, Ruth slipped her wet coat off and hung it on the coat stand as Nana came to her feet and wandered across the shop. Ruth smoothed her wet hair from her face with the small hand towel her grandmother passed to her, refusing to rub it. It would only dry in an instant and stand up around her head like black dandelion fluff.

She cast Nana a sideways glance. "I don't understand how he got here—he's very lucky he never drowned."

"Well dear, we would never have known about him if he had."

That was a consideration which drew unreasonable fear into her heart as though she would have missed him. She folded the towel and placed it in a neat square on the back of the chair, her movements slow and considered while her heart beat like the wild flutter of a bird against her rib cage.

"I wonder who he is." Ruth slipped a pack of tarot cards off the counter and placed them back inside their wooden box. Her grandmother loved the cards, but she never put them away.

"He's the writer."

"The writer? The one due to stay at Joan Hawthorne's bed and breakfast for the whole of the summer?" She swiped crystals up one by one and placed them in their velvet-lined box as she spared her grandmother a quick glance for confirmation.

"Aye, poor wee beggar, that's the one."

"But didn't they contact him after Joan died to say he could no longer stay there?"

"They tried. Apparently, he'd already started out, and dinna pick up the message."

"Och what bad luck. I wonder what he'll do." She imagined there'd be a fierce quarrel amongst the villagers once the word was out as to who most deserved his custom.

She cast her grandmother another quick glance before she applied herself to wiping the counter down. The black glass top was always smeared with fingerprints.

Silence filled the room and suspicion curled through Ruth's stomach. She darted her gaze back up to the other woman's guilt-ridden face.

"No, you dinna." The delicate shrug of her grandmother's slight shoulders confirmed Ruth's barely formed thought. "No, Nana. Please say you didn't invite him to stay with us."

Regretful wrinkles curled around her grandmother's cheeks as she pursed her lips. "What could I say?"

"You could have said no." Ruth pressed her hand to the erratic thrum in her chest as she recalled the huge figure dressed in black, with muscles that flexed with incredible energy. "Or you could have said nothing at all. You didn't need to offer. We're not a bed and breakfast."

"Joan's poor widower sent him here, to me." Her grandmother's lips pursed in a tight moue of close-knit wrinkles. "There was nowhere else at this short notice."

There were numerous places, and her grandmother well knew it. Her crafty gaze slid away to dart around the room.

"I suppose he'll stay a couple of days, and then make alternative arrangements?" The hope in Ruth's heart escaped through her voice, a dream which Nana trampled.

"Well, no. He needs somewhere for the whole summer, my bonnie lass."

How did Nana think they could home him? Another mouth to feed when they barely had enough for themselves. They weren't prepared for visitors, and they had no experience in running a guest house. A man such as him, in an expensive leather coat, and exuding American wealth with ease, would expect far higher standards than they could offer.

Ruth's gusty sigh earned her a flash of disapproval from her grandmother who'd gone from apologetic to defensive in the blink of an eye.

"I'll have none of your attitude, young lady. As you well know, money is tight."

Ruth opened her mouth to protest, then closed it again. There was no point arguing. Nana was right. The situation was dire, and with another poor summer without tourists, there was no way they could maintain their way of living and manage to keep the old manor house. They already had to cut their coat to suit their cloth.

The position of first flute she'd been offered with the Scottish Orchestra in Edinburgh was what she wanted, what she'd studied and practiced for all those years. They'd shown patience and compassion allowing Ruth until the end of the summer to give a decision. One she found difficult to make when money wasn't the only factor which influenced her decision. Comfort and security for Nana were her main concerns. Then there was the sneaky little trickle of fear. Something she'd yet to define. A dark, indecipherable quiver of panic which took hold each time she thought too hard about leaving the island. A tug of instinct which kept her close and raised her hackles of protectiveness for no apparent reason.

Her stomach fluttering with guilt, she ducked her head to scrub a little harder at the irksome scratches on the surface of the counter caused by too many crystals placed directly on it. Nana really should use the velvet mats, but she all too often forgot. Ruth concentrated on them while her grandmother continued. "I sent him on ahead, he had a heavy rucksack he didn't need to carry with him, and the weather was setting in."

Ruth hadn't noticed his rucksack when she'd barreled into him, her mind had been too filled with his heady scent, her vision distracted by the squareness of his sexy chin, but her grandmother's words brought her head up. "What if he robs us blind?"

Rusty laughter filled the small shop. "Eeeh, I seriously doubt there's anything left in our house anyone would wish to steal."

Only all the old heirlooms which were worth a small fortune, but Ruth bit her tongue and kept quiet. Her grandmother had already made up her mind that they didn't have enough money to sustain themselves, and it would have been a cruelty even to suggest they sell one of their artifacts to ease their lives a little.

Ruth's mind wandered as she buffed the surface to a shine. A man was not currently her priority, although she understood her grandmother's desire to see her happy. Romance was something Ruth found when she buried her nose in a book. Okay, the tall, dark, mysterious man she'd bumped into sent little shockwaves through her system, but he would only be a distraction from the decisions she had to make.

The icy touch of her grandmother's fingers urged her to take both frail hands in hers to warm them with her own pitiful heat. "What will he do until we get home?" Ruth asked.

"I told him to make himself comfortable and put on the shepherd's pie I'd made for us for tonight."

Ruth opened her mouth to reply and closed it again when her grandmother sent her an arch look. "I'm sure we can make do with what we have in the fridge, Ruth."

What they had in the refrigerator was a sorrowful nothing except for a few limp vegetables, until supplies arrived from the mainland. They might have to eat beans on toast, with a little scraping of grated cheese, if they were lucky and the tall guy didn't help himself to those too. With the size of him, the shepherd's pie wouldn't fill his boots.

What they needed was for the damned ferry to come in. Even when it did, they wouldn't have sufficient funds to restock their freezer and larder, but at least they'd be able to get some provisions.

With a reassuring squeeze of her grandmother's hands, Ruth let go and turned away so the older woman couldn't see the concern on her face. Her heart broke at the thought of leaving Nana once the summer was gone. Ruth couldn't just nip back for a quick visit to check on her. The island was almost cut off during winter with high winds and choppy seas.

She steadied herself before she replied. "You're right…we could do with his money. I'm sure it will go a long way over the summer."

"Aye, it will. I negotiated twice the rent when I threw in the incentive of breakfast and evening meals too."

Ruth's stomach sank. Just wait until he found out how poor his breakfast of porridge, and evening meal of potatoes and mutton were. She and her grandmother were both excellent cooks, but there was only so much one could do with meager ingredients. Their vegetable garden hadn't fared well, the weather too wet to bring the vegetables on. Last summer's crop had rotted in the ground before it was even part-way grown, the potatoes blighted, and their cabbages hadn't fared any better. They'd never had a time like it, and according to Nana, summers had always been long and hot until constant talk of the jet stream had moved the weather front, so they were besieged by rain all year long. Nana blamed it entirely on the power of the media.

A crack of thunder had Ruth whipping her head around as the entire sky lit up. A combination of sheet and fork lightning streaked across the blackened clouds while the god of thunder hammered on his drums loud enough to shake the ground.

She gave a soft snort of regret as she stared out of the window at the torrential rain. She'd give him a week to take in the elements, sample the food, and taste the loneliness before he took his lanky cowboy frame off their island and back to America.

No matter how much heat pulsed off him when she'd stood in the circle of his arms, he'd be a block of ice before Ruth and her grandmother returned to their chilly stone house.

»»»•«««

Green eyes glittered with feral threat from the other side of the huge, rustic kitchen. Three pairs of them. Stuart paused in the doorway. He'd seen some strange sights in his time, but domestic cats the size of small pumas gave him a moment of concern. The old lady hadn't warned him about them, but he had to presume they lived there.

He had a choice. He could back the hell out of there and wait outside in the torrential storm for Clarisse to get home, or he could do as she suggested, go into the kitchen and help himself to some of her home-cooked shepherd's pie. Reheat instructions neatly tucked in his shirt pocket.

With a small turn of his head, he took a cautious peer out of the window into the black of the storm while he kept an eye on the feral creatures in the corner of the room.

The deep rumble of his stomach over the sound of the thunder decided him.

He was prepared if they attacked. His full-length leather coat offered some protection. He removed his sodden Stetson, made a slow stretch forward to place it on the drainer next to the sink and froze mid reach to check them out. If their gazes hadn't glittered with evil intent, he might have mistaken them for statues. All three of them sat in a perfect line-up. Until one of them yawned, exposed bright white fangs and finished off with a malevolent grin Stuart suspected was designed to send him running. Interesting concept. He'd never run in his life, not from anything normal or paranormal. It might disappoint them, but he wasn't about to go anywhere.

If they attacked him, well, he'd be sorry to see the demise of his coat, but he'd be willing to sacrifice it to make a getaway.

He studied the trio of cats. If he'd had any doubt about whether he'd walked into the correct house, their intense stares chased it away.

Their eyes were just like hers. An exact replica of the young woman he'd met in the village. Not too dissimilar to the old lady's either, although time had faded hers. Hers were less emerald, and more a gentle sage. Strange that her character was more of a sage as well. She'd been kind and thoughtful when he'd explained his situation, and he'd appreciated her sweet suggestion to board with her.

He swept his gaze across the cats again. Both the women were related to each other, but the surprise came with the similarity in eye-color to the cats. In the chill of the big, old kitchen, the skin on the back of his neck prickled a warning. He might not have accepted Clarisse's invitation to lodge if he'd known he was about to walk into the devil's parlor. Then again, he'd hardly been left with a choice. There was no way back to the mainland and not another person around in the deserted little village, as though they'd holed up against the imminent storm.

He cast the troublesome trio a quick glance, shrugged out of his coat, and hung it behind the door, conscious as he did of the drip, drip, drip onto the quarry tiled floor. He needed to find something to mop it up with before the old dear returned and slipped on the puddle which had formed on the floor.

He rubbed his damp hands on the knees of his jeans while he glanced around the kitchen at the countless cupboards.

A little tick of sadness mingled with unease at the death of the other old lady. Maybe his expected arrival had caused her demise, but there was nothing he could do. He blew out a gusty breath. The last thing he needed was another death on his conscience. It appeared the fates wanted to play games with him, throwing a few curve balls to detour him on his quest. A quest he'd been sidetracked from several times. Death wasn't an alien concept on his journey, and the supernatural was his life's pursuit with overt and public demonstrations under his pen-name to disprove and annihilate supernatural theories. As a journalist and author, he was ruthless in his determination to root out the impostors, the charlatans, quite comfortable to throw them to the lions like offerings to the true gods. As a desperate and fearful man, he'd made it his mission to seek out the supernatural in the certain knowledge that it *did* exist, and it held the lives of his loved ones to ransom.

He chewed his bottom lip as he studied the fur balls a moment longer, their gimlet stares enough to make a grown man cautious. Perhaps they were the three fates. With a self-deprecating laugh, he shrugged off the fantastical concept, opened the cupboard under the sink, kneeled, and grabbed a cloth. It had to be the spooky old house together with the electrical storm raging outside that had him on edge. Just slightly off kilter. That, or the unexpected response he'd had to the young woman outside Clarisse's shop. The unguarded smile that had beamed out of her had knocked him back to leave him speechless for a moment while she filled his arms, all subtle scents and wild, curling hair. Paired with the deep beauty of her eyes, she'd managed to stir something inside of him.

As he backed out from under the sink, the hairs on the back of his neck gave another uncomfortable prickle. With a slow turn of his head, he came face to face with one of the cats.

"Hi."

Its loud purr rumbled through the kitchen. Stuart followed the line of its gaze and glanced back under the sink. Not a stupid kitty by any means. He reached in and pulled out a tin of cat food while he listened to the automatic reverberation of the cat's happy anticipation.

"Score!"

Unsure how much he should feed them, he turned out the entire contents of the tin into the dish on the floor and watched while the three animals consumed it with delicate nibbles. If it kept them from eating him, he was all for it.

Strange, they didn't seem quite as big as they had when he'd entered the house. Perhaps the dim light and shadows made the ebony figures appear much larger and more of a threat. Or more conceivable, he'd allowed his imagination to run wild at the thought of entering the premises of a supposed witch, albeit with her permission.

A witch. That's what he was there to find, and as luck would have it, it looked as though he'd fallen straight into the witch's den. At least that's what the recently widowed Scottish gentleman told him before he'd sent Stuart to find her. The local white witch, he'd called her. Stuart had seen too many witches in his life. Too many who purported to be, at least, but the longer he searched, the more his cynicism grew.

The sweet old lady who'd offered him the luxury of her home had been just that—sweet. Although not altogether stupid. With a guile and shrewdness, she'd managed to persuade him to pay far more than he'd expected for a four-month stay. She'd hardly cast a spell on him, though, and he could well afford the money. The self-contained cottage he'd meant to stay in would have been far cheaper. On the bright side, he no longer had to provide his own food, nor keep the place clean and tidy. The old dear would feed him, vacuum the carpets, clean the bathroom and change his bed linen, while he could concentrate on the reason he was there. To break an age-old family curse. And write. He could write.

He swung open the refrigerator door, and his heart joined his stomach. Virtually empty except for several blocks of what seemed to be paper wrapped butter, and three clear bottles of milk. He glanced at the cats as they licked their lips. It appeared they were better off than their owner in the food stakes. His mouth twitched as the felines leaped on the milk he poured for them. He turned back to the refrigerator as his stomach howled with hunger, sure he'd averted their desire to feast on him.

He pulled forward a covered dish and removed the foil lid. The shepherd's pie the old lady had told him to help himself to, he assumed. He poked his finger into the potato layer just to make sure while his stomach gave another unholy grumble.

In the scramble to get onto the fishing boat earlier, he hadn't managed to grab himself any breakfast. The old fisherman had made it clear it may be his only chance to get across to the island before the storm set in, which could last for days. He'd already had to kick his heels for two days at the dock while they'd decided if it was viable to send the ferry across. With the lack of passengers, the decision had been made, based less on the weather, and more on the financial aspect.

Stuart ducked his head back into the fridge to take another look at the shepherd's pie. It looked good. He sniffed at the food. It smelled good too. Very good. A fair size portion. Enough for him. His stomach gurgled and did a slow roll over as he sighed. Or about enough for two small ladies.

He stared at it for a long moment before he tucked the cover around it and pushed it back inside the fridge, ignoring the vicious clench of his stomach.

As he bent over to inspect the few items of vegetables in the bottom container of the refrigerator, the distinct sound of kitty pleasure rumbled while one of the black cats wound her way between his feet in gracious appreciation of the food he'd served them.

"Yeah, smitten, since I'm the one who fed you, I guess." He scratched the top of the cat's head and let it butt up against his hand. Perhaps it thought to lull him into a false sense of security before the three of them went for his jugular. He hunkered down and scratched some more, chuckling as she squirmed with joy and flung herself on her back for him to rub her stomach.

Well, there you go. Never judge a book by its cover. The aloof sentinels were nothing like they'd first appeared.

Stuart sank his fingers into the cat's thick, black pelt, his lips curved at the way she writhed on her back for him. There'd been a time when he was younger that he'd had a dog, part of a past he could barely recall. He'd been on the road so long that there'd been no point. He swiped one last stroke along her back and off the tip of her tail before he came to his feet, closed the refrigerator door with a little shrug of regret, and wandered through the kitchen. He touched his fingers to the various cupboards, opening them one after the other.

Clarisse had said to help himself. Fascinated, he opened one virtually empty cupboard after another, until he came across one with several items.

Jars of pickled stuff in a neat, straight line. Red cabbage, onions, tomatoes, asparagus. He reached in and took out a jar of asparagus, set it on the counter while his stomach protested yet again. Beetroot. He scanned the shelves, surprised at the range of food as though the old lady had to have one of everything, but more than one would be too much. Fennel. He picked out the jar and put it next to the asparagus. When he opened the next cupboard, he grinned to himself. Not so badly stocked with canned food. It appeared fresh food was in short supply. No wonder they pickled so much. It made sense on a little island. The cans were everyday items. Two cans of baked beans. He reached in and pulled one of them out. It would do nicely if the old lady had some bread he could toast.

»»»•«««

Sick to death of canned vegetables, Ruth tried not to heave the deep sigh which threatened in case her grandmother overheard it. The ferry hadn't delivered fresh food in almost two weeks. The last time it had arrived they'd only been able to afford a small amount, not enough to sustain them until their vegetables were ready to pick or dig. It wouldn't be long, once summer deigned to honor them with its presence. The amount of meat left in the freezer wouldn't go very far if her grandmother decided their new visitor needed it all, and the loss of the shepherd's pie weighed heavily on Ruth's conscience. She knew she should be gracious, but it proved hard to whip up a little charity when there was so little food of interest.

With a weary groan, Ruth tugged her boots off in the porch, wiggled her stockinged feet, and swung open the back door into the kitchen. With one step, the quick suck of icy water filled her woolen socks to send her skidding across the tiled kitchen floor. Her breath exploded from her lungs as her body slammed into the solid form of the tall cowboy dressed in black. His hard, muscular arm whipped around her waist to steady her. Her head snapped back, just in time to catch his quick flash of surprise.

Embarrassment battled sheer shock while her heart thundered in her chest.

"Twice in one day." The rumble of his voice sent a flare of heat through her body. All she could do was cling on. "Must be an omen."

Omens were not something she was happy to invite into her life.

She took the opportunity to inspect his face without the concealing shadows of his hat. As her eyes met the metallic gray of his, her world ground to a painful halt. Her blood pounded, thick and primal to roar through her confused mind.

Recognition burned its way into her consciousness, sending a pulse wave of dark clouds to flood her senses and drown her defenses. Weak, she sagged against him. The last thing she wanted in the world was to show weakness, but she had no choice. The sheer beauty of his eyes had robbed her of all strength.

His unexpected tenderness took her by surprise as he swept the damp tendrils of her hair away from her face, then trailed long fingers over her icy skin to cup her cheek in the warm palm of his hand. It took all her effort to convince herself to pull away, but he tightened his arm around her waist to make a prisoner of her.

"Are you okay? Did you twist something?"

Only her heart. Perhaps her soul. But the fog in her head wouldn't allow a cognitive thought to transform into speech, so she clamped her mouth shut and continued to stare into the torrid depths of his stormy eyes.

With as much apparent fascination as Ruth, the cowboy stood in utter stillness while the solid rhythm of his heart pounded against the palm of her hand where she rested it against his chest. Drawn toward him, she swayed closer, her chilled fingers absorbing his warmth.

"Ruth." The rusty tones of her grandmother's voice slashed through the mush in her brain. "Let go of the boy now and get a cloth to wipe up this wet before someone slips over."

"I'm sorry, Clarisse, it was my fault." The tension in his arm never relaxed. His jaw was solid, but he didn't appear to have any difficulty squeezing words out. His gaze still bored into hers. "I meant to clean it up, but I got distracted by food and the cats."

"Nayru, Din, and Farore." She had no idea why the cats' names popped out of her mouth when she'd been unable to say anything else, but the dark twitch of his eyebrows lightened her mood. It seemed he had no idea who the three were. A little joke between Nana and herself from her childhood when Zelda had been a video game addiction she'd discovered when she was at school on the mainland, and the three goddesses had stood for power, wisdom, and courage. She could have enlightened him, but the desire to open her mouth again seemed to have deserted her.

With her arms still wedged between them, one hand on his chest, the other turned numb from being trapped, Ruth wriggled her fingers and braced against him to put a little distance between herself and the dark cowboy. Her knuckles encountered the unexpected hard ridge of his erection as she pulled back.

His breath hissed in through his teeth, and his body went rigid as she whipped her hand out from between them and grabbed his arm for balance.

Cheeks flaming, she dropped her gaze and stepped back as he loosened his hold on her, not entirely letting her go. His hand still rested on her waist while he slipped the other to her shoulder and sent a wild thrill over her skin.

"Are you okay?" The concern in his voice couldn't tempt her to meet his gaze as her face glowed.

With a brief nod, she stepped back out of the circle of his arms, aware of the solid flex of muscle beneath the sleeve of his shirt as she released him. With the absence of his heat, the chill seeped through, and she gave him a pained grimace. "I'll get a cloth."

Her thick socks were sodden, and as she paced across the kitchen, the squelch in them turned icy.

There before she could make it to the cupboard under the sink, he took her by surprise as the three cats curled around him, with flirtatious flicks of their tails and wistful hope in their eyes. "I'm sorry, it's my mess, I'll clean it up." He ducked his head into the cupboard but still managed to stroke the cats in a natural move as he retrieved a cloth.

On his hands and knees before her grandmother, he mopped the floor at her feet, drying it as best he could. Not flustered, not subservient. Anything but. A man in control.

As he came to his feet, the curtain of his black hair swept back to allow his eyes to meet Ruth's again. She found this time when their gazes locked, heat rushed to her cheeks, and a desperate tremble filled her heart.

The soft clucking sound from her grandmother pulled her back. "We don't put wet clothes here, for obvious reasons. We would normally hang our clothes in the scullery when they're droukit, but you'd not know better, until now."

His dark brows twitched, a light of confusion flitted across his features at her grandmother's strong brogue, deepened by her annoyance. With difficulty, Ruth kept her face sober as she stepped in to translate. "We hang the soaking wet items in the utility."

He nodded as he dumped the saturated cloths into a bucket. Ruth sucked in her bottom lip. She had no idea a man could exude sex appeal in the act of domesticity. Her heart stuttered as she curled her toes into her icy, wet socks. The cowboy slipped his hands into his pockets, but the interest in his eyes hadn't faded. Rain hammered on the windows behind him as the sky turned from gray to black.

A soft sweep of warmth carried the scent of wood-smoke as it filtered through from the lounge.

"Did you light the fire?"

"I did. I hope it's okay. Clarisse said to make myself at home, but home is so much warmer than this."

She flicked a glance over him. In his shirt sleeves, she'd bet he was used to central heating. Whereas her grandmother and herself normally donned at least three layers of clothes against the bitter bite of the cold on spring evenings. The inefficient rattle and burble of their ancient heating did little to warm the place through. They were never short of wood for the fire, with plenty of woodland on the island of which they were all entitled to take their share. Ruth ensured she kept their store well stocked. She balled her hands up to tuck away fingers roughened from using an axe to split logs. Fingers that should be smooth and delicate.

She craned her neck so she could see through to the lounge, a soft whimper escaping her at the heavenly sight.

A fire roared in the hearth, the likes of which she hadn't ever been able to muster despite her abilities. So fierce, it surprised her that he hadn't set fire to the chimney. The heat pumped out through the intersecting hallway into the kitchen, to wrap around Ruth like a favorite blanket.

The last two summer seasons had been so poor, the damp had barely cleared from the old stone house before winter set in again. With an appreciative sigh, she murmured, "It's wonderful."

"I'll replace the wood I've used."

"No, it's fine."

"I may have used too much."

"It's okay," She glanced at him again and smiled at the flicker of concern on his face. "If there's one thing we have on this island, it's plenty of wood."

"Excellent. But I'm sure someone needs to chop it. I'll make sure I do my share while I'm here." He threw the cloth in the sink and rinsed it through, washing his hands while Ruth stood rooted to the spot.

Confused laughter rolled out. "You do know you're paying for this?" She waved her hand to encompass the room in general.

His cheeks creased as he accepted a towel from her and wiped his hands. He shrugged his wide shoulders and made her mouth water as his black T-shirt stretched over well-defined muscles. "Bed and meals are what I paid for, but I'm sure I've already used far more wood than is acceptable. No offense but it's damned cold here, and if you're happy for me to load up the fire to keep my butt warm, I find it acceptable enough to chop a little wood, rather than pay extra for the privilege of having it supplied by you."

At a loss for words, Ruth shook her head while her grandmother moved off into the scullery to hang her soaked coat to dry.

The savory aroma of shepherd's pie teased Ruth's senses and reminded her of the meal her grandmother had donated to him. As she followed her grandmother into the scullery to hang her coat, she glanced over her shoulder at him. "I'll prepare something for dinner if you're hungry." She raked her gaze over him. He seemed like the type to be forever hungry. His long limbs and defined muscles certainly showed no evidence of food deprivation.

His lips did a strangely attractive one-sided quirk. "Dinner's already in the oven when you're ready."

Speechless, she stared at him for a long moment before she broke eye contact and turned to look at the oven. How she'd missed the pale golden glow from the inner light, she had no idea, but she'd assumed the smell had been from when he'd eaten earlier. Evidently, the scent was from more recent fare.

She cracked open the oven door to peer in. The hot waft of air almost took her eyebrows off, but the juices in her mouth ran riot. Her stomach let out a raucous growl. Convinced she could eat the entire meal herself, she slipped the door closed again to shut the temptation away before she headed for the scullery.

She stripped off her coat and hung it beside her grandmother's in the close confines of the scullery. "He's prepared our tea, Nana," Ruth whispered.

Her grandmother's gray eyebrows twitched up while the wrinkles around her mouth flattened out into a smile. "Looks like I may have made the right choice, dear, allowing him to stay." She patted Ruth's hand as she walked back into the kitchen, a superior tilt to her head and enough of a jaunty step to give Ruth a little jolt as it occurred to her, her grandmother may just have been far wilier than expected.

»»»•«««

The food was more delicious than the simple fare should have been, but being ready and piping hot made all the difference. The bottle of Merriweather damson wine her grandmother retrieved from the cellar had certainly been a welcome addition, as was the apple crumble Ruth whipped up herself with the last of the apples they'd stored over winter.

"Nana tells me the reason you missed your message about Mrs. Hawthorne dying was because you were on your travels."

The smoky velvet of Stuart's deep eyes glittered at her in the firelight as Ruth sank onto the squishy sofa opposite him, replete after her meal.

"I was." He placed his wine glass on the spindly table next to him and leaned back. His broad shoulders spanned the width of the old armchair. "I'm doing research, and it takes me to some pretty remote places."

Unable to suppress her curiosity, she tucked her legs under her, desperate to delve into the exciting life of a well-travelled man. "Like where?"

His smile was slow to spread as he opened his hands to encompass the room. "Like here."

Feeling a little foolish, she let out an embarrassed laugh. If he'd been closer, she might have punched him on the shoulder for teasing her. "Before here. Where did you come from?"

"Zambia."

"Oh, how wonderful. I'd love to go." She shifted over as Nana lowered herself onto the sofa next to her. "What did you do there?"

"I met the people. Fascinating."

"Third world."

"Indeed."

His whiskers rasped as he rubbed his long fingers over his chin. The deep rumble of his voice soothed her. "Not just third world, but the deeper into the country, the farther from civilization, the more amazing they become. There, where development hasn't yet touched them." He shifted, sat forward in his chair. "In a village where the men wore nothing but loincloths, and the women wore even less, I met a man. A young, strong, healthy warrior, his skin black and shiny as jet." He leaned forward, his face compelling in its intensity. "But when he stood on a scorpion, and it stung him, he was a dead man."

Tension rippled over her skin and Ruth slipped forward in her seat to meet him halfway. "He died."

"He should have."

She could tell from the way he swept his hand over his face what it had cost him to witness the event. "We threw him in my truck, got him to a Dutch field hospital where the doctor did everything he could for him. By the time we arrived, the neurotoxins had sent his body into spasm, and despite the antivenin, the warrior continued downhill. His skin turned a strange gray ash color, dull despite the layer of sweat covering his body. The doctor told me this was the way of things out there." Stuart screwed his eyes shut. "The young warrior's face contorted so unnaturally, and his screams were inhuman."

Ruth shuffled closer, placed her hand on his knee. "Oh God, what happened?"

He opened his eyes and smiled. "He lived."

"He lived? How? How did he live? You just told me he was dying."

"He was. But not from the venom."

"Then, what?"

"The belief."

She flung herself back in her seat, almost bounced her silent Nana from the cushion next to her. "But you said he was stung by a scorpion."

"He was. And it didn't have sufficient venom to kill him. There aren't many deadly scorpions in the world, and certainly, the one that got him wasn't. The blood tests proved it."

"I don't understand, why was he dying?"

"Because he *believed* the scorpion had taken his soul."

Stunned, Ruth stared at Stuart before she wet her lips and continued. "You said he didn't die. So, what saved him?"

"Not what, but who. The witch-doctor from his village."

Surprise struck her silent as he smiled and shook his head as though he still couldn't believe it himself. "He'd followed the truck, barefoot. Eight hours it took him to reach us."

"What did he do?"

Stuart let out a low laugh. "He showed the warrior a scorpion, claimed he'd hunted it down after it had stung the young man. Then he wrapped it up in a white cloth and flung it into the hospital incinerator. It went up in a tiny ball of flames."

""What happened next?"

"Color flooded back to the warrior's face, and within minutes he was on his feet. He declared the witch doctor had returned his soul to him."

"Did you believe him?"

Stuart quirked the side of his mouth up in a wry smile. "No, but the warrior did."

"Huh." She tipped her head back against the seat and crossed her arms over her chest. "Amazing."

"Yeah. The power of belief."

"Aye." Nana shifted next to her. The older woman's gruff voice cut through Ruth's reverie. "Or the witch-doctor found the scorpion who stole the poor wee man's soul and cremated the little bugger, so it returned to him."

Stuart's laughter rolled across the room. "If you believe in witchcraft."

"Aye, if you believe." Clarisse came to her feet, a little unsteady in her frailness. "It's time for me to get off to bed. I've a shop to open tomorrow. If you'll excuse me."

In a smooth move, Stuart rolled to his own feet and dipped his fingers into his pocket to remove a small slip of paper. "Before you go, Clarisse, I'm sure you'd appreciate me paying my way for a lovely meal, and welcoming home."

Ruth thought Nana's heart might give way as the old lady stared hard at the piece of paper. The violent tremor of her fingers had Ruth on her feet by her side, but when she pried the check away before it became too crushed to save, her own fingers trembled at the sight of the amount he had written it for. The entire amount, up front for a four-month stay. More money than they'd earned in the previous year from their gift shop.

With a proud lift of her chin, Clarisse eyed Stuart for a moment, then gave a regal nod as though he hadn't just knocked the wind from her. "There was no need to pay it all at once. You may find we dinna suit." As Stuart opened his mouth to reply, Clarisse folded the check and tucked it into her skirt pocket. "If that's the case, I'll issue you a refund."

Stiff ankled, Clarisse made her way to the door. "You've chores in the morning, Ruth. Dinna stay up too late listening to wild tales."

"No Nana. I'm coming now."

With a sigh of regret, Ruth pushed her hair back from her face. If only she could have listened longer, but Nana would be waiting for her. "Aye well, it's time for my own beauty sleep, but I hope you'll tell me some more another night."

The cats moved as one from the dark encompassing shadows thrown up as the flames guttered in the fireplace, and wound their bodies in sinuous circles around her ankles. Determined not to trip over them, Ruth concentrated on every step to the door only to realize he was right beside her, his voice smooth in her ear. "Will the fire be safe?"

Ruth glanced back at the smoldering embers as she turned off the lights. "Aye. It's low enough." But as he preceded her out of the door, she wafted her left hand to encourage the fire to peter and die. Instead, much to her disgust, it threw a nasty little fireball in her direction and with a loud *whoof* plunged the room into darkness.

··•··

Regret shimmered through him as he flopped onto his side. He'd enjoyed regaling the ladies with tales of his exploits. The old lady had remained quiet, the faded jade of her gaze lost none of its intelligent inquisitiveness as she'd kept her attention on him, but he'd felt Ruth's interest deepen with every word he'd uttered and it was just a matter of time before she started to ask more pressing questions. His exhaustion was genuine when he'd followed Clarisse up the stairs.

The moment his head hit the pillow, though, all signs of fatigue disappeared, and his mind flooded with thoughts of Ruth. Her wide emerald gaze, full of fascinated curiosity; her soft, pouty mouth, with its lower lip slightly fuller than her top one, and the sweet little nose she wrinkled when she stopped to give something he'd said consideration.

She'd taken him by surprise with the deep undertow of sexual attraction. The first time she flung herself into his arms, it had been an automatic reaction for him to grab her tight, but he'd found a strange reluctance to let her go.

The fresh smell of sea breeze and freesias had caught him unaware to pull at a long-lost memory he'd been unable to pin down. In an instant, she'd wound herself through his senses with a wild and carefree temptation she appeared oblivious to.

The woman was a danger to him. Too curious. He gave a little thought to the pert nose of hers. Imagined it crinkling as she laughed, and again while she stuck it in his business. Questions. She'd had a million, her bright mind probably stifled by the isolated life the two women led. With no man in the house, Stuart had to assume the old lady was a widow and the young one not married or otherwise. There'd been no mention of a man in her life, and he'd done his own gentle prying. A little less obvious than her, it hadn't taken too much effort at dinner to prize information out of the two of them. Then again, he had the distinct advantage with his background in journalism. His job was to find answers.

They'd not mentioned they were short of money. Why would they? They were proud women, but he'd hazard a guess there wasn't too much readily available. That's why he'd written the check out for the entire stay. As for Clarisse's theory that they may not "suit", he had no intention of leaving, and he might as well make his visit as pleasant as possible.

He rolled onto his back and stared up at the ceiling even though darkness obscured it and he could barely see six inches in front of him. The waft of clean linen with a hint of sea breezes reminded him of Ruth, and his body stirred. Just as it had when he'd found his arms full of her for the second time that day.

She wasn't short. The top of her head reached eye level. Her crazy hair tickled his cheek when he'd held her close, the subtle scent of it winding through his senses. But he could imagine her willowy figure would break in the first high wind. How had she survived so long in such bleak conditions?

She'd felt his instant attraction when she'd brushed her hand over his unexpected erection. Her eyes had darkened with shock as she'd sucked in a swift little gasp.

But something more than just shock lurked in her eyes.

His own embarrassment at the incident had been swept to one side at her soft, sweet blush. The combination of her bright mind and wild beauty lured him.

He couldn't remember the last time he'd been in a relationship, but it didn't mean he had to leap on the first unsuspecting female he came across. In his line of work, women weren't hard to come by. They were attracted to his career, seeming to find it romantic. Journalism brought with it an abundance of advantages and disadvantages. Moving around, he met a variety of women. Being transient, he rarely had an opportunity to develop a relationship with them.

With a huff, Stuart bounced over onto his side again, curled his arm under his head and tucked his knees into his belly. His feet were warmed by the hot water bottle which had been placed in his bed. He needed to heat up the rest of his body before he froze to death. How did they live without an electric blanket? If this was spring, he couldn't imagine how they'd survived winter. He shuddered again, reached down and drew the rubber bottle up to his stomach. If he could get his core warm, he'd maybe live until dawn.

He closed his eyes, and the image of Ruth filled his vision. The awareness in her sparkling emerald stare, her delicate touch, had his emotions raging.

He wasn't there to get involved on any level. He was there to do a job before time ran out. It would be best to avoid contact with Ruth, although with living under the same roof for the next few months, it might prove impossible. He curled tighter into a ball, hugged his knees and tucked his chin under the covers to stop the frantic chattering of his teeth.

He knew of ways to warm himself up and smiled as he visualized Ruth. She'd be a distraction. He blinked his eyes open and stared into the darkness. There was no time and no reason why he should want to be distracted. He'd not come there for her.

Her grandmother interested him, though. She was the reason he was there. Provided she was the only witch on the island.

Within moments of him entering the gift shop, she'd offered to do a reading of her tarot cards for him. She wasn't insulted when he refused… she'd just given a small incline of her head and carried on as though she'd never extended her services.

There was no fear of what he might see in the tarot cards. His refusal had been a simple lack of belief. He'd dealt with a lot worse than a reading in his time. Much worse. None of them had ever borne any significance to his life. Every reading he'd ever attended, séances, palmists, they'd all been bullshit. Well, most.

He stretched himself out and flung himself back over again, irritated with the twitch of his over-tired limbs and the insistence of his mind on staying awake to prod at him with little knives of doubt and guilt.

All his adult life he'd sought out the spiritual, the supernatural, and never found hard evidence to show it existed. Yet he knew it did. He'd experienced the unexplainable, witnessed the impossible. His family was living proof of it, and all he wanted was to follow the trail, track down the truth before time ran out. Time for yet another generation to be blighted. Time for his brother and nephews to suffer further.

With another sigh, he flipped over onto his front and buried his face in the pillow. He could still smell Ruth. Her delicate scent permeated the covers, the room, and the house.

It didn't seem to carry the smell of her grandmother, or perhaps his senses had latched on to Ruth's aroma and were unwilling to let go.

Her grandmother was the one he was there to investigate, not Ruth, but the younger woman's presence dominated his thoughts to distract his mind from his real purpose.

His body stirred again until he rolled over and threw back the covers. He came to his feet in a fluid motion so he could pace to the large window. He pulled back the curtains and stared out over the silvery hued landscape to the mystical sparkle of moonlight on the water where the land met the sea in a small cove beyond the house.

The storm had ceased to rage just a short while before to leave a clear night sky as though it had never been ripped apart by a thousand blazing strikes of lightning and the cruel battle of blackened clouds hadn't crashed out their fury to culminate in a violent crescendo.

Stuart traced his gaze over the rain-soaked beauty of the shadowed land.

Doubt curled in his mind. This was where his path had led him to find the supernatural, but so far, his instincts had given him nothing. No hint there was any substance of real magic anywhere.

He narrowed his eyes as three black feline shapes extracted themselves from the deeper shadows of the garden, heads lowered as they stalked their unsuspecting prey.

The chill of the night soaked into his skin and tempted him to jump back under the covers, but he hesitated. Paranormal or not, whatever made all three cats freeze like statues, then turn their heads in unison to peer up at him with glittering green stares sent a shudder through him.

He'd quite possibly come to the right place to find what he searched for. He hoped to God he had.

This was where he bet his brother's life he would find it. He had no option, as that was what was on the line, and the only way he could save him was to find the goddamned witch. A real witch, not a two-bit hustler, not a tarot card reader, but a fire-breathing, spell-busting, devil-driven witch.

Chapter Two

Pale peachy hues daubed Ruth's bedroom in a gentle persuasion for her to open her eyes and greet the morning.

Reluctant to move, Ruth took a moment longer to languish. She'd barely slept. She'd been quick to drift off, warm and replete, but vivid images had woken her from a dream she couldn't recall which had left her restless and irritable. The only memories were of storm clouds rolling in to make a pewter filled sky.

With a sense of trepidation, Ruth swung her legs out of bed. She expected the naked oak floorboards to send an icy nip up her feet, but the floor had lost its chill. Quick to throw off the dream and get herself ready for a day of work, Ruth flipped open the bedroom curtains and stared at the brilliant bronzed sunrise. A clear sky streaked with orange and peach to bring the promise of a beautiful summer's day greeted her, coaxing a smile from her as she leaned against the window frame.

Vibrant green rolled over the hillside into the cove below where it met the small golden beach which slid effortlessly into the water.

Her heart stuttered as her gaze locked on a tall, rangy man dressed all in black with a Stetson perched on the back of his head. He paddled barefoot in the surf. Black jeans hitched up to his knees, he kicked at the white spumes and leaped backward to avoid the roll of the tide from lapping too high up his calves. Carefree, he threw back his head and, she imagined, laughed. He might look carefree, but she could bet his feet were blue with the icy wash of Atlantic water.

Ruth tugged her gown closer and folded her arms over her chest as the imagined chill gripped her and goose bumps stippled her forearms. The iciness of the Atlantic sea, even in the height of summer was enough to give anyone hyperthermia.

It did her heart good to see a grown man, a handsome man, with such enjoyment.

Her pulse unsteady, she blew out a breath while she watched, and a smile played across her lips. Just the sight of the man as he waded back into the water tripped her heart and tempted her to run down and join him, despite the threat of cold feet.

Once again, he jumped back from the waves and as he did he turned side-on to expose his face to her and give her the opportunity to study him unnoticed for a long moment. His face wreathed with a smile, eyes crinkled at the corners, he threw back his head again while his bare feet sank into the sand and she knew for certain this time he let out a wild laugh.

Tempted to open the window to listen for the sound of his laughter, Ruth let her fingers curl about the brass handle ready to push the window open, and then pulled back in a hasty retreat as the smile dropped from his face. He whipped around to scan the house like the intensity of her gaze touched him.

Her cheeks heated. She swallowed to clear the dryness which threatened to close her throat while she rubbed her damp hands against her gown. She hadn't meant to spy on him. He just happened to be there when she'd opened her curtains. Yet guilt curled in her stomach, followed by the embarrassment of being caught in the act of spying.

She stumbled from the window, whirled away, dashing to the bathroom. Her heart skipped while a secret thrill coursed through her veins. He was gorgeous, handsome. Had he any idea how attractive he was?

She closed the bathroom door and leaned against it, a heated flush warming her face. Gorgeous and dangerous with a strength she hadn't imagined to accompany those long limbs, the muscled definition of his calves quite took her by surprise. She cupped her hands under the running tap. Little shocks of desire tickled her senses while she tried with desperation to cool her overheated cheeks with generous splashes of icy water

Perhaps he was best avoided as the temptation proved a little too much. The vision of his tanned legs sent fire racing through her veins and dispelled any memories of the bad dreams which had disturbed her sleep. Aware her breath had become a little erratic, just like Nana's the day before, she drew it in slow and controlled, then released it one long, breath out. Good Lord, she had no control over her desires, and the man wasn't even within touching distance. The temptation to grab him and snog the life out of him was strong, but fine tendrils of unexplained apprehension wound through her stomach.

She didn't know if he was married or spoken for and here she was weaving romantic kiss scenes in her head. Still, long distance lust couldn't harm, provided he didn't realize.

With another delighted shudder, she dropped her wrap to the floor and stepped underneath the scalding water of the shower to dispel the image of the man from her mind.

Pale blue jeans took a little persuasion to hitch up her still damp legs, but she slipped the fine cotton shirt on with ease over her white T-shirt. Layers. The rule was always layers. She yanked a sapphire blue woolen jersey over her head and tugged it into place as she made for her bedroom to grab a pair of thick socks from her drawers. The bright sunshine might promise a warm day, but still, early in the year, the weather could turn in the blink of an eye.

With no sign of the handsome writer when Ruth stuck her head through the kitchen doorway, the pull of disappointment left her flat. She'd hoped to have caught him, perhaps spend a little time before she left for work.

The scent of smoked bacon clung to the air.

She opened the fridge door and peered inside. Her thoughts wandered as she stared at the interior of the virtually empty fridge. He'd softened her too much by leaving enough bacon for breakfast for both her grandmother and her. He must only have had two paper thin slices and an egg. For all his quiet mysteriousness, the man displayed a thoughtfulness to surprise her. He'd paid his way; he should expect more than he seemed to.

She checked the status of the bread Nana had put to bake the night before and realized he must have filled up on it and plenty of their freshly churned butter from the farm next door.

It warmed her heart to think he'd considered them, especially her grandmother, when he'd taken his food and left enough for them both.

She stared out of the window at the calm, cloudless sky. Gratitude surged through her heart.

Today the ferry would come. Today they would get their supplies. With the money Stuart had given them, they could afford to pay for enough food to see them through until they became almost self-sufficient again, provided their crops didn't fail. She could get out into the garden, start to turn the heavy wet mud in the raised vegetable gardens and hope it would soon turn back to decent soil with the heat of the sun and the sea breeze to dry it out. Then she could plant. If Mother Nature felt gracious, they'd soon have their own crops again. Ruth scanned the pure cerulean blue sky and offered up a silent prayer for it to continue to grace their little island for more than just a few pitiful weeks. Stuart's money was great, but the independence Nana would have once the vegetables started to grow was of as much importance.

Ruth turned from the fridge, and her three familiars were there, ready and willing to wind themselves around her ankles until she fed them.

"He's already gone."

Ruth glanced up at the rusty sound of her grandmother's voice. "Aye, Nana. He helped himself to his breakfast. It appears he's quite independent."

"That he is. I would have made him a decent breakfast myself if he'd waited, but he was in a rush to get on with his day."

Ruth had the strange sensation her grandmother frowned on his independence. She rather thought Nana would have preferred to spoil him, tending to his needs, for which he'd paid. Before she could make comment, her grandmother continued. "I'd have made him a fine, thick porridge to line his stomach for the day, not just a frivolous bit of bacon." Ruth moved away to the kitchen sink to fill the kettle, a fleeting smile curved her lips at Nana's concern for the cowboy. Her mind filled with romance and music while she absorbed the beauty of the shaft of golden light through the window. Ruth half listened to Nana chatter on with her instructions.

"We'll have tourists today." A situation her grandmother always approved of and one which would make her happy. "You'll need to get the supplies, while I keep the shop open. I've written a list."

"What about the check?"

"You can place it in the bank, but with the security it provides, we'll have enough money to cover what we want."

The mere thought of it had taken the lines of stress from Clarisse's face, to smooth out her wrinkles and soften her jawline.

"Aye, and there should be plenty of fresh fish today, with the seas calmer." Ruth stroked an affectionate hand along Nana's arm and gave a gentle squeeze. "I'll drop down to the dock and pick us some up for our supper tonight."

Excitement at their ability to replenish their stocks put a bounce in her walk as Ruth made her way through the village down to the docks. Her stomach, cheerfully replete had invigorated her entire body. At least that's what she told herself, convinced it could have nothing to do with the handsome cowboy who'd taken up residence in their house. Ruth lifted her face to let the thin strains of sunlight warm her skin.

With idle curiosity, she wondered where Stuart had gone, but, determined to concentrate on the jobs at hand, she pushed all thoughts of him from her mind. She wouldn't dwell on those tanned legs and those storm-gray eyes which stirred her blood and sent her heart into overdrive.

With a flick of her unmanageable hair over her shoulder, she took cautious steps over the fishing nets laid out along the dock.

"Good morning Bill, and how well did the fish bite today?"

"Well enough." Bill pushed his cap back from his weather worn forehead and gave Ruth an intense stare through his squinty eyes. Not always at ease with the way Bill focused on her when he had something he considered important to say, Ruth afforded him the time and patience he needed to speak again. He drew air in through his nose. "We had the Yank here."

It appeared she couldn't dismiss the man from her mind after all. She should have known better, he'd be the talk of the island, and she and her grandmother were not going to escape the gossip. On the contrary, they would be in the middle of it as everyone would want to know what they knew. So far, it proved relatively nothing.

"I don't think you'll find he's a Yank. He's from America, but from his accent possibly more southern." She didn't really know; she'd only ever heard the gentle drawl of Southern gentlemen on the television. She was no wiser than anyone else, but she'd taken exception to the way Bill had said it as though he didn't trust Stuart.

"He's been asking questions."

"Questions?" He was a writer. They were renowned for their nosey natures and enquiring minds. With a dismissive shrug, Ruth glanced down into the box of ice and fresh fish. After all, she didn't want to join in the gossip, but it wouldn't harm if she listened to it. As well as the cod and ling, Ruth noticed skate. A rarer fish, but one she preferred. She pondered the selection with the concentration it deserved.

"Aye, he asked me if I'd ever heard of a selkie."

Despite her resolution not to become involved, she whipped her head back up to see if Bill was being funny, but the old boy had never been funny in his life.

Why would Stuart ask about selkies?

Somehow, she'd not expected the author's questions to take that direction. She had no idea what he wrote about. From his appearance, she'd had an idea he may write fiction. Thrillers. Deep and dark with a touch of illicit sex…

She shoved the errant thought from her mind and concentrated on Bill.

"What did you tell him?"

Bill snorted. "I said who hadn't heard of selkies? You're in the Hebrides, son, not only have I heard of them, but most people on this island will have encountered one or two in their lifetimes." He leaned forward and gave a yellow-toothed grin. "I told him some of our residents even have selkie blood in their veins." Bill reached into the box and hauled out a decent size skate, knowing what her choice would be, and flicked it onto a piece of white paper. "I told him I had stories could make his hair curl."

Ruth chuckled as she let her gaze wander out to sea with the unconscious thought of seeing selkies frolic in the white froth from the spumes thrown up by the Atlantic.

Somehow, she doubted such stories would make Stuart's shoulder-length, straight, black hair curl. He didn't give the impression of being overawed by strange tales, his calm demeanor and cool stare told of a lifetime of experience.

She'd not always been convinced by talk of the sightings, despite being brought up with tales which had been woven into her family's history. Easy enough for visitors and newcomers to mistake the white roll of the tide as something other than waves. A person's imagination could easily lead them astray. Her imagination had been vivid when she was younger, but not since she'd returned from university in Edinburgh had she fancied she'd seen anything mystical.

Ruth squinted into the bright reflections of sun as it sparkled across the surface of the water. The vision of Stuart paddling in the surf tickled at her memory while Bill flicked another skate on top of the first, then screwed his face up while he studied Ruth. "Enough for you?" She peered down at them. The fish were a good size. One would be more than enough for her and her grandmother to share, and the other would go part the way to fill Stuart's flat, muscular stomach.

Ruth jerked her head up from her contemplation of the fish and rid herself of the insidious thoughts which trailed through her mind. How he'd had the power to transplant sexy thoughts there, she wasn't sure, but she couldn't possibly be responsible for the tiny licks of lust she experienced.

"Yes, thank you, Bill. I'll take some cod too while I'm here. Nana can freeze it for when she wants to make her fishcakes."

Bill squinted up at her and licked his lips. He threw a huge cod onto the scales and smiled as he made a drastic reduction to the price. "Tell your Nana I'll look forward to my share when they're ready."

She smiled back as she handed over her money and took her neat package from him. A widower of many years, he was quite capable of looking after himself, but when it came to fishcakes, it proved a little beyond his culinary capabilities, and he always appreciated a donation from Nana. Fair exchange was no robbery, and the man often donated a piece of cod for the pleasure of Nana's fishcakes.

Ruth folded her arms about herself, the nip in the air still sharp. The wicker basket she held by its handle tucked neatly into the crook of her elbow bumped against her hip as she moved along the dock where fresh fruit and vegetables were unloaded from the small ferry. A sprightly old gentleman, Mr. Low, directed proceedings so he could sell his goods before the ferry made its return journey to the mainland.

Satisfied with her provisions, Ruth held out her money for Mr. Low and accepted the change with a grateful nod.

"I hear you've managed to persuade the Yankee to come and stay with you."

Ruth whispered a curse under her breath at Nancy's bitter tones. Typical of the woman to sidle up for a sly dig. Ruth straightened her shoulders, took a long, deep breath and turned to look Nancy Belmont in the eye. "I'm not sure he's a Yankee, but I believe he's from America."

"That's what *he* said." Nancy's stance reflected Ruth's, but her generous bosom spilled over bare arms thickened by years of laundering for the islands' population.

"I'm sure he's right."

Ruth didn't wish to engage with Nancy whose surly nature was more the reason why tourists didn't return to her bed and breakfast establishment. She turned to walk away. With a violent jerk, Nancy grabbed her arm, her fingers dug deep, and she whipped Ruth back around to face her. Unable to stifle the quick yelp of surprise, Ruth took in the woman's flushed face and desperate gleam in her eyes. It wasn't the first time her claw-like fingers had taken hold of Ruth. The last time, Ruth had only been a young teenager, and the woman had frightened the living daylights out of her.

Nancy's accusation all those years ago had been that Ruth had turned Nancy's son's brain into a mindless, sodden mess by bewitching him. Unfortunately, Nancy's son had just entered puberty, and anything with female hormones would have turned his brain to mush. A fact that seemed to escape his mother. Ruth hadn't been well-enough informed to have realized as much back then.

She'd made it her habit to avoid the woman ever since, not an easy accomplishment when there were only a couple of hundred people on the island.

With as much decorum as she could muster, Ruth raised her chin, met Nancy's gimlet stare head on and gave a cool one of her own, surprised to find there was no longer any fear. She was an adult, and the woman could no longer hurt her. "Was there something else you wanted?"

The woman's grip never lessened, but a brief flicker of shock crossed her features at Ruth's immovable stance before she continued regardless. "You took our custom. By rights, he should have come to us, and you know it. We've a proper bed and breakfast, registered with the AA and featured on Trip Advisor. Your Nana caught hold of him and would nae let him go."

Ruth raised her eyebrows and let a slow smile slide over her face, pleased to see a wary flicker in the other woman's gaze. "You know, I think Nana took him in out of the goodness of her heart when he was sent to her, but why don't you take the matter up with Nana and see what she has to say about it?" She knew full well the other woman would never risk the wrath of Nana. Nancy was a typical bully, too frightened to take on a real challenge, and Clarisse had never been considered a soft touch, unlike her granddaughter.

With slow reluctance, Nancy released the tight hold she had on Ruth. Her eyes grew round until they almost popped out of her head. "She'd probably turn me into a frog."

Ruth took a deliberate lazy perusal of Nancy from the top of her square head, down past the rolls of fat squished around her short neck, over her hunched shoulders and bulbous body. She skimmed her gaze to the hem of Nancy's thin skirt, took in the woman's skinny alabaster legs, and then tossed back her head to give the brightest smile she could find.

"I'm not sure her services are required."

Crimson washed up Nancy's chest with a fiery rush to continue over her neck and through her face almost bursting from her hairline.

Satisfied she'd managed to defend herself against the other woman's rudeness, a secret thrill at her braveness curved Ruth's lips. She flipped her curls over her shoulder, and before she was tempted to cast her own little spell, she whirled in the opposite direction.

And smacked straight into a black-clad body; the warm spiciness of him instantly recognizable. The V of his sweater exposed the tanned flesh of his neck and sent a torrent of lust through Ruth's veins. She inhaled his scent while the temptation to slide her fingers over the taut muscles of his chest proved almost too much. She tilted her head back to allow her gaze to meet his. Her smile stretched a little wider in the desperate hope he couldn't read her thoughts, aware of his fingers as they tightened their grip on her shoulders. Power she'd not noticed before sprang up between them and stirred a kernel of excitement in her chest.

One dark eyebrow rose in a wicked arch and made her wonder if he could read her mind. "We seem to have made a habit of bumping into each other."

Not such a bad habit. She could get used to the touch of his hands on her shoulders, or any other part of her he cared to lay them.

The storm in his gaze captivated her, sending a rush of desire through her system to jumble the words in her head and leave her speechless. She parted her lips, but no sound came out. His dark gaze heated with intimacy and slipped down to study her mouth with such intensity it silenced the world, narrowing it down until there were only the two of them. The chaotic thoughts in her mind stilled. Little breaths hitched through her lips and stuttered in the back of her throat while she took in the dark beauty of him, listened to the sound of each breath he took through firm, straight lips. Lips she had the desire to touch with her own. She angled her head, and her lashes fluttered closed.

A rough hand yanked her around, and before Ruth could clear the fog of lust from her mind, Nancy shouldered past her and stood squarely in front of Stuart. She slapped one plump hand on her rounded hip and leaned forward from the waist. "I hear you've been speaking to people about all things peculiar and weird." The flesh on the underside of her chin wobbled as she shook her head at him. "It looks like you may have chosen the right place to stay with a renowned witch under the same roof."

"A witch?" His deep, quiet voice was laced with coolness as he studied Ruth before he returned his attention to the other woman. The chill of his scrutiny should have frozen anyone with half a brain, it certainly gave Ruth pause, but it appeared Nancy had even less as she barely broke her verbal stride.

"I don't mean Ruth. Everyone knows Ruth can't weave a spell worth shit."

Stuart's jaw flexed as he perused the other woman, his hands hung loose by his side. "Why would Ruth weave spells?"

Nancy dipped her head, lips tight and eyes narrowed to sly slits. "Because her nana's a witch and her mother was a witch. By rights, Ruth should be one too, but she isn't. She hasn't been able to perform a single spell since birth without it going awry."

Ruth curled her lip at the other woman and noted, despite her words, fear still lurked in the depths of her mucky hazel stare. "Nancy." She'd never used the woman's first name before out of respect for her age, but respect flew away on a frantic wing. She jerked her chin up. "You may be a little confused as you've contradicted yourself. Either I enchanted your son, or I'm not a witch. I can't be both."

Cool air replaced the intimacy she'd shared with Stuart a moment before as he took a small step back, his distaste palpable. It couldn't be helped if the man didn't like witches, but a worm of regret wriggled through her.

"It's just not my thing." She flashed him an apologetic smile, but his features remained cool until the desire to give a deeper explanation hung between them. People were wary of witches, whether or not they believed them capable of casting spells as Nancy had proved. With a careless shrug, Ruth stepped back out of the small circle the three of them formed, convinced the attraction between her and Stuart, so thick in the air just moments before, only lived in her imagination. She spread her hands, amused at the quick jerk of Nancy's head as if she thought Ruth was about to cast a spell on her.

"They go wrong. My spells. I haven't tried for years. Too much bad happened."

He raised his chin in a small acknowledgment, but his gaze never faltered. "You're a witch."

More an accusation than a question, Ruth's stomach clenched to remind her of her poor night and the vague, uneasy dreams winding through her disturbed sleep. She licked her parched lips and gave a quick glance around to see who else may have overheard their conversation, aware of the superior lift of Nancy's chin as she gloated. No one else paid any attention in the hustle and bustle of the busy dock.

Stuart's attention never wavered from her as he let the coolness of his gaze sweep over her in a wave which sent an icy tingle up her spine.

Not everyone was at ease about Nana and her being witches. All the islanders knew, of course. They came to Nana for tarot readings and small, harmless spells, as did the tourists. Most of the visitors thought of it as trickery, a little fun. Take a potion, weave a spell. Go back to the mainland and laugh about the quaint little old lady who believed she was a witch.

What none of them knew, would never know, was the extent of Clarisse's abilities.

Ruth forced another smile as her jaw clenched while she refused to give in to the temptation to apologize. She swiped her manic curls back from her forehead and side-stepped him, so she no longer had to look into his inquisitive face.

"I'll run along now. I need to get our supper in the fridge." She lifted the fish to indicate what she meant and swung her raffia basket full of vegetables.

"Ruth?"

She paused, turned her head so she could face him once more while Nancy's gaze sharpened with interest and the older woman stepped a little closer. "Yes?"

"Perhaps we'll talk later."

"I'm sure we will, but right now I have work to do."

She put a bounce in her step, so no-one would know about the sick churn of her stomach.

Irritated with her own stupidity, Ruth snapped her spine straight. She should never have allowed her mind to weave a little romance into their encounters. The man was beyond beautiful with his intense gray stare and sculptured lips. She'd enjoyed the touch of his hands on her, would have liked a little more contact. She'd even thought her interest had been reciprocated. What a fool. She'd failed to consider most people were still scared of the idea of a witch.

With a little groan of embarrassment, she kept her chin up and her head determinedly facing forward.

He hadn't seemed the sort to run scared, but he'd certainly stepped back as soon as the word *witch* had been associated with her. She'd had it all her life, the wariness all the islanders exuded. The only place she'd never suffered had been when she'd attended Edinburgh University, where she'd deliberately kept her heritage a secret.

As sexy as the cowboy was, she'd known when he realized the truth, it would be her who got hurt. Her who would bear the brunt of disappointment as yet another man turned from her, afraid of her supposed powers. Useless, pathetic powers.

Determined not to allow them to see how upset she was, she swung the basket a little too hard and suffered for it when it cracked against the back of her knee, almost sending her to the floor in a heap. There was no laughter from behind her, but she refused to turn just in case they watched her.

>»»•««<

The coincidence was too much. How could he have landed on the island and walked straight into the shop and later the house of two supposed witches?

Of course, he'd found his fair share of impostors and con artists during his time as an investigative reporter of the paranormal.

He'd made it his life's ambition to strip each and every one of them of their fraudulent cloaks and expose them, so the world could stop being deceived by them.

Shocked at how many people were willing to be misled, he'd witnessed those who desperately sought out reassurances that were simply not true. They settled because they wanted the comfort, but when the comfort was a blatant ruse for some charlatan to profit from another person's desperation, he couldn't accept it.

He hated it.

He'd never found anyone he'd ever been entirely convinced was genuine.

Yet he knew they existed. On countless occasions, he'd come across people, who, although they had no significant power, they seemed genuine about offering assistance to those in need. The relief they offered was worth far more than the paltry coins they asked for in exchange. Those, he left alone. Sometimes their spirituality offered enough to others, but he wasn't looking for that.

So, he continued his quest. Each assignment scraped a little more at his hope and rolled his cynicism into a hard ball which stuck at the back of his throat.

Fear and determination still drove him forward, but he'd started to believe he would never find what he searched for.

Time was running out. For him; for his brother; for his two young nephews.

Stuart picked up the rucksack he'd placed on the ground when he'd approached Ruth. The other woman's aggression had been tangible, and he'd had a brief moment when he wondered if she'd been about to strike Ruth. Her color had certainly been an unhealthy puce when he approached, but by the look on Ruth's face, she'd pretty much handled the situation.

With a casual move, Stuart slung the rucksack over his shoulder. "Keep away from her."

He turned his attention back to the squat little woman, and in lieu of talking, he raised his eyebrows.

"Ruth. Keep away from her. She'll bewitch you. She bewitched my son, and he's never been the same since. We had to send him to Glasgow to get away from the power she held over him."

He leaned closer to the woman to listen carefully to her words through the thick Scottish brogue. Unlike Ruth's gentle cadence, this woman's was much harsher and more difficult to understand.

"Thank you. I'll bear it in mind."

"She may deny her inheritance, but some believe she's far more powerful than her own nana. She just hasn't let her powers come forth yet."

"I see. Thank you for your information."

Stuart gave her a dismissive nod before he turned to make his way toward the gift shop. Most of what he'd heard from the locals had been about Clarisse's magical skills, very few had spoken of anything else other than some interesting tales of mermaids and selkies. Strange that no one else had mentioned Ruth's abilities or lack thereof. No one other than Nancy had spoken of her.

Perhaps he should take Clarisse up on her offer, determine how skilled she really was. At least spend some time with her to garner some insight into the way she worked.

Typical of the mystical shops he visited, a sweet little bell chimed as he let himself in. He glanced around at the over-full shop, bulging with tourists. Their excited babble drowned out any thoughts he had of starting his investigations, and he backed his way out again. It could wait. Perhaps Clarisse would oblige him with a tarot reading after dinner at the old mansion. Thick with atmosphere, it provided the ideal place for conjuring magic.

He turned to make his way back to the house. Jet lag had woken him early, and he'd had a good start to his research, fascinated with the old boys who'd returned from their fishing expeditions, but tiredness dulled his brain and dragged at his legs. The weight of them slowed his pace. He'd benefit from a short catnap before he wrote up his notes.

In the absence of anything magical apart from the selkie tales, Stuart let his attention wander as he idled his way through the village until he found himself at the start of the dirt track leading to the house. The weak sunshine did little to warm him, but the wind had dropped from the previous day, the cold no longer bit bone deep. He'd known before he arrived it wouldn't be warm. The Inner Hebrides were renowned for their winds and cooler climes, although they didn't seem to suffer from the frosts of the Highlands. Still, he was used to warmer temperatures. Zambia had almost melted the skin from his bones.

A wave of tiredness swept over him as he rounded the corner of the house and came to a standstill.

She was there. The lush grass under her naked feet, the brilliant sparkle of sunshine on the water behind her almost blinded him, while the white-streaked sky framed her dark beauty. Her wild locks churned in the wind as she fought the sheet she attempted to put on the line until she could pin it down with wooden pegs.

Unable to tear his eyes from her willowy form, he waited while his heart thundered and his pulse raced.

The brightness of the day just served to make her stand out against her background as she bent to retrieve a pillowcase. Her struggle far less than before, she bent once more, flicked out the last pillowcase and punched the pegs onto it to tether it to the line.

Fascinated, Stuart crossed his arms over his chest and squinted against the glare of the sun reflecting off the water. Pleasure rippled through him at the simplicity of her actions, the fluidity of her moves. Somewhere in his hesitant thought process, he recognized the surge of passion which had his blood thundering through his veins. The swift rush of it filled his ears until he could hear nothing. He couldn't attribute it to jetlag, but to the undeniable beauty of the woman who drew him to her with her quick, efficient moves.

As the wind whipped her long hair over her shoulder and she turned in his direction, she froze at the sight of him. Her green gaze glowed from a face as pale as porcelain.

Storm clouds rolled in thick and furious behind her to blot out the brightness of the day. The wind lashed at her long, dull brown dress and made a vicious grab at her hair. Stuart's stomach lurched in confusion and his vision tunneled to narrow in on the apparition before him. Water churned thick and fetid, rising over her ankles to drag at the material of her dress.

Her gaze entranced him while she reached out a ponderous hand, ragged nails blackened with dirt clawed the air in an entreaty. Emerald eyes pleaded with him as they swamped with tears. Her full lips quivered while she begged without words for his help and wrenched at a little part of his consciousness like a memory dredged from deep within.

Dizzy, he raised a hand to his forehead and blinked, convinced he'd lost his mind. He sucked in a deep breath and fought the confusion, pushing back on the darkness.

"Stuart?"

The picture flashed negative in his mind's eye followed by a blaze of vibrant green grass, bright sparkles on the white spume of the sea, and a clear azure sky.

Tempted to shake himself, he ducked his head to stare at his feet as a wave of nausea struck him. It had to be jetlag. There was no other explanation. While he hauled in another lifesaving breath, powerless to stop her move toward him, he swayed on his feet. Perhaps all he needed was to rest in a darkened room, rid himself of the powerful vision still vivid in his mind.

"Stuart? Are you all right?"

Not yet ready for her, he raised his head, his pulse raced fast and erratic.

He wanted to ask her how she'd done it, but the look of genuine concern made him falter.

Whatever she'd done to him, it had left his mind in a pure fog and evaporated his ability to speak. He raked his gaze over her with narrowed eyes and felt the ground solidify beneath his feet again. "I'm fine." His voice thick and rusty, he gave a small cough to clear his throat.

"Are you sure? You've gone very pale." She reached out one elegant hand, clean nails clipped square, and touched her cool fingers to his cheek. He may look pale to her, but fiery heat rushed to his face, to scorch his skin so only the gentle graze of her touch could cool it.

With no thought to his intent, he pressed his hand against hers to hold it against the blaze of his skin. Her fingers gave an almost imperceptible spasm, but instead of removing them, she brought her other hand up to cradle his face.

Lost in the misty depths of her sea green contemplation, Stuart took one of her dainty hands in his and placed a kiss in her palm.

She curled her fingers inward and tucked the kiss inside, warming his heart with the simple action.

Time slowed down so when he dipped his head, he knew without a doubt in his mind he was about to kiss her sweet, lush mouth, which curved in secret invitation.

So secret, it appeared Ruth had no idea of his intention as she dropped her light hold on him and stepped back.

"I think you should sit down before you fall." She gave a flick of her fingers in an airy wave at the picnic table and bench, but her accent had thickened through the husky tones of her voice. "I'll make you a cup of tea."

She was gone. In the blink of an eye, she disappeared. Bereft he gazed after her.

He dipped his fingers into his pocket and drew out a hair elastic, then scraped his hair back from his face and tethered it at the nape of his neck. The fresh wind cooled his skin, and he closed his eyes, tipped his head back, and breathed in the scent of the ocean. The sound of it filled his head and brought peace back to him.

What had she done?

He opened his eyes to stare up at the cloudless sky.

He strode over to the small picnic table, flipped his notebook out of his back pocket onto the table before he sat on the wooden bench. Consumed by the thoughts racing through his head, he grabbed the pencil from his shirt pocket and started to write.

Questions.

How did she implant the vision of herself in my head?

How did the sky become so black, so fast?

Where did the storm clouds come from, just to disappear as rapidly?

Why did Ruth's eyes glow an ethereal green?

What era did her dress come from?

Had hypnosis been used?

Determined to push aside the distraction of her beauty, he rubbed his fingers over his lips, flipped over a couple of pages and started to sketch with frantic lines. He concentrated on the style of dress before it faded from his memory, shading it in with fast, rough strokes of the pencil. It had to be as accurate as possible so he could research it.

While his fingers were occupied, he mulled his first question: how had Ruth managed to conjure the image in his mind? The one that refused to leave. Each time he blinked he could still picture the woman. Ruth, but not Ruth.

"I've brought you a cup of tea." Her silky voice soothed him, and he raised his head as she placed a tray laden with fine china and cookies. "Perhaps a biscuit will make you feel a little stronger. You turned waxen." She slipped onto the bench on the opposite side of the table, pushed up her sleeves, and reached for the teapot.

He skimmed his gaze over her finely woven blue woolen sweater and studied her as she concentrated on pouring the tea.

Her untamed curls danced around her head in the light breeze. She glanced up, a flicker of surprise lit her face before she handed over the teacup with a slight rattle against its saucer. Aware he'd made her feel awkward with his intense scrutiny, he couldn't persuade himself to look away. Ruth wasn't quite the same as the image in his head. She was far more beautiful.

He reached out. His hands too big against the fragile china. As frail as eggshells, he was quick to place it on the table in front of him. When she offered him the cookies, he took one.

"Did you bake them yourself?" They looked homemade.

"Nana did before she left this morning."

The texture melted in his mouth as he bit into it. "Nice cookies."

"Biscuits."

He smiled at her correction, but in his mind, they were cookies. Biscuits were a whole different thing where he came from, and he'd eat them with thick, meaty gravy.

"I don't normally drink tea."

She froze, her own cookie halfway to her mouth. "I'm sorry. I never thought. Tea's very good for you if you're not feeling well."

"I'm fine, but coffee's my drink of choice."

She placed the little cookie down on her plate and wiped her fingers against her pale jeans in a self-conscious move. "I'm sorry. I never thought to ask. We don't have any coffee in the house. Nana and I only drink tea." She rolled her lips inward, and guilt washed over him while the insult he'd dealt her lay between them. He realized just how rude he sounded.

"It doesn't matter." He picked up the delicate cup, smiled, and took a large mouthful of tea to pacify her. The strong, smoky flavor hit his taste buds. His throat spasmed and he gulped at the liquid, desperate to move it on before it burned his throat at the same time as he reached for the cookie again. Without wanting to appear greedy, he rammed in as much of the cookie as he could to disguise the foul flavor of the tea. "I'm good with tea."

"I'll get you some coffee. They'll have had some delivered, although I'm not sure how much choice we'll have as it's not a popular drink here."

"It's okay. I'll be fine with tea." He stared into the cup. At least she'd given him a small one. "I'm sure it's an acquired taste." He swigged back the rest of it. His eyes watered, but he forced it down and cracked another smile as he placed the empty cup back onto the saucer with a clip before he shoved the rest of the cookie into his mouth.

Ruth looked as if she was about to say more, but she picked up her own cup and took a delicate sip. Her eyes closed while a brief flicker of pleasure crossed her pretty features. If anything could persuade him of the benefits of tea, her perfect expression could.

The sun kissed her pale features and emphasized the smattering of golden freckles across her nose and cheeks. When she opened her eyes, he had to resist the temptation to fall into the ocean depths of them.

Her mouth curved into a smile and Stuart's attention was drawn to the deep cut of her cupid's bow. His mind hazed over, hypnotized by her presence. Overwhelmed by the quick rush of adrenaline, Stuart stared at her lips, inclined to take a taste of them and find out whether they were as delicious as they appeared.

She leaned in, and he moved to meet her halfway, his breath caught in the back of his throat as she gave an answering gasp.

"Oh my goodness, did you draw this?"

Before he could recover, she'd slipped the notebook from beside him and pulled it toward her, turning it so she could study the picture he'd drawn of her.

"Oh, but you're very talented." The mellow voice and soft brogue smoothed away the fizzle of irritation at being thwarted once more. He almost laughed. He thought she'd been going to kiss him. Again. She was too much of a temptation, but it was evident she had no idea what effect she had on him. Despite her untamed beauty, her sweet innocence warned him to stay away.

Mad curls slipped over her shoulder to obscure the rounded curve of her cheek. Stuart reached out to push them back. But before his fingers could touch her, she whipped up her head and stared at him, her green gaze turning darker.

"What made you draw this? It looks like me, but it's not."

The cynical twist of his mind sneaked through, and he dropped his raised hand and leaned his elbows against the wooden table. Clever lady. Perhaps his earlier thought of hypnosis was right.

"It just came to mind earlier when I saw you hanging out the washing. It conjured a vision of an old-fashioned era."

Her alabaster skin flushed to the roots of her black hair, and the pulse at the base of her throat fluttered.

"I thought you were a writer, not an artist."

"I am a writer. This is just a sketch. I often use them in my work. It helps me visualize what I want to write."

"Oh." She glanced down again, to study the drawing in front of her with such intensity he wondered if she'd forgotten he was there.

She clawed her hair back and twined her long fingers through it as if they had a hope of containing it. "It's amazing. Perhaps you should turn professional."

"I prefer to write."

Ruth pushed the notepad back toward him and reached out for her cup of tea once more. "What do you write?"

"Paranormal."

There was no evidence of surprise in her direct gaze, which meant people had already talked about the questions he'd asked. Small town folk were quick to get word out, and Nancy had mentioned he wrote the weird.

"Fact or fiction?"

He sputtered out a laugh. "Paranormal is only ever fiction."

Her eyebrows tweaked downward. "Do you think so? You don't believe strange things happen?"

"I do."

"Sometimes there's no explanation for certain powers and abilities."

"There's always an explanation."

"What if there's not? Have you never heard of anything which defies explanation?"

"Like you being a witch?" The fog in his brain cleared with a rapidness he could hardly attribute to the beneficial effects of the tea, but more to the subject matter which had him intrigued.

She shuffled on the hard, wooden seat and reached for a cookie, took a nibble.

"I'm not much of a witch."

But she didn't deny she was a witch. Interesting. Did she believe she was? Or did she want him to believe she was?

"What makes you say that?"

"Because any magic I try goes wrong."

"So the toad-like lady inferred." Pleased to coax a smile from her, he leaned in. "In what way does your magic go wrong?"

"Well, for example," She placed her cookie back on the dainty plate, lifted her hand and clicked her thumb against her forefinger. A tiny blue flame like a pilot light flickered from the end of her thumb.

A cheap parlor trick he'd seen many times before. She'd just come from the kitchen where she'd had plenty of opportunity to prepare the little stunt, but he'd humor her in her obvious attempt to entertain him. Perhaps she was just like all the others. Maybe she craved the attention she could get for her clever little skills, but the difference was, she was bashful, and perhaps that's what worked. Maybe it gained her more attention, rather than less. After all, Nancy's wariness had been palpable, despite her protestations about Ruth's lack of skill.

Stuart reached out to take hold of her hand, moving closer to peer at the end of her thumb. The moment his fingers encircled her wrist, an electric fission buzzed through his skin. The nerves in his hand contracted and tightened in spasms. The tiny blue flame leaped up, burst into a brilliant inferno which flashed golden for a split second before it shot skyward, close enough to singe his eyebrows. He dropped his grip on her and flung himself back away from the blaze. He swiped at the burn on his eyebrows, while he gasped for breath as the heat seared his skin. Before he could draw in another lungful of oxygen, a deluge of cold liquid slapped him in the face.

"What the fuck…?"

"Are you okay?" She always seemed to be asking him if he was all right. "I'm so sorry, so terribly sorry." She swiped at his face with fingers not quite as delicate as they appeared. With frenzied movements, she brushed away the droplets of milk as it dripped from his hair, the cold slide of it running down the side of his nose.

A tea towel replaced her frantic fingers as she dabbed at this face with ferocious enthusiasm. He squinted up at her, not knowing whether to laugh or run screaming from the woman. It was madness, sheer madness.

"Stop, Ruth. Stop."

She halted with a suddenness that left him speechless, her concerned eyes held the glint of tears, and she twisted her hands together until her knuckles turned white.

The speed with which she'd launched herself around the table to get to him surprised him. It seemed slender and willowy was also quick and agile.

He reached out with both hands and grasped her fingers to still the infernal twist of them. "It's okay. I'm fine. There's no damage." He hoped to God there wasn't. He couldn't tell if she'd scorched his eyebrows from his face. He poked out his tongue to catch a drop of milk at the corner of his mouth. At least it tasted better than the tea.

With a helpless look, she held still while he peered up at her. And tried for humor. "Do I have any eyebrows left?"

She raised her hand, stroked one fingertip along the line of his brow, a twist of regret in her shy smile.

"You do, but a millimeter closer and you could have lost them altogether."

The stench of her fireball still lingered, but he couldn't detect the scent of lighter fluid. He encircled her wrist with his fingers once more, careful this time to direct her thumb sideways so she couldn't repeat the action. There wasn't a mark on her thumb, nothing to indicate she'd just used it as a flame-thrower, no residue, not even a hint. He leaned in, sniffed, but there was no odor to her skin, just the soft coolness of it and a vague whiff of freesias.

The hot zap of passion had evaporated, but desire still simmered low in his belly, ready to sear her again, given half the chance. A chance he was reluctant to take until he had a few more answers. She may be beautiful, but he wasn't about to let her distract him.

"How did you do it?"

She withdrew her hand from his grasp and stepped back to the bench. She slid in behind the table and picked up the pot of tea to refill his cup. She dipped her head to avoid his scrutiny—her beautiful lips gave a tiny downturn at the corners.

"I told you I was no good. Nothing ever goes right with my magic."

He narrowed his gaze to study her. Guileless, she poured his tea. Did she really believe she was capable of magic?

"You should see what Nana can do." She offered the cup to him, and he resigned himself to having to drink more of the foul brew.

She leaned forward and plopped two sugar cubes into his cup, and handed him a teaspoon. "You may find it more palatable like this."

He took a wary sip. Sweet nectar coated his tongue. How the hell had two sugar lumps transformed the flavor from arsenic to ambrosia? He frowned at her over the rim of his teacup while he took another sample of his tea. Was this another trick? She gave a careless shrug and turned back to pick up her long-ago abandoned cookie.

He held the little teacup in the palm of his hand to let the warmth seep through his skin. "So tell me, what can your nana do?"

Her wide smile brightened to illuminate her face with enthusiasm and left him wondering whether she'd experienced any of the sharp teeth of desire that had bitten him. From her demeanor, there was no hint, but he'd seen the shy looks, and he wasn't mistaken about the simmering heat over her skin when he held her.

"Her magic is supreme."

He leaned forward to study the conviction in her gaze, but his cynicism got the better of him. "She sells it?"

Doubt flashed across Ruth's face, and he knew his tone had been one of disapproval. When he spoke with people about the art, he kept his tone even and non-judgmental, but there was something about this woman that stripped him of his caution.

She swallowed some tea, her lips tightened. "Aye, she sells it. Along with her potions and her crystals from her gift shop. You sell your books, I assume?" One slim black eyebrow arched, and he accepted the challenge, was happy to rise to it.

"Yes, I do, but it's different."

"It's no different." She shot back. "There's no difference between selling your talent or your gift. You write a book, people presumably buy it, read it, enjoy it, or not as the case may be."

Offended by her implication his writing may be no good, a little spark of irritation lit in his stomach. "But what if you sell false hope?"

"*You* sell fantasy."

He didn't correct her. He based all his work on reality. He didn't write fiction, he wrote cold, hard facts about cheats and liars, but she wasn't to know, and he wanted to get his point across. "People understand it's not real."

"Not necessarily. People believe what they want to believe. If your written word captures their imagination to such an extent, then they live in your world, the one you have created for them for the expanse of time while they're reading your story. When the story is over, they don't necessarily leave it behind. It can be implanted in their memory." Impassioned, Ruth stabbed her finger at him. "Something *you* created could have captured them for all time, changed their lives. *You* may have given them hope. Not *false* hope. Something you created may have an effect, changed someone's way of thinking. Inspired them."

Her fervent speech tugged at his emotions, but it wasn't him who inspired people. It wasn't his job to fill them with hope. His job was to crush the liars, the deceivers. To expose them to the world and stop them from taking advantage of the weak of mind, the frail of spirit and those desperate for succor that would never come. He protected. Not inspired. His duty was a serious business.

He gave a wry smile and glanced down at the table, reached for another cookie, and took a bite. "People know when they buy a book they're buying a fantasy. It's different," he insisted, although his argument didn't hold as much weight as it had a moment before.

"No." Her hair bounced when she shook her head, her eyes wide with conviction. He wanted to reach out, take a curl and wrap it around his finger, watch it twine itself until it took possession of him. "Nana sells hope. People know she does too. She doesn't deceive anyone. They know what they come for. She doesn't tell lies."

From the stubborn lift of her chin, he'd not convince her otherwise. Her passion didn't make her less attractive. Instead, it sparked a hot ball of desire deep in his belly. "What does she do?"

"Tarot cards. Has she offered to conduct a reading for you yet?"

"Yes, she did, but I declined." He shrugged. "She told me perhaps we'd do it another time."

Ruth's eyebrows twitched upward. "Okay." She picked up her own cookie, nibbled at it. "She has the power to heal."

He didn't believe it for an instant, but he kept his features neutral. He'd listen to what she had to say about Clarisse's powers, and if he continued to interject with cynical questions, there was a risk she would withdraw. He needed to allow her to talk about her grandmother's gifts. She believed in them. He desperately wanted to, but experience and the cold slap of reality held him back.

"People come from a long way for her help. She can't stop someone from dying. It isn't possible. The three fates wouldn't allow that kind of intervention, and in any case, if it was possible, governments would have harvested her power and others like her long before now."

Stuart took another taste of his tea. Perhaps he could tolerate it.

"You believe there are others like your nana?" He smiled at her over the rim of his delicate teacup, an invitation for her to declare she was just like Clarisse.

"Of course there are. Many."

She really believed it. She was sold on the whole witches' power and fates. She bought into the whole shebang. God, so did he. He knew it existed. He just had to find the proof.

"She uses aura readings." Ruth shuffled forward, intent once again. She reached out her hand as though she was about to touch him, but hovered her palm just over the back of his hand. "Aura readings make use of energies. She lays her hand on people's heads."

He nodded. He'd heard of it, many times, but never witnessed a true healing.

Whether the power of suggestion was responsible, or the heat from her fingers, Stuart's skin tingled, and warmth flowed from the back of his hand, up his arm. Determined to ignore the sensation, he held her gaze with his own. "What about love potions?"

Ruth's emerald eyes widened, her thick black lashes gave an almost imperceptible flutter before she removed her hand. "It's a sticky area." She gave a light shrug and smiled, her full lips tempted him to lean in and capture them with his. "Nana refuses to do love spells. It's not something many witches would do these days."

He could tell her there were many he'd met who did just that.

"You can't bend another's will to suit one person. Very dangerous. Again, it works against the fates, not with them. No. She wouldn't entertain such a dangerous pursuit. The Wiccan rede is to harm none." She fluttered her fingers. "'An Ye Harm None, Do What Ye Will.'"

The fine shudder she gave stippled her arms in goosebumps. Ruth glanced away, over the sandy bay, across the sea. Her voice, when it came, was vague and distant. "No one can force another to love them. It's a terrible violation."

Reluctant to lose her, he turned his hand over from where it rested on the table near hers and enveloped her long-fingered elegance in his palm.

She jerked her head around to face him as though he'd disturbed a deep sleep. Her eyes darkened to jade as she stared at him for a long moment before she visibly gave herself a shake.

"It's the same with curses. She won't ever direct them at a living being. After all, we believe in the rule of three. You get back three times what you dish out."

It seemed like the infamous witch was reluctant to use many of her powers. He'd met so many keen to show off their abilities and it surprised him Clarisse should be so reticent.

A thought occurred. If Ruth was working her way through the thirteen powers of the witch, then at some point, she had to have knowledge of what had occurred earlier.

"What about command of the weather?"

"Och, aye. She can do it all right, but weather's a dangerous and temperamental beastie to deal with. We've had appalling weather for the past three summers. There's nothing Nana can do to help, she's been asked by many an islander to intervene, but the weather is fickle, and interference with it can have far-reaching consequences."

Amazed by her convictions, Stuart leaned in to watch the expressions flit across her face. She'd left her hand under his, and the cool fragility of it turned warm with their contact. Her eyes sparkled with interest, and her fine mouth tilted up at both edges in a tentative smile. It wasn't Nana's powers he was interested in so much as Ruth's. Nana was at the gift shop. Was it possible she could have invoked any kind of image or hallucination from there? He doubted it.

Besides, he smiled at the lovely woman opposite as she continued to speak, Ruth's powers were on a different level. He dealt with the strongest power of all, the power of attraction. Unsure whether she was aware of how beautiful she was in a wild, untamed fashion, Stuart skimmed the pad of his thumb over the fine skin of her hand and repressed a smile as her voice stuttered for a moment before she continued as though it had never happened. But her pupils dilated, her emerald eyes darkened. Yes, she was damned well aware of him. He'd known from the very first moment they met when she'd gazed into his face with such intensity in her cat-like stare.

Her other hand gave a nervous flutter as she spoke of astrology, but she made no attempt to remove the one he already held captive in his.

He stroked again. Her voice stilled. Her generous lips parted. The pull of invitation too hard to resist.

Careful not to spook her, he raised his hand to brush aside the wanton curls from her cheek. They sprang around his hand, twining themselves between his fingers. He used them to his benefit and gave a gentle tug to persuade her closer, the mild ache in his chest spread until he knew if he didn't kiss her, he would go mad.

The black of her pupils expanded to fill the feline tilt of her eyes. He never took his gaze from her until the moment he touched his lips to hers. He closed his eyes and gave himself over to all his senses.

He sipped the sweet honeysuckle from her soft lips, indulged in her perfection, and lost himself in her heady scent. The downy hair at the nape of her neck coiled about his fingers and imprisoned him while he made his tender investigation.

He touched the tip of his tongue to her closed lips. A deep moan broke free as she opened for him, allowing him access. The inside of her mouth tasted like nectar.

Warm desire deepened in his belly to spread like wildfire through his veins, setting his pulse alight, so the gentle lap of surf at the nearby cove filled his head.

His mind went blank as desire, deep and dangerous whipped through him to make him forget. Forget everything. Who he was. Why he was there. He dove deep, tangling his tongue with hers to savor her rich taste. Desperate for more, he staggered to his feet, reached over the small table and snaked an arm around her waist to hoist her over onto his lap as he slapped back down on the bench.

Her screech reverberated through his mouth to pierce not only his ears but fry his brain.

He jerked back, breath hissing through his lungs as he took in her glazed expression and flushed cheeks. She'd damned near deafened him.

"I'm sorry, did I hurt you?" He needed to ask even though all he wanted to do was drag her back and kiss her blind. He swept a tender hand across her forehead and watched with fascination as her curls bounced straight back in wild abandon.

Her lips parted, and he dipped his gaze down to stare at her lush mouth, swollen from his desperate kiss. It curved up at the edges tempting him to haul her back into his arms again and ignore any protest.

"It's just the two broken ribs."

Laughter stuck in his throat as she rose from the bench with an unhurried, elegance. She pushed her hair over her shoulder to no avail as it sprang back again and coaxed a smile from him. She leaned in. Head still in a spin, he waited for her to climb into his lap. Disappointment warred inside him as she reached for his empty cup and stacked it with hers on the tray. She swiped the whole lot up in a quick, efficient move and twirled in the direction of the house, calling over her shoulder. "It was a lovely interlude. Thank you, but I need to get back to work now before Nana comes looking for me with a stick in her hand to beat me for my laziness."

Astounded by her careless abandonment of him, Stuart gaped at her receding form. Bloody hell if she'd glanced back, she would have thought she'd just left the village idiot rocking in a corner.

Interlude! It hadn't been an interlude for him. It had been a screamingly passionate moment which she'd missed.

The woman was oblivious of the effect she'd had on him, or he hadn't moved her in the least. Her casual saunter out of sight indicated the latter, but he was pretty damned sure her lips had been as keen as his when he'd kissed her.

He stared at the back door of the house where she'd disappeared. Was she always as casual with her kisses? The woman at the dock said Ruth bewitched her son. Maybe the young man wasn't the only one she'd enchanted, but perhaps it had less to do with her being a witch and more with how free she was with her favors. A woman with such stunning good looks wouldn't find it hard to entice men.

He raised a clenched hand and scrubbed the taste of her from his mouth. He didn't need the distraction, no matter how beautiful and free-spirited she was. He had a purpose, and if he wasn't careful, time would run out. Perhaps he'd had a lucky escape because once caught by her enchanting wiles he'd be hard-pressed to get on with the job at hand.

He surged to his feet and swiped up his pad and pencil. He needed to ask more questions in the village, get down to the nitty-gritty of things and see if this so-called witch had any real kind of power.

With one last glance over his shoulder, Stuart shook off the wrench of regret and made his way to the gift shop to investigate Clarisse.

»»»•«««

Spaghetti legs was the only clear thought that came to mind while Ruth leaned weak and limpid against the kitchen door. The man had turned every bone to jelly leaving her in a liquefied pool of overheated wax.

Oh boy, could he kiss? She'd never been kissed like that in her life, and she'd had a few good kisses. This was one to write home about. The man had seared her soul with the mere touch of his lips on hers, but when he'd slipped his tongue inside her mouth, the temptation to drag him upstairs to her bed had almost gotten the better of her.

She wasn't one to drop her panties in the blink of an eye. If anything, she erred on the side of caution. She'd not had many relationships. One, while she was at university, couldn't be considered excessive. Only one since, but he'd long left the island with neither of them having any regrets. Her main problem had always been the fear they showed once they knew she was a witch. The hurt she suffered at their withdrawal. But Stuart knew she was a witch. She'd sensed the recoil, the doubt mixed with passion. His little whip of insult about his writing had amused her.

Ruth drew in a shaky breath and pushed herself away from the door so she could place the tray on the kitchen top before she dropped it.

If it hadn't been for the sharp jab in her ribs as he'd dragged her toward him over the wooden bench, she may never have made it up to her bedroom. The invitation of the lush green grass may have been too much and the distance to the house too far.

Breathless, she glanced out of the window, her heart beating too fast as she watched Stuart gain his feet. Would he come after her? The secret thrill of it scorched through her veins.

He raised his head and stared at the house for a long moment while the pulse of hope thrummed in the base of her throat. Another breath hitched in. What would she do? She barely knew him. He'd only arrived the night before. She stuttered out a laugh, what would he think if she wrenched open the oak door and flung herself down the garden path at him? She held her jittery stomach with both hands. She could rip his clothes off him and roll naked in the cool, green grass.

Would he think her a slut?

The islanders would. If they heard about it. Which they would. Everyone knew each other's business on the island. Why wouldn't they?

She preferred the anonymity of the mainland. The privacy she longed for was never available on the island. She couldn't have a clandestine affair without it being common knowledge. She'd not even had a mild flirtation with Nancy's son when she'd been accused of witchcraft. In fact, she'd never even kissed him. She wouldn't have dreamed of kissing him. He'd been a sloth of a spotty teenager back then, and by all accounts, there'd been no vast improvement as he'd reached maturity.

She couldn't imagine her and Stuart having a clandestine affair, more a torrid, tumbling one if the passion in his expression and the fire in her blood was any kind of measure. But she wasn't sure an affair would be enough for her and the fear of how much more she wanted, kept her there.

She blew out a breath before she peeped out of the window again, shamed by the disappointment that welled up as Stuart turned and strode off toward the shore. It would have been quicker to get to the village if he'd passed the house, and she may have been tempted to open the door and lean with feigned casualness against the frame as he walked by. He may have stopped to indulge in another kiss. She could have invited him upstairs.

The opportunity slipped by as he disappeared from view.

Chapter Three

The chance to kiss the little witch again hadn't presented itself, nor had he gone out of his way to search her out. Instead, Stuart spent a couple of days with the islanders as he coaxed stories of the supernatural from them. Not much coaxing was required as most of them were all too happy to impart their stories. Tales passed down through generations, predominantly of water spirits, kelpies, mermaids and selkies, sea monsters and loch monsters. Most of which was to be expected, he guessed, on an island with little else to concentrate on.

Sea-mists and storms played their part in the mysterious and mythical beings. Many of the stories were of the same creatures, with a different embellishment. Most of them were folklore he could have researched on the Internet, but the fascination with their wonderful accents and animated versions kept him occupied for more time than it should have. Some of the stories from the older folk almost required a translator as they slipped from time to time into the Gaelic which more than half the islanders spoke as a matter of everyday life. In deference to his American accent, many of them slowed their speech and enunciated in English when they remembered, or when he prompted them.

Fascinated by the information they plied him with, his interest lay in witchcraft, but none of the islanders had tales to tell other than of Ruth's sweet old nana who used her herbalism and spiritual abilities to aid the islanders and entertain the visitors. She couldn't be classified as a dark shadow on the earth. None of them had anything to say about Ruth, nor were any of her abilities ever raised, even though he tried to edge a couple of folks around to the subject of her.

Disappointment sneaked its way through his initial excitement to damp it down. He'd expected far more. From the research he'd conducted before he'd arrived, he'd expected to meet a fierce and powerful witch on the island. She alone held the key to what he searched for. The evidence he'd gathered for years, researched, studied, poured over, all indicated this was where he would find her.

He glanced out of the window to watch the sun shimmer over the calm sea, tempted to sit and daydream, but he had work to do. Time was against him and doubt gripped his gut. What if he was wrong?

What the hell did he do? He'd put every last bit of hope into his research.

He picked up the now empty package the postman had dropped off earlier. It had taken far longer to get to him than he'd anticipated while it went through customs. He hadn't been able to risk smuggling it out of Africa, but he'd put his faith in his find, knowing if he'd made a mistake it would cost his brother his life. His investigations to break the family curse and end the death of generations of men in his family had led him there. Whether or not he'd taken the wrong avenue was yet to be established.

Frustrated, Stuart crushed the cardboard in his hands, aimed it at the black waste bin under his desk, and missed. With a huff of disgust, he straightened. He needed to focus, not crawl under furniture to tidy up.

Stuart slipped the file off his desk and flopped onto the bed. He flicked the pages over one by one but found no point in re-triangulating his location. He'd already made his calculations a dozen times before he'd arrived there and a dozen more since. Yet still, he came up with the same island, the same answer. The location was right.

He'd tried to delve deeper into the history of the island, but according to the locals, there'd only been one family of witches. Clarisse, her daughter Claire, and Ruth. Claire had long since died, but he quashed the grinding doubt she'd been the one. He refused to believe the possibility. If she had been, then his brother's life was over just as surely as hers. It meant the next generation, his nephews, would have to pursue the resolution to the curse. The only way it would happen was if Ruth gave birth to the next witch.

He surged to his feet, ripped the tie from his hair and paced closer to the window to stare out over the ocean. If he squinted, he could see the next island on the horizon, almost close enough to swim to. Although he'd probably die of hypothermia if he attempted it, judging from the ice-cold of the water he'd experienced a few days before. It had taken his feet until mid-afternoon to warm through again after he'd paddled in the surf.

What if he'd made a mistake and the witch was there? On the next island, or the one closer inland? He leaned his forehead against the cool windowpane and closed his eyes while he rid himself of the insistent doubt.

He wasn't wrong, but it meant he only had one choice. The old lady. Clarisse.

With a rough snort, he pushed himself away from the window again. She wasn't an all-powerful witch, and without further evidence, he was reluctant to do what was required to break the curse.

He broke out into a cold sweat.

He slid the top drawer open in the fragile antique table and removed the small wooden box he'd placed there together with a bundle of documents that had accompanied it. Documents he'd studied that afternoon as horror scraped across his nerve endings, and bile rose again in his throat.

He kept the key to the box on him at all times. He blew out a gusty breath while he flexed his fingers. Worn and aged, he needed to give the key a gentle jiggle in the lock before it scraped around in the barrel.

The resinous jade luster glowed up at him from the nephrite handle of the ancient knife, to remind Stuart of Ruth's deep green eyes. He touched his fingers to it, smoothed them along the glassy, polished surface of its perfection.

With a hard swallow, he took hold of the handle and raised the knife from the black velvet bed of the box, little shards of ice stabbed his gut with the new revelation the documents had brought him.

How was he supposed to plunge the blade deep into her heart? *With but one strike, straight and true.* His breath unsteady, he stroked his thumb over the handle. In his opinion, murder was still murder even to achieve the essential means to an end. He'd come this far. All his life had been focused on this point, and yet he hesitated. What if he was wrong? What if the entire research his family had conducted for generations proved inaccurate, and he was ultimately wrong?

Not only would it be murder, but murder of an innocent.

Torn apart by doubt, he stared at the yellowed documents. Disgusted by them. There was no proof Clarisse was a witch. She was just a kind old lady who happened to meddle a little in the occult, not a black-hearted witch re-born through generations.

Disgusted with himself, he replaced the knife and clipped shut the lid, irritated with the tiny key for refusing to turn this time.

Why couldn't it have been clearer?

In his naiveté, he'd expected to arrive on the island accompanied by thunderbolts and lightning to point the way straight to a diabolical fiend. Not an old lady, who the entire small population loved.

Despite the thunderbolts and lightning that had driven Ruth into his arms, there'd hardly been any other indication. Ever since the day he arrived, the weak rays of the sun had warmed the small island and filled it with light and hope.

He closed the drawer to block out the sight of the box. Dear God, what was he to do? He'd never expected to have to kill someone. In his ignorance, he'd thought he just needed to find the woman, and somehow, she'd have a solution, put it all right and break the curse with an elegant swipe of her little black wand.

Confused since his arrival, he needed to ground himself in reality, instead of wallowing in the mystical realms of the island. He needed to phone his brother.

He scrubbed his hands over his face in frustration, then stared at his cell phone. The service was appalling on the island, and he only had two bars on his cell, so it wouldn't be a clear phone call. Ian should be awake by now, but Stuart could never be quite sure as Ian's sleep pattern had become more erratic as his brother's health deteriorated. With the time difference, it should be about 8:00 am.

Stuart swiped a finger across the cell's screen, selected his brother's number and tapped his fingers while he waited for the line to connect. The distant buzz indicated it had started to ring at the other end.

His brother's gruff voice came over the line. "I'm still alive, but only just. I take it you haven't slain the dragon? Or better still, the witch."

Typical of his brother to use his acerbic humor to cover up his anxiety.

"You're not going to die, Ian. Not if I can help it."

"Have you found her?" Hope laced his brother's voice, and Stuart's heart grieved for the information he needed to impart.

"No. At least, there's a supposed witch here, but I'm not even sure she's as convincing as any of the previous old ladies I've exposed for fraud. She doesn't seem to do anyone any harm. She reads tarot, sells crystals, herbs, yah-de-yah-de. You know the drill. I've seen no evidence of flames pouring from her fingertips." He stuttered on his last words as memory of the fireball that almost singed his eyebrow off sprang to mind; of Ruth with a tiny blue flame dancing on her fingertip, and confusion in her cat-like expression.

"Stuart, are you there? Is everything okay?"

"Yeah. Everything's fine." He hesitated while static crackled down the line. He didn't need to mention irrelevant details. Nor could he bring himself to impart the information he'd just come across. In all honesty, if his brother truly believed Stuart was to sacrifice another human, he'd call off the search. There had to be another way. "How're Susie and the boys?"

"Yeah, they're good. Susie works too hard. School will be out soon, so the boys will kick around here all day long." Quiet static filled the silence. "She worries too much about me."

"I know." Stuart raked his fingers through his loose hair. "I know Ian. Tell her I'm working on it. I'm so close. It won't be much longer." He wasn't sure he believed his own reassurances.

"It better not be buddy, Ryan's ten soon, so by all accounts, I'm a dead man on his birthday. You have until the end of the summer."

"Yeah." All too well aware of the life leeching away from his brother, Stuart could give no more comfort.

"Stuart?"

"Yeah?"

"When I'm gone, you'll keep searching, yeah?"

"Ian, you're not…"

"But if you don't manage to find her before I'm gone, you'll not give up. For the sake of the boys."

"Of course I won't. I'll look forever. Until my last breath."

The deep sigh on the other end of the line wrenched his heart. He rubbed the pain in his chest and wandered back over to the window, cracked it open to allow the sea breeze into his room, and stared out at the waning light. "I'd better go. I've more to do."

"Yeah, take care. Don't let the witch catch you unaware."

Stuart snorted, knowing his brother only half joked. "She won't. I never take my eye off the goal."

The black shadow of one of the cats raced through the undergrowth of the garden in pursuit of some prey. A poor mouse, in all likelihood. Stuart watched as he swiped disconnect on the screen, fascinated as the creature paused, its lithe muscles bunched before it pounced.

"Nayru." Ruth's voice, filled with reproach, floated up from beneath the window and Stuart opened it wider so he could see her. She scooped the black cat into her arms and deftly whipped something from its jaws. "What have I told you about eating birds? They're not for you to kill. It's plain bad manners, young lady." She held the cat under one arm while she raised her other hand. She held the little bird high while the cat snickered in bad temper. She opened her fingers, but instead of taking to the skies, the bird perched on the palm of her hand.

Stuart supposed it could be in shock, but he leaned farther out of the window to watch it turn and face her. A trill song emitted from its beak before it spread its wings to flutter above her head, its perfect melody filled the quiet evening. Still fascinated, he found he couldn't move from where he stood as the bird came level with his bedroom window.

"It's a skylark." Her voice floated up from below the window.

He glanced down at her upturned face. Both the cat's eyes and hers glowed a brilliant green as the pale light of the dying sun slanted over them.

"It's a lucky skylark." His interest in the bird evaporated, as the woman below the window stole his attention. Dazed by her beauty, he stared down at her. Urgent need moved through him.

"It is." She placed the cat on the ground, then straightened. She tilted her head to gaze up at him, her face a perfect alabaster, the long line of her neck a sweet temptation for him to taste, if only he'd been closer. She swiped back tendrils of hair caressing her cheeks and smiled at him as his blood warmed. "I've spoken with Nayru about this before, but she needs a reminder every so often."

The plaintive song of the bird ceased as it flew heavenward.

Stuart leaned on the windowsill, the simple pleasure of talking with her through the open window swelled his heart. She was safer where she was. At least he wasn't tempted to get an armful of her. Not entirely true, the temptation was there, but she was well placed out of arm's reach. A little harmless flirtation wouldn't go amiss.

He rested his chin on his hand and grinned.

"So, the other two are called Din and Farore. Did you get them all at the same time?"

Her warm chuckle floated up to him. "Of course. Can't you tell, they're sisters? We had their mother, but she died a couple of years ago. They're thirteen now."

Nayru wound her way between Ruth's feet as though she knew they spoke about her, the loud rumble of her purr carried, only to be joined by another, then another. At different pitches, the three cats came together to greet each other with delicate touches to each other's noses, followed by a tender stroke against their mistress's ankles.

Curious, Stuart leaned out farther. "Where did you come up with their names?"

She smiled up at him while she bent to smooth a hand over the cats' backs. "A video game called Zelda. I used to play it when I was at school on the mainland. They're three goddesses with enormous powers."

"So, you're a fan of Zelda?"

"Of course. Who isn't?"

He watched her. The light softened to a warm golden hue while the sun dipped toward the sea. It bathed her in a shimmering glow until he fought the temptation to climb out of the window just to be near her, aware he should keep his distance.

"You want to go for a walk?" The words were out of his mouth before the conscious thought even formed in his head.

Thick black lashes fluttered while surprise skimmed over her face at the rapid change of subject. She dipped her head. He assumed to compose herself for a moment before she tilted it to look back up at him. Little brackets in her cheeks deepened as her lips curved upward and he let out a breath he hadn't been aware he'd held for too long.

"That would be nice. I'll check with Nana, but she said supper would be a little while yet. I hope you don't get fed up with fish. We tend to eat quite a bit of it here. There was a good haul of cod today, so she's making fishcakes, the best you'll ever taste."

"I look forward to them." Not as much as he looked forward to a romantic walk with the vision of loveliness.

"We'll have about half an hour."

Half an hour. It wouldn't be enough. The thought flashed through his mind that no amount of time with her would ever be enough.

He straightened from where he leaned against the windowsill. "I'm on my way."

»»»•«««

Heart aquiver with excitement, Ruth dashed into the house to grab a shawl. Once the sun was gone, it would be too cool for the thin blouse she wore.

"Nana, I'm going for a walk with Stuart."

Her grandmother turned, no surprise in her expression as she skimmed her perceptive gaze over Ruth before she gave a brisk nod. "I'll see you in half an hour."

"Aye, we won't be long."

"I dare say."

Nana pursed her lips. Ruth swiped her shawl from the back of the door, wrapped it around her shoulders while she listened for Stuart coming down the old staircase. She lowered her voice in case he heard. "Is there something wrong with me walking out with him?"

Her grandmother cast a look above as she too listened for his movements. "No, but I feel a storm brewing."

Ruth glanced out of the window. No sign of a storm, the sky was clear, orange streaks raced across it to meet the sea.

"I don't mean the weather. Something in the air, something's changed." Her grandmother, in her irritation, picked up a cloth and wiped her hands on it. She opened her mouth, then closed it again as Stuart breezed through the open kitchen doorway. Black jeans clung to his muscular legs, and the layers of T-shirt, shirt, and pullover in the same color still managed to define his broad chest.

Ruth snatched her gaze away from him, a rush of heat scorching her cheeks as she refused to meet his eyes. Guilt swarmed through her veins. Guilt for whispering about him, and deeper guilt that the first thoughts she'd had as he stepped into the room were not fit to have in front of Nana.

"Are you ready?" His voice never hinted of any suspicion they'd been talking about him, but he narrowed his eyes as he looked from Nana and back to her.

"Aye." She tucked her shawl in closer and picked up a flashlight before she stepped out into the shadowed evening with a determined stride. "We'll not have to go far, but I'll show you something for your research into the selkies and such."

He snapped the door shut behind them and followed her down the two steps onto the lawn. She headed for the beach then took a diversion to the right. Aware he'd wandered the coastline, she knew that unless he'd looked for it, he'd have not come across the place she wanted to show him.

"I thought we weren't going to be long." The husky quiet of his voice smoothed over her senses to wash away the doubt her grandmother had managed to inveigle.

"We're not."

"Why the flashlight?"

"You'll see."

She stepped into the small wooded area with trees gnarled from years of exposure to the battering winds. The arc of her light played across the vegetation as she stepped through a small gap and followed the path as it wound away from the lights of the house.

As Ruth continued, the trees became dense, leading them away from the coast. The sparse grass thickened to a lush carpet and the night crept in beneath the canopy of leaves above them.

She shone the beam of light over the surrounding area. If she'd been alone, she wouldn't have needed the light. She'd brought it for his benefit. She knew the way, day or night, as well as she knew her way through the old house.

Aware he'd come to a standstill beside her, the fresh smell of soap and underlying leather bathed her senses while his calm, steady breath whispered across her cheek. So close, if she turned her head her lips could meet his. She hesitated before she played the beam of light around the small circle of stones. It would be a mistake to take that route. A big mistake.

"You've heard the tales of selkies?" Her voice wasn't quite as controlled as she thought it would be. The tremble in it not from nerves, but desire.

"Many of them."

"Aye. There are many. Folks reckon half the population here has selkie in their blood."

"Do you?" Doubt laced his low whispered question.

It wasn't an obscure prospect, given the history of the entire island, but there was no selkie in Ruth's blood. "No, but you may not have heard this tale yet." Not many of the islanders repeated it. They found it too close to the truth rather than a mythological fantasy. Uncomfortable with it, most folk steered clear of her. Rather than let little hints of gossip taint his view, she decided if there was to be anything between them, as she knew there must be, then the tale should come from her. The truth as she knew it.

With a light step and hope in her heart, she moved into the circle of stones and sank onto the soft, cushiony ground. The moss so thick and cool, it gave underneath her, like a downy pillow.

Stuart joined her, tucked his knees up to his chest, and wrapped his arms around his legs. As he wasn't used to the cold, she should have warned him to wear warmer clothes. Her woolen shawl kept out the chill and fell to well below her knees, so when she sat, it kept the icy dampness of the ground from soaking into her backside.

He waited in silence for her to begin, so she switched off the flashlight and let the last rays of weak light filter through the gaps in the thick umbrella of leaves above them. The gloomy shadows of the trees deepened by the moment. Relaxed in the darkness, Ruth drew in a slow breath before she started.

"For generations, my family have passed this tale down from mother to daughter. As far as I'm aware it's still as accurate as the first telling, although I imagine you understand from your own studies how stories can get twisted out of shape."

She gave him a sideways glance and tucked her hair behind her ear, so the curls didn't bounce about her face to obscure her view of him. He appeared relaxed enough. His hands dangled from where he rested his forearms on his knees. Shadows deepened to give a sinister appearance to his handsome features and made her wonder if it would have been better to keep the flashlight on.

His slow nod encouraged her to continue, but the air thickened in her lungs. She glanced away at the surrounding stones to get her balance back. She was safe there. Nothing could harm her within the circle of stones, although she hadn't cast her circle in deference to his obvious doubts about her magical abilities. She had no physical fear of him, which was why she'd invited him within the protective ring. She was more concerned about the damage he could do to her heart.

The salty evening air settled in a heavy blanket around them, but his scent wrapped around her to heighten her senses. His closeness she felt just as sure as if he stroked her skin.

She scraped her fingers through her thick mop of hair to stop it falling across her face, and with determination, turned her attention back to the story.

"The year was 1672. This tiny island was virtually uninhabited—a mere handful of people. Some say they came from shipwrecks, some that they were escaped criminals from Edinburgh jail." She gave a shrug and peered through the shadowy light at Stuart to see the glitter of his eyes in the shadows. "They were all of them, strong people. For whatever reason, they'd survived, and they banded together for safety and company. Strange bedfellows so to speak. No one knew how many lived here, not many I imagine, from the small numbers we currently have. Counting probably wasn't their strong point." She smiled, but he remained motionless, his silence an indication of how intent he was on the story. She paused for a moment while she gathered herself for the next part, but Stuart remained still as she continued.

"One night a squall blew up. We have many storms, but this particular one raged for three nights. I would imagine not dissimilar to the storm which accompanied your arrival." She gave an embarrassed laugh and then continued before he could ask any questions and distract her from her story, but it seemed from his silence she'd captured his attention. "The islanders believed the fury of the gods punished them. Food became short because they couldn't fish in the torrid seas and of course, in those days, it was the mainstay of their diet. The wind was so strong they feared to go outside of their little stone houses in case it whipped them away." Absorbed by her own story, Ruth stared at the stones. Each one touched the one next to it. None had ever been moved from where they'd laid for centuries. "On the fourth morning, the storm broke, the sky cleared, and the sun shone through. A few of the islanders went down to the water's edge to forage, desperate for food and fresh water. Shipwrecks brought in a good haul after a storm. Pirates were rife in these waters in the 16th and 17th centuries, and their bounty could be rich." She raised her head and stared through the dusk at Stuart's impassive face again. Could he be bored, or did he listen intently? She squinted into the dark shadows obscuring his features, but he never moved a muscle. Only the subtle sound of his light breath could be heard in the silence.

She took a breath before she continued.

"What they found, though, was not what they'd expected. Among the debris lay the body of what they first believed was a woman. Long flowing hair, sleek and black. It covered half the naked body. Where the hair ended, the rest of the body appeared to be that of a seal."

"Frightened to approach, they edged forward, none of them brave enough to touch the woman, but a pitiful cry emitted from under the swathes of hair and seaweed. One brave young girl picked up a stick and lifted the heavy weight of the hair from the half human, half seal. She exposed the body of what they later described as a selkie. It was, in fact, a male. Beautiful beyond belief."

Ruth paused, waiting for a response, while the air thickened and grew heavy with tension. She leaned in, quieted her voice in the stillness. "The story goes the young girl fell in love with him in an instant. In his arms, he cradled a tiny bairn. A newborn with its umbilical cord still attached to the placenta. Its pathetic wail enchanted the young girl, so she leaned in and took it from the circle of the selkie's arms. As she cuddled the bairn to her breast, the selkie opened his eyes." Ruth closed her own to envisage the scene better as though it were her own memory and not just folklore. "Liquid black gazed up at her to melt her heart. Afterward, she claimed he'd spoken, but no one else heard his words, just the muffled sound of an animal in pain. What they were witness to was her swearing to protect the little one for all time. A human baby girl with hair as black as night and eyes as deep green as a summer sea."

As the night turned pitch black Stuart never moved, but she felt his attention on her as the air between them sizzled with his interest. They sat so close she realized it must have been her who had shuffled nearer until their knees touched and their faces were separated by a mere sliver of air.

Aware his interest lay in the story, she swallowed to ease the dryness of her throat before she continued, conscious her brogue thickened as she slipped deeper into the story. "After the bairn was removed from the haven of his arms, and he'd gained the promise from the young woman, it's said the selkie turned back into a seal and died. Legend has it he'd clung onto life until he knew the bairn was delivered into safe arms. It's said that his descendants have continued to grace these shores with their presence, protectors for generations of the wee bairn's kin."

The rustle of Stuart's clothes drew her attention in the silent circle as he moved for the first time, shuffled even closer to her. His interest was palpable. "What happened to the baby?" His warm breath puffed across her cheek.

"The young woman raised her as her own. She never married but lived to a ripe old age. They say she never fell in love again but died content that love had touched her soul."

"…and the child?"

She had to lean away from him for her own sanity, but her voice thickened as she replied. "She grew up, married and had a daughter of her own." She loved the romance of the story. The whole idea intrigued her of being rescued and living a life loved by the people who surrounded her.

"Where did she come from?"

Ruth shrugged, it didn't really matter to her. It had been centuries before and who would have been able to tell in those days? "It could have been a shipwreck."

"Could she have come from the mainland? From Scotland?"

It seemed a strange thing to question. Why would she have come from Scotland? The crossing for a baby would have been too far, too cold. She would have died. The only logical explanation was she'd been in a shipwreck, and the selkie transported her to the nearest island. The magical powers of the selkie were well known, but would one have been able to cast such a powerful net of protection over a newborn to transport it so far?

Ruth puffed out an impatient breath, unsure why she felt so irritated by his line of questions. There was no logic. It was folklore, a tale. She'd related a story; it didn't mean she had all the answers. "I suppose, but it's more feasible to be a ship in those storms."

"Was there nothing to indicate where she'd come from?" He placed his hand on her thigh and shot heat straight through to her heart, avid in his attention, unaware of the effect he had on her.

"No. She was naked as far as the tale goes. A wee newborn. Nothing to indicate she came from anywhere but the sea."

"But she wasn't a selkie herself?"

"No." Heat rose up her neck, to stifle her until she jerked her leg away from his hand and came to her knees in front of him.

Oblivious of her discomfort, Stuart shuffled closer. "How can you be so sure?"

"Because she would have turned into a seal at some point and from what happened with the male selkie, certainly when she died."

"No one ever saw her change?" He also came to his knees and leaned in until the heat from him touched her, washed over her until she thought she would suffocate with his tangible annoyance. A shard of dusky light highlighted his features so she could once more see the depths of his piercing pewter eyes. She faltered for a moment before she replied. He seemed desperate for her to agree the young bairn had been a selkie, but she couldn't bring herself to weave that kind of ambiguity around a tale she'd lived with all her life.

"Not in any of the tales I've ever heard. It's never been questioned before."

"Perhaps she managed to hide the fact from them."

Angry now, she shot to her feet. All she'd wanted was to please him with her tale, steal a kiss or two in her magical place, but he'd spoiled it with his insistent questions. She flicked her shawl tight around her and jammed her hands into the woolen folds.

Her throat had become so dry that the next words she spoke came out on a strangled breath.

"There would be no reason to. Everyone knew she'd been delivered there by a selkie. One who gave his life for hers. Besides, everyone knew she was a witch."

His harsh intake of breath accompanied his quick leap to his feet.

"You never mentioned she was a witch."

Offended by the accusation that she'd deliberately withheld information, Ruth leaned in until her nose almost touched his, and the air between them sizzled to life. "Well, I tried to tell you a story, Stuart. You interrupted. Several times. I was getting there."

This time she was left in no doubt he was as irritated as her as he flung himself away from her to trace the stones around the circle's inner edge, his back to her.

"What's the stone circle got to do with it?" He touched his toe to one of them and her muscles bunched in anticipation of him kicking them.

It may have had no connection, just a place where she liked to find contentment, but Ruth knew there was strong magic there. Ancient magic which drew her constantly, and she had no desire to see it desecrated because the control on his temper had slipped.

In an effort to appease him, she softened her voice. "The story goes the young girl insisted they bury the selkie here. She asked for a humble stone cottage to be built for her and the wee bairn."

He stared down at the stone his shoe touched, hands on hips, silent but for his breath drawing in through his teeth, no longer it appeared in anger, but disappointment. The warmth she'd gained from his closeness had turned to ice. Regret slammed through her. What had she done? What had she said? Her heart trembled in her chest. Distressed, she stared at him. He'd taken her words to heart, and somehow, she'd managed to hurt him.

"Stuart?"

He whipped his head up as though he'd forgotten she was there. "Yeah?"

The dark pits of his eyes were unreadable, and Ruth realized time had flown since they'd arrived. She had no desire to hurt him anymore, nor would she allow him his way with the story. She couldn't change it to suit him, and the best course of action seemed to be to back off. She hugged herself and stepped to the edge of the circle. "I think it's time for supper."

He rubbed his hand over his mouth, then turned and stepped over the stones to stride away in the opposite direction.

"Stuart? You're going the wrong way. Supper will be ready."

"Ask Clarisse to keep mine warm. I'll be back later."

"But it's dark. You might lose your way."

"It's a goddamned island, Ruth. How wrong can I go?"

As his temper whipped back to slap at her, she had no idea what she'd done to annoy him, but she wasn't tempted to apologize or grovel. Dammit, she thought he'd want to hear her tale. He'd been fascinated by everyone else's. What was wrong with hers?

Never easy at the thought of hurting another, she called out in the dark. "Do you want the torch?"

He'd already disappeared from view, but his voice drifted back to her. "I'll be fine. Go home, Ruth. Go back to your nana."

The strange flutter in her stomach distressed her. She hadn't meant to upset or annoy him. She'd hoped he might hold her hand on the way back, maybe press his lips against hers again. A sweet promise of more to come.

She bent to pick up the flashlight, and a blue flame shot skyward as her fingers reached for it, wrenching a high-pitched squeak from her. She slapped a hand over her mouth and peered into the darkness, grateful Stuart had departed. She didn't need him to witness yet another pathetic pyromaniac accident.

She swept her hand over the flame and doused it with ease, and then stepped out of the stone circle to make her way back to the house. With a small shudder, she switched on the flashlight to light the way. She wouldn't normally bother, but tonight the chill raised goose bumps on her skin and created little shudders in her stomach.

Movement in the undergrowth didn't concern her overmuch, but when Din and Farore leaped at her from the bushes, her heart almost exploded from her chest.

"You bad cats."

By the time she reached the house, she was flustered. She paused outside the kitchen door to gain a little control, annoyed she'd allowed his attitude to rile her. He couldn't blame her. She couldn't make the damned tale fit his expectations. He was a writer. He could weave it whatever way he wanted. Writers didn't have to tell the truth, most of what they wrote was made up from their vivid imaginations anyhow.

She smoothed her hair back from her face, gathered her composure, and swung open the old oak door in the hope Nana wouldn't notice she was out of sorts.

"The laddie upset you, did he?"

The old woman hadn't even turned from the stove and she knew.

Ruth tutted with disgust and placed the flashlight on the kitchen top. "No, I think it was the other way around. I angered him."

"Aye, well, it's to be expected. The man seeks answers, but they're not always the ones he wants to hear."

Nana turned with two plates in her hands. "I've put the lad's in the stove to keep warm until he decides to come home."

"How did you know I would come back alone?"

"I didn't, but I did know only one of you would come through the door."

"How?"

Nana set the plates down on the table while Ruth washed her hands, a little smile curved her lips. "I saw the blue flash of lightning fill the sky. I knew you were upset."

Ruth blinked as Nana took a seat at the kitchen table. She'd not seen lightning, only the blue flame which shot into the sky.

She closed her eyes for a moment, but when she opened them, Nana's serious gaze was still on her.

"I'm sorry, I lost control."

"There's no need for you to lose control, Ruth."

"I'm a terrible witch. I have no control."

Nana picked up her knife and fork and cut into the fishcakes to allow the steam to escape from the middle while the inviting smell filled the kitchen. Her eyes narrowed on Ruth. She waggled the knife at her. "You know Ruth, I've told you before, when you start to take yourself seriously, you'll be surprised by how much control you have."

"I don't. I'm a rubbish witch."

"Pish." A rare hardness filled Nana's gaze. "If you'd stop guddling around and concentrate, there is nothing you cannot do with magic."

Panic laced Ruth's voice as she met Nana's gaze. "I can't do anything. It's beyond me. I always mess up."

The sharp clatter of cutlery as it hit the wooden table jerked Ruth upright. She'd never seen Nana so cross with her.

"You can and you should, Ruth Alexandra. I have never said this to you, and I think I may have been far too easy with you, but you, my young lady, are too powerful by far. You need to concentrate if you want to harness your powers, otherwise they are wasted, and there was no point you being born."

The hurt cut her to the quick. Shocked at Nana's attack, Ruth stared open-mouthed across the table at the other woman she barely recognized.

"You've never said before." Her voice croaked out, the choke of tears filled her eyes and clogged her throat.

It only served to harden her grandmother's expression and tighten her mouth until the feathered lines cut deep into her skin.

"No. I'll take the blame, but it's time you made more of an effort with your life. You've fiddled about all too long doing nothing to better yourself and even less to use the gifts you were born with."

Offended, Ruth reared her head back to meet Nana's hard stare with a shocked one of her own. "I went to university."

"And what have you done with your qualification? Your talent. When folk are crying out for you to join them."

"I…"

"Nothing." Light bounced off the knife Nana pointed at her and sent reflections to spin around the room. "Nothing whatsoever. You should be ashamed of yourself." Her voice thickened with tears as she pinned Ruth with an angry frown. "It's as much my fault as yours. I should never have let you get away with it. I've allowed you to float through your life with no direction since your mother died. Well, she was my daughter and believe me when I say, she was not the easiest child in the world, but at least she remained true to her heritage instead of making a mockery of it."

Ruth opened her mouth to deny it, but Nana slashed the air with her knife; her color rose up her neck to flood her cheeks and threatened to explode from her hairline. She'd never seen Nana this angry. Not since Ruth's father packed his bags and hovered at the doorstep, desperate to leave.

Nana had never given him the chance. She'd literally thrown him down the porch steps with a quick burst of energy from her fingertips. They'd watched as he'd charged down the dirt path, his bags lay forgotten on the doorstep.

Pain from the memory choked her. It had been a week after her mother's death, and he'd gone. Deserted her and Nana. Disappeared from their lives and allowed Nana to raise her single-handedly. At the age of eight, Ruth had already been devastated by the death of her mother, but her father's desertion had broken her heart. At the age of twenty-six, she still couldn't understand how the man had walked away from his own flesh and blood without a backward glance. It had taken years before she'd stopped hoping for some kind of contact; a letter, a phone call.

Nothing came.

Too proud to try and trace him, Ruth let him go.

This wasn't like then, though. She stared into Nana's face, confused by the anger there. She'd stayed because she didn't want Nana to be alone.

Clarisse sighed and put down the knife, reached across the short expanse of the table to lay her hand on Ruth's.

"It's time, Ruth. Time you grew up and started to believe in your powers."

Ruth shook her head. "I'm terrible."

"Terrible because you have no faith."

"Aye." There was truth in what she said, but the reason she had no faith was because she'd always been so poor with her magic. It always went wrong. The day she'd turned Puddle Jackson's guinea pig into a frog and couldn't turn it back was the day she'd stopped trying.

With a quick squeeze of her hand, Clarisse let go and pulled herself erect in the wooden kitchen chair. "Don't you tell me about Puddle Jackson, child. You were twelve years old and far too young to give up."

Guilt swamped Ruth because it wasn't just about her poor magic, but the desire she'd had to impress Puddle Jackson. Just like the desire she'd had to impress her long-gone father.

She picked up her knife and stared at the fishcakes on her plate. The desire to eat had deserted her. "I know. Perhaps I should try again."

"Without a doubt, you should."

"I'm sorry."

"Yes, you should be too. If you're given a gift, it's a sin to turn your back on it. You need to use it, develop it, perfect it. You've been blessed with two gifts in your life, neither of which you've done justice to. It's time to show the world what you're capable of with the first gift and for you to embrace the second. You've done nothing but act as though being a witch is a burden and an embarrassment. How do you think it makes me feel? Every woman in our family has been born a witch with the abilities and powers at their disposal to do with as they please. Not look down their noses and pretend they're above such things. You, young lady, have more power in your index finger than I was ever blessed with. I've had to work hard for every morsel of control, practice to perfect my techniques, and yet you have the audacity to sit on your laurels and pretend the magic doesn't exist."

Ruth raised her head to stare at the other woman whose eyes were red-rimmed with age and regret. Sick remorse clenched at her stomach. Her appetite gone, she laid her knife and fork back down.

"I'm sorry Nana."

"Stop apologizing. I'm a witch. You're a witch. The best way to make amends is to acknowledge your fate and open your heart to the real you, Ruth, and stop turning your back on your heritage." With a little sniff, Clarisse raised her fork to her mouth and took a delicate piece of fish cake. The fury and fear dissipated from her eyes as she nibbled. She'd made her point, and Ruth's grandmother had never been one to hold onto her anger for long. With one last nod, she sliced the next fishcake in two. "You know I've never been able to command the skies the way you do. Perhaps next time you set them alight, you should take notice and acknowledge it was your doing, no one else's, not even Mother Nature's."

Regret rode high, amongst the other emotions dashing through her. Fear, doubt, excitement. She picked up her own silverware and cut into her dinner. Maybe Nana was right. Perhaps she should take her advice and do more than dabble. She needed to acknowledge her inheritance. The time had come for her to prepare for her own future both in terms of her magical and musical abilities. First, she'd deal with one, and then resolve the other.

Chapter Four

The snug living room with a bar in it and a roaring fire could hardly be classed as a pub, but it had pulled him in when he could think of no other place he wanted to be.

His mind a turmoil, he nursed the Edinburgh crystal glass in the palm of his hands while bright shards of light spun from the golden liquid. A single malt whiskey from the Isle of Skye. He savored a sip, held it in his mouth to appreciate the pungent earthiness of bonfire smoke. When he swallowed, the heat curled in his stomach to chase away the chill Ruth had managed to put there with her tale.

He'd intended to get drunk, but the hard-eyed stare of the old man behind the living room bar had made him think twice about ordering the full bottle of twenty-year-old whiskey. The old boy would consider it sacrilege to use such an excellent whiskey for the buzz and forgetfulness it could bring. Stuart raised the glass to study the amber contents. For that purpose, he might as well take a trip down to the dock and see if the fishermen had any cheap rum or gin aboard their little boats.

He took a glance around the room and estimated most of the fisherman were already there, drinking the good stuff. When it came to whiskey, it appeared a Scot didn't lower their standards.

Hand a little unsteady, he took another sip, let it wash over his tongue while he let out a quiet moan at the pure luxury of it. He breathed out through his nose, the heat scorched, and he mused if he could set light to the fumes and become a dragon.

"Aye laddie, there's nothing as fine as a single malt at the end of a long day to warm yer innards, if yer ken what I mean."

Stuart stared as the old fisherman raised his own glass in a salute before he took a healthy mouthful, moved his jaw in a slow sucking motion while he held the whiskey for a long moment to extract every last morsel of taste before he swallowed it.

The fiery liquid didn't appear to have quite the same effect on the fisherman, but he'd probably supped it from birth.

Stuart smiled at him and nodded his head as the old boy indicated with a motion of his glass he wanted to sit in the spare armchair next to Stuart's.

They sat in silence for a moment longer while they both took another mouthful.

"I saw you down at the dock a few days ago, with Ruth."

Stuart gave a weak smile. He knew who the fisherman was—he'd extracted a reluctant tale from the man earlier in the morning when he'd only just tethered his boat and started to unload his catch.

"Bill, isn't it?"

"Aye lad, it is."

The old boy's squinty-eyed stare pinned Stuart until he looked away into the flames of the fire. The hushed tones of male voices filled the small room, and as the heat seeped through his body, Stuart realized how little it would take for the strong whiskey on his empty stomach to have the effect he'd set out to achieve.

"Clarisse makes a fine fishcake."

Stuart rolled his head against the high back of the chair to glance back at Bill. "I wouldn't know, I haven't sampled them, yet."

Bill leaned forward, narrowed his already squinted eyes. The left one rolled around a little in an effort to focus, then it settled and seemed to stare somewhere just beyond Stuart's ear, while the right one concentrated on his mouth. He lowered his voice, "I'm surprised Clarisse hasn't availed you of some, me lad. I've already licked my plate clean from the one's she sent Ruth with earlier. I could not imagine she would let you go without." He leaned back into his chair and grinned while he rubbed his belly with one hand. "They're the best you'll ever taste in your life, and if you've done something wrong that would put Clarisse in a rage, I suggest you go put it right, laddie, and quick, if ye ken."

The broad Scottish brogue washed over Stuart. If he attempted to translate every word the old man said, he'd have confused himself with the complexity of the language, but the gist of it was unquestionable.

"I never angered Clarisse."

"Ruth, then?"

"No." He hadn't angered her. He'd insulted her and annoyed himself. What business was it of the old man to pry? He glanced around the room, imagined every one of them there knew each other's business.

He helped himself to a healthy gulp of golden liquid and realized his mistake as molten fire shot down his throat to burn its way into his belly. Surprised not to see fire shoot from his mouth as he spluttered out a cough, he leaned forward to rest his elbows on his knees while he drew in gulps of air to douse the burn, attracting the attention of the entire room for his efforts. None of them laughed but knowing smiles were tossed his way as he swiped the back of his hand across his mouth and wheezed in a long breath past the fire in his lungs.

"Perhaps ye should take more water with it."

He glanced at Bill, then down at the drink he still held in his hand. "There's no water in it."

Bill sucked in air through his teeth with a sharp tsking sound. "Aye, you should always take water with it, lad. They say the best is from the water used to make it, but we settle for our own fresh spring water here on the island. It's just as good and pulls out the flavors to their full."

"You water your whiskey?"

"Aye laddie, if you dinna wish to suffer the burning fires of hell in yer heed the next morning, then water is the way ye should go."

Stuart gave a light snort and drained his glass just to prove he was no kid, nor old man who needed to water his drink down. He was more than capable of holding his alcohol, and after his encounter with Ruth, he was perfectly entitled to get drunk.

The woman drove him crazy. The scent of her whirled through his senses while the story she'd told made no sense, and her irritation at his rational questions had raised his hackles. What made her believe she could place her hand on his thigh, slide it up higher and not gain some kind of response from him? Did she believe he was a freakin' statue?

The wrinkled old man behind the bar, with a remarkable resemblance to Bill, except for the squint, lifted a bottle from the counter and made his way over with a flat-footed gait. With a heartfelt grunt, the gentleman bent forward from the waist and topped up Stuart's glass.

"If the wee laddie wishes to drink, Bill, let him drink. He may have matters that do not concern us he wishes to forget for a wee while."

"Ach, haud yer whisht, auld man and leave the bottle behind."

Stuart grinned through the mild haze of cigarette smoke and alcohol. "What did you say?"

Bill stared at him for a moment, then topped off his own drink with equal parts water and whiskey. "I told him to be quiet." He raised the glass to his mouth and smacked his lips against the liquid. "So," he scanned the room, then let his gaze wander back to Stuart, "someone upset you."

Stuart laughed again, this time a little louder. The man was nothing if not persistent. "No."

Bill screwed his eyes almost closed but kept silent.

"Not really." Stuart wriggled in his chair and couldn't remember a time when anyone had made him feel like a stupid schoolboy. He pushed his hand through his hair and realized it hung loose and ragged since he'd wrenched the tie from it and left his Stetson back at the house. The woman had made him lose his mind. He placed his glass on the small table between him and Bill, then scraped his hair back and tethered it with the small tie he always carried. The old man sipped his drink and waited with undeterred patience.

Stuart gave a stiff shrug. "It was Ruth."

Without a sound, Bill managed to convey his surprise as his white eyebrows shot up his wrinkled forehead. Stuart grabbed his drink and took a deep slug of its contents, this time the fiery liquid burned all the way down in a welcome trail of fire. "She told me a tale."

Bill inclined his head for him to continue, but instead, Stuart held his tongue while he stared into the flickering flames of the fire. The heat of the alcohol seared away the irritation and made him see more clearly. "I wanted it to have a different end." He raised his head to scan the silent room. Every eye was upon him while they waited for him to continue. With no justification for his emotions, he shrugged. "I wanted the baby to be a selkie, but she wasn't, she was a witch."

He'd hoped with his entire being she'd not been a witch, but no matter how hard he'd tried to get Ruth to change her tale, she'd been insistent what she told him was true. He skimmed his gaze over the old fishermen, half a dozen in all, every one of them waited for him to continue. He downed his whiskey and placed the crystal glass onto the table with a sharp clip, much harder than he'd intended.

Bill leaned forward to refill his glass and Stuart attempted to raise his hand to indicate he didn't want anymore, but his muscles had turned to butter, and he found he hadn't the inclination to decline. The glass was pushed into his hand, and he relaxed back into his seat, allowing the heat to wash over him. The warmest he'd been since he'd arrived on the godforsaken frozen hellhole of an island. How could it be spring? The temperature hadn't raised its head above freeze-your-ass-off point.

His eyelids turned heavy and fluttered closed while he sipped a little more to make him feel better. Another while longer and he'd head back to the house. Perhaps apologize to Ruth for his churlish behavior. He rolled his head against the downy cushion of the chair back and blinked the bleariness from his eyes.

It had been a mistake to drink on an empty stomach.

"I was looking forward to the fishcakes."

An agreeable grunt rumbled throughout the room, and Stuart swept his gaze about to see the attention of the entire place was still on him. What was it they wanted from him? He gave them a sloppy grin, raised his glass and took another swallow. "But she chased me off, made me lose my appetite. For food and the kiss I wanted to coax from her."

"What did she say to make you lose your appetite?"

The old men all leaned forward to better catch the words which fell in an uncontrollable rush from his loose lips. "She told me the tale of the selkie and the babe." To his own ears, it sounded as though his accent slid into a gentle Scottish brogue. He hiccupped as he took another sip from the crystal. "How would she know the bairn was a witch?" He flicked his hand in a dismissive wave. "We're talking about centuries ago, how can a tale have retained any accuracy over such a length of time? It's folklore, fantasy."

If he'd expected masculine support for his derision of her tale, he received none. Silence hung heavy in the over-heated room while his head started to spin. He needed to get out of there, get some fresh air, but his rubber legs refused to untangle from where he'd stretched them underneath the spindly coffee table.

He squinted at his legs, crossed at the ankles, then jerked at them, insistent they do his bidding. The small table flipped over, and before he could move, Bill shot out his hand and saved it from hitting the floor.

Surprised at the speed of the old man, Stuart blinked at him in the burnished orange glow of the fire. The corners of the room retracted and darkened, encroaching on the light, so it narrowed down until his vision was only of the dying flames and Bill's age-ravaged face. The old fisherman's squinty expression widened to morph into soft black liquid orbs which gave a slow, easy blink. The wrinkles cleared, his face lengthened to form a long snout which bore thick white whiskers, and a shiny black nose. For one brief moment, Stuart stared into the features of a huge gray seal.

Breath lodged in the base of his throat. He counted three heartbeats, four, then five before he managed to draw in a little oxygen and give his head a pathetic shake. "I think I may have had too much to drink." His tongue thickened while the whiskey turned to oil in his stomach and spun the room in sickening spirals. Desperate to get out, he lurched to his feet.

The dark receded as flames leaped up the chimney breast in a wild blaze of bright sparks as a log settled. The low murmur of voices filled his head once more, and when he glanced at Bill, wrinkles spread across the old man's concerned face, his faded eyes narrowed almost to slits.

"I'll see you home laddie."

"No." He gave a little stagger, held his hand out to rest on the chair back while he gained his equilibrium. "No thank you. I can manage."

Bill inclined his head and raised his glass to his lips, his wild eye spun before it settled on Stuart once more. "Be careful how you go." He gave a brisk nod. "Take more water with it next time."

Stuart's faltering footsteps echoed in the empty cobblestone streets as he weaved his way back to the house. He'd no idea how much time had passed since he'd first started to sup the whiskey, but what he did know was he could no longer see the hand in front of his face. Darkness blanketed the houses, with no lights from the small windows to even give a hint of the way through the village.

Mind spinning, Stuart lifted his gaze in the direction he believed would lead him home. Home. When had he even begun to think of it as home? He snorted out a laugh as his feet decided to take him on a sideways jig, in a mad detour into the gutters which bordered the street.

His eyes gave a wild roll in his head while he let out another raucous laugh to echo through the empty streets. Perhaps that's why Bill's eyes looked in different directions. He'd pickled himself in single malt over the years, and they'd loosened in his head, just like Stuart's. Maybe they'd never be the same again.

He lurched to a standstill, flopped forward to rest his hands on his knees and gain his balance, but the world still spun in sickening circles. He squeezed his eyes closed, but his stomach lurched. Heat rushed up his neck, he slapped a hand over his mouth and jerked upright fast enough to make his spine crack. He gulped down the nausea and stared wide-eyed as the sky above him illuminated in giant waves of color. Emerald and sapphire undulated in great flags, interspersed with sheets of violet and fuchsia. The colors swirled, intermingling with each other to produce richer, deeper shades before the entire display streaked up toward heaven to leave long streamers of jewels to light his way.

Hypnotized, Stuart willed his feet to stay still while he gazed into the night sky, his neck craned until it ached. With eyes desperate to close, his whiskey soaked brain refused to let him turn away from the miraculous display of colorful ribbons God had kindly sent to light up his world.

Not that he believed in God, but the Devil had been sent to torment him in the guise of a sweet innocent with an abundance of black curly hair and deep emerald eyes, as rich as the swirling display in the sky.

With a languid blink, he flung his arms wide and watched Ruth, the supposed witch, dance in the kaleidoscope of color, and prayed to the God he didn't believe in she wasn't what his pathetic and inefficient research pointed to.

Stuart sniffed and ratcheted his neck back down to look at the wet cobblestones, shiny reflections of the fire in the sky. The burn of muscles in his shoulders hinted at the length of time he'd stood in the middle of the village with his face turned upward, his brain still a sludgy mess. His heart even sludgier. She'd done that to him. Damaged him.

With a small stagger, he lurched his way up the incline until Clarisse's house was in view, aware with every step he took his limbs became heavier and his eyelids more insistent on closing.

He swung open the kitchen door, shushed it as it rebounded off the wall, and danced sideways through the opening before it closed on him again. The night air had done little to un-fog his brain, but the invitation of fishcakes convinced his delicate stomach he should eat.

He peered into the old kitchen Aga at the covered plate Clarisse had left for him. His mouth watered as he reached in. He whipped his hand back as a hot little spurt scorched his fingers. He grabbed a towel, folded it in four and hauled the plate out.

It didn't matter how long the food had been kept warm—he didn't care. With the cover she'd put over it, it hadn't dried up too much. The taste melted on his tongue, fragrant and savory. It filled his stomach, dampened down the swirl of oil in his gut. He scooped in mouthfuls of fish and potato, accompanied by the fresh white bread and pickled onions she'd left on the kitchen table. He hesitated before he popped the first pickled onion into his mouth, waited for the taste to explode over his tongue, and then took another. A strange combination of food, but it worked.

Desperate to remain upright, Stuart rinsed his empty plate and silverware, wiped down the kitchen counter, and then made his unsteady way upstairs.

He hesitated for one split second outside Ruth's bedroom door, even raised his fisted hand to knock before sanity overruled the whiskey. His apology could wait for the morning when he could conduct it with some decorum and a lot of sobriety.

Without switching on the light, he climbed under the bedcovers fully dressed, his eyes already closed. The whiskey still swirled in his brain and warmed his body against the night chill that seeped through the old stone house making it colder inside than outside.

Bright flashes lit the inside of his eyelids, but the effort to open them once more proved too much.

·•·

Ruth hadn't attempted to conjure up the elements for so long that she wasn't sure if she remembered how. She'd taken care to cast the circle with salt and simple chants before she composed herself in the middle. She had faith there was little there to harm her, but even a poor witch knew to protect herself from evil forces. She'd learned that much from her mother and Nana from when she was a girl, and she'd accompanied them both to that spot.

Cross-legged on the cool moss carpet, Ruth persuaded her muscles to relax. She rested her hands, open palmed and loose-fingered, on her knees while she took the time to become centered, to rid herself of the lingering annoyance with Stuart. He still hadn't returned by the time Nana and she were ready to retire to bed.

Instead of following Nana up the stairs, Ruth had given in to the pull of magic which tempted her to return to her circle.

With each controlled inhale, she opened herself up. Slow and rusty, the exercise was nevertheless familiar. The memories of lessons learned since childhood flooded back.

On her exhale, the connection built. She tipped her head back, tilted her face to the clear, starlit sky to harness the power of the elements which surrounded her.

No longer a surge of uncontrolled energy, as it had been in the past, but a slow build-up of power thrummed through her veins and warmed her insides. A ball of heat built deep in the core of her and spread its flames outward to tingle with restrained power through her extremities until she turned her hands palm upward.

For the first time in her life, control remained steadfast despite the burgeoning force that vibrated through her.

She raised her left hand level with her chin, called upon the elements and sent a gentle puff of breath over her palm. A tiny blue flame leaped from her hand to spear at the stone directly in front of her. Then it danced through the circle to ignite each stone in turn until she was surrounded by a low, flickering fire with flames of emerald and sapphire.

The quick leap of fear she'd expected that would send her running back home, never came. Instead, excitement fluttered its delicate wings until elation filled her heart. She could do it. She'd done little more than light candles and set the small fire in their hearth in the past, reluctant to attempt more of a challenge, but with knowledge came instinct. This craft she'd feared for so long was nowhere near as uncontrollable as she'd believed. Perhaps Nana was right. The time had come to embrace her skills.

A small smile curved her lips. She was ready to accept it.

She raised her arms as the moon rose higher and watched the flames chase away the night sky with streaks of neon violet and jade. The circle of fire obscured her view of anything beyond the perimeter of stones.

Ruth squinted against the brilliance of the flames, raised her hands higher, and watched with satisfaction as she bent the fire to her will. The cool of the summer evening was singed away with the heat of the blaze, but she continued to wield her influence over her chosen element. Fire. Shoulders flung back, arms outstretched, the power surged through her body.

Not dissimilar to conducting an orchestra, she imagined, not that she'd ever conducted an orchestra, but she'd been in one, many times, and she understood the rhythm.

Accelerato, accompanied by a quick flick of her wrist, and the flames whipped up the tempo, making her thrill at her control. A calmness bathed her world as she made the fire dance to her tune.

Calando and the blaze fell away, quietened until it flickered low over the tops of the stones in shades of gold and burnished orange.

The power settled, and she rested the backs of her hands on her knees while her body relaxed and absorbed the gentle heat from the flames. Content she'd achieved so much for her first time, she allowed herself to drift within the safety net of her protective circle.

The gentle press of his lips against her forehead sent a warm wave to bathe her heart and wash away her anxiety while frissons of nervous excitement skittered over her skin to awaken her innocent flesh with a secretive tingle.

The cool touch of his mouth skimmed the tip of her nose and slipped down to meet her lips in a brief kiss, enough to entice and make her crave more.

"I love you. I will always love you."

From the deep husky timbre of his voice, she knew he spoke the truth, even without the textured, smoky silver depths of his soulful eyes which begged her to trust him. The passion vibrated through him to convince her of his love.

She angled her head to allow him better access to her neck, with no attempt to disguise the delicate shiver raising goose bumps on her skin in case he should mistake her reaction for fear or revulsion, neither of which could be further from the truth. She wanted what he wanted, to satisfy the desperate desire of their two bodies in a union to sear their hearts.

To her satisfaction, he glided the heat of his fine, skillful hands down the sides of her neck to rest them on her naked shoulders. He pressed the pads of his thumbs into her flesh and traced a pattern along the top of her bodice where the material dipped low over her bosom. For one long, shimmering moment she stilled, her vision faded into a soft swirl of colors while she anticipated his next move.

Her breath came in short, desperate hitches while he pressed another kiss to her open mouth and dipped his tongue inside to shock her senses with the erotic masculine taste of him. A taste she'd never had the pleasure of experiencing before; the unexpected invasion of his tongue a secret delight. She leaned in, drew his tongue deeper into her mouth so she could sample it further. The musky scent of him washed over her senses to leave her languid and compliant until her body melted against him.

"Stuart."

Liquid fire shot through her nether regions to weaken her legs as he scooped his thumbs under her bodice and grazed her taut, stiffened nipples making them ache for more. More of something she'd never experienced, nor could she imagine. She could only place her trust in him and allow him to do what he desired. He loved her. He'd care for her. Their circumstances no longer mattered, for love would always come first.

Her muscles turned to water, and she knew the only solution was to lie down, but he would think she was too promiscuous should she suggest it. He swiped his thumbs again, then circled them around her nipples, each stroke quickened her pulse and shortened her breath. Heat spread molten between her thighs, and she gasped out his name once more as her legs refused to hold her up and she sank weightless to the floor.

Before she connected with it, he scooped her up with arms of iron and carried her to her small cot. With a gentility which belied his size, he laid her down. Desperate and stormy, his pewter eyes met hers as he raised his hands and wrenched her bodice apart straight down the middle to reveal her tender breasts to his greedy gaze. Jolted out of her dreamy compliance, she snatched in a gasp of air. No longer as gentle and slow as he'd been, he dipped his head and drew one pebbled nipple into his mouth and suckled it deep until her body bowed and her heels thrashed against the flimsy cot. Trapped by his fiery passion, she curled her fingers into his thick, black hair to keep his head in place while heat flooded her body and a moist warmth slicked between her thighs.

She stiffened at the touch of his hand on her naked legs, her heartbeat stumbled, lost in the pleasure he offered as his persuasive stroke convinced her to allow him to sweep her full skirts aside. The whisper of sensation threaded its way through her heart to set it free as the waning sun slanted its amber magic through the small window to bathe her skin and turn it into spun silk.

Without lifting his head from her breast, Stuart skimmed his fingers up her thighs, his movements ever more frantic. Despite her trepidation, she allowed her legs to fall open at his insistent touch, exposed her most delicate parts for his delight and her education.

Fear of the unknown stiffened her limbs as she thought to protest, but the moment his rough fingers brushed at her swollen flesh, she was powerless to stop the flex of her hips. She quivered under him while a desperate keening wail burst from her lips to be echoed by his low, appreciative groan which reverberated through her chest.

He raised his head to gaze down at her. Passion etched shadowed lines on either side of his mouth in the dance of the firelight in the darkened room. His black brows dipped low. Intense, his face filled with avid concentration as he pushed two fingers deep into her hot, wet center. Pleasure burst from her while a storm of desire raged in his eyes as his lips hovered over hers. "Moya."

Ruth's eyes sprang wide open. Her heart thundered in her chest, and she couldn't seem to get a grip on her wild breath. The pulse in the base of her throat threatened to burst free while her gaze darted around the inner circle, desperate for some tangible essence to center on.

Flames rocketed skyward in a wild, frenetic dance of golds and scarlets to cut through the milder swathes of ultra-violets and aquamarine while she gasped for air, steeped in passionate desire. She drew her legs up to her body, wrapped her arms around them and rested her cheek on her knees while she battled to control her desperate panic. Her entire body was aflame as much as the fire which surrounded her and just as consumed. A hot tingle washed her skin, and she was aware as she huddled herself of the swollen wetness between her thighs and the unfulfilled hunger that throbbed its desire.

As she reeled in her senses, she blinked. Each time her eyelids closed, the image of Stuart's face filled her vision. Storm-filled lust swept through his gaze in a dream so real she could still smell him, taste him. He'd set her on fire in a way she'd never experienced before. Although their stolen kiss in the garden had hinted at how hot they could be together, this took it to a whole different level.

Around her, the flames continued to rage out of control, but she centered herself, concentrated on drawing the fire back down as her breath evened out. The sensations never waned, but hazed her vision while need dipped its vicious claws into her flesh.

She stared above the lowering flames into the pitch black of the night, surprised by the density of it. How much time had passed since she'd first cast her circle?

A swift flash of movement from outside the fiery ring caught her attention and caused the flames to flicker scarlet and jump for a brief moment in perfect harmony with the stutter of her heart. Determined to keep control, she harnessed her power. She reached out with her senses, and as her spirit touched another, she parted the flames and allowed a dark shadow to slip into the protection of her circle.

Two more forms whipped in close behind.

"Nayru."

The cat slinked past, circled around the back of her, and stroked its silken fur in slow, sinuous movements against her body while it wended its way around to the front again. Ruth reached out to run her hand from the top of the cat's head to the end of her tail.

Reassured by the cats' presence, Ruth relaxed as Nayru climbed into her lap and settled between her legs with a contented rumbling purr. The other two stationed themselves either side of her, like guardians of the night.

Dawn broke to flood the earth with deep golden hues that nudged her to stir. Calmer now, centered at long last, Ruth blew a cooling breath out over the top of her upheld palm and extinguished her ring of fire.

Legs numb from sitting for too long, she pushed herself up and ignored Nayru's quiet, insulted hiss as she deposited her on the ground. She stood while sharp pins and needles shot through her feet and up her ankles in a heated rush to throb at her knees.

No harm had come to her, but without a doubt, what she'd experienced had not been a dream, but a memory. With sharp claws, it had forced its way into her consciousness, insistent she witness the event.

She raised her hands and pushed her hair away from her face as she stepped beyond her stone circle. The cool chill of the morning air touched her skin and raised fine goose bumps to make her shiver.

Strange, she'd watched through the other woman's eyes, experienced through her body as though it was her, but it couldn't be her. Her head a whirl of confusion, Ruth made her way through the small woodland and over the lawn back home with the memory of Stuart's face, his body, his passion foremost in her mind. It was him. It was Stuart, she wasn't mistaken, they were his features, but he'd spoken with a deep Scottish brogue, and his clothes had been from another era.

Confusion warred with the desperate desire that still singed her body.

The house came into view through the shrouded mists of early morning, and she glanced up at Stuart's window. His curtains were wide open and the man, naked it appeared, from the waist up, leaned on the sill of the open window, his straight black hair fell in a wild mess to his shoulders. Her gaze clashed with his deep, turbulent one, but she barely missed a step as she continued on her way with the pretense she hadn't spotted him.

With her experience so vivid, so real, she half expected him to be there, waiting for her, but she wasn't ready to face him yet. The vision had been too wanton and passionate.

For a long moment, she waited outside the back door, unsure what to do. Should she tell him? He was the one who sought out strange tales. Perhaps he would know and understand how it had happened. She was pretty sure he wouldn't have heard much stranger than the memory she'd invoked.

With shaky fingers, she pushed back her hair.

Should she speak with Nana? She huffed out a breath. There was a conversation she wasn't prepared to have, with either of them. With a derisive snort, she pictured their faces as she regaled her memory or her dream of wicked, frenzied lust and sex with their lodger.

Perhaps that's all it had been. A desperate desire to be in his arms, tear up his sheets.

She covered her face with her hands and shook her head in denial. Once again it appeared her powers had run amok, but this time she wasn't convinced her lack of control had been responsible, merely her inadvertent brush against a power far more tangible than a dream.

With a deep sigh, she scraped her hair back from her face and gave in to the persuasive nudge of her three black shadows to take them into the kitchen and feed them.

··•··

Wrenched from the passionate embrace of the woman's arms he'd been wrapped in, Stuart had bolted upright in bed. His lungs worked like bellows to suck in air like he was a drowning man.

Every muscle vibrated with tension while his erection strained with painful awareness. A vivid recollection of him skimming his tongue over a tender breast pushed its insistent way into his mind.

Sweat beaded across his upper lip, then broke out over his entire body until he threw back his covers and leaped, naked from his bed. He flung open the curtains and dragged in great gulps of air. The watery pink tones of dawn brought with it the promise of another beautiful day.

A dream. It was just a dream, but it had felt so real his heart still pumped with erratic enthusiasm. He raised a hand to rub unsteady fingers over his lips while he hung his head out of the open window. The satin smoothness of her skin still glided against his, the taste of her lingered in his mouth, the liquid heat of her slipped through his fingers.

He raised his head to stare out of the window at the serene view. The sea, as calm as a millpond, didn't help to soothe his irregular pulse nor drown out the conviction he'd experienced something far stronger than a mere dream. The honeysuckle scent of her still filled his nostrils as he breathed in the cool dawn air.

The sight of the three guardians as they trotted across the lawn in formation dragged his attention back to the real world, only to be catapulted through time and space as the woman of his dreams stepped out of the tree line. Dressed in the jeans and wrapped in the shawl she'd worn the previous evening, she glided with smooth elegance over the small beach and across the lawn.

The same woman he'd held in his arms not so long ago. Her body arched, delicate and quivering under his. Her hands in his hair as she'd pressed him closer to her breast while his fingers had invaded her body. And yet it couldn't have been. Once again, she'd been garbed in clothes from another era. Clothes he'd had no hesitation disposing of.

Restless, he shifted, recognized the deep green of her eyes as she tilted her head back to stare straight at him. Her step faltered for one almost imperceptible moment before she continued on her path to the house as though she'd never seen him. But was that a flicker of awareness he'd caught in the deep sea of her gaze?

He stared into the distance.

More than just a dream. Without a doubt, Ruth had consumed the whole of his restless night while flashes of lightning filled his room and the heat of summer passion burned his skin.

But it wasn't her name on his lips as he'd been rudely jerked from his whiskey induced sleep.

The name he'd grated out hadn't been Ruth. It had been Moya.

As the adrenaline receded, he sagged against the icy wall of the deep window recess. His stomach clenched and a thousand woodpeckers hammered out their enthusiasm in his fragile head.

The rude awakening had almost swept away the effects of the alcohol, but it appeared the whiskey was to have its revenge after all. Stuart tangled his fingers through his hair to persuade it back from his face and dragged in a deep breath. It had been a long time since he'd consumed so much alcohol that memories of the night before hazed into a kaleidoscope of confusion and jumbled visions.

His thickened tongue protested as he attempted to swallow. He needed water. That was what old Bill had told him the night before. *More water with it, laddie.* A low groan of regret rumbled through his chest as he hauled on a pair of gray joggers and made for the bathroom.

The chill of the water he splashed on his face did nothing to make the pain recede. If anything, his whole brain rapped against the inside of his skull as he bent over the sink.

He scrubbed the furry coat from his tongue and brushed his teeth until they ached. He was never going to drink again. He risked cracking open his eyes to gaze at himself in the fogged-up mirror. Dark-haired, it never took much encouragement for his beard to sprout. He preferred to be clean-shaven, but the effort was too much, and he wasn't sure his over-sensitized skin could bear the scrape required. The grit in his eyes hadn't cleared, and while he gave rapid myopic blinks back at himself, he inspected the red-rimmed puffiness which surrounded them. If his liver had suffered as much, he was in deep shit. He needed coffee. Damn, but he needed coffee more than his life. His stomach rebelled at the thought of the fragrant tea that would be on offer. It might just have to be water. Water, and a bacon and egg sandwich. The memory of late night fishcakes stole into his mind and clenched his stomach in a vicious twist.

He curled his toes up in defense against the frozen tiles under his feet and then padded out of the bathroom back to his own room to haul on some woolen socks for protection against the hypothermia he was about to suffer.

His preference was to return to bed, curl up for the rest of the day, and nurture his wooly brain, but even through the thick mist of his hangover, he had questions he needed answers to.

A watery image of a large dark seal swam before his vision, followed by swathes of colored lights which could be an indication his brain was about to ignite, but he had a vague recollection of the sky lighting up in the prettiest of colors.

Yeah, he needed answers.

The pungent smell of coffee almost persuaded him the alcohol had fried his brain beyond help, but when he stepped into the kitchen, he could have wept at the sight of a brand-new percolator filled with rich, black, aromatic coffee. A large pottery mug had been left beside it, and despite the way he'd treated her the previous evening, he offered up a silent prayer to Ruth for her sweet consideration in buying him the coffee.

It took the entire contents of the coffee jug and two fat slabs of fresh white bread overflowing with greasy bacon and eggs before Stuart garnered the energy to leave the quiet house and venture down to the dock.

Despite Ruth's dawn sojourn, it appeared she'd returned to bed, and her grandmother had not yet risen.

Stuart's thickened brain rifled through the chaotic mulch of memories while he sorted through the questions he needed to ask. He took a moment to find his notebook amongst his overfull pockets and pulled out a pencil to write things down before he managed to forget them. Quick visions flashed through his mind like a film reel on fast forward.

Shards of white light pierced his eyes to stab at the dull throb behind them and make him appreciate he'd never known pain until the moment he attempted to look out to sea from where he crouched on the dockside.

He pressed the heels of his hands deep into his eye sockets and rocked while a shameful, high-pitched mewl escaped his throat.

"Water next time, laddie. We all learn our lessons the hard way." Bill peeled one hand away from Stuart's eye and pushed a glass at him. "This'll cure you."

Stuart eyed the white fluid with suspicion. It wasn't possible to feel any worse than he did. He downed it in one gulp. Instant regret slapped at him as a thick slide of snot-like texture slid down his throat with the rest of the liquid and his stomach gave a violent contraction.

The rusty chuckle from the old man seated next to him didn't help, as Stuart's stomach heaved until he gagged.

"If you can keep it doon, ya'll be fine by tomorrow." Bill cackled like an ancient old crow. "Clarisse sent it for you when I told her how much you'd drunk. I ken you'd need it."

Stuart kept the back of his hand pressed firmly against his lips while his mouth produced copious amounts of saliva to make his throat contract in a desperate attempt to keep the contents of his stomach down.

"What the fuck was in it?" He gasped from behind his hand.

Bill hooted with laughter and applied a sharp slap to Stuart's back, almost achieving the very thing Stuart wanted to avoid.

"Doona ask me. The only thing I know for sure is there was a raw egg involved." He chortled again as Stuart gagged. "Aye, you consumed a lot. It'll take a while for ye tae recover from such an indulgence."

Stuart raised his head as the waves of nausea subsided. "It'll take a sight longer before I drink again." As the silence hung between them, he peered up at Bill. "I didn't think I drank so much."

"Aye, ye did, laddie." Bill's sly squint rolled in a mad circle before it settled on him with a serious stare. "Ye had enough to do damage if'n you continued, but we packed ye off home and watched ye through the kitchen door, safe and sound."

Stuart blinked as he tried to wrap his mind around the fuzzy events of the previous night. There were some things he struggled to hold on to, and some he remembered with clarity. "I told you I could make it home on my own. I thought I left you behind in the bar."

The fisherman's face creased as he flashed a gummy smile and bobbed his head in agreement. "Aye ye did, but we dinna wish to risk ye falling in the sea. Young Tod and I watched ye home."

Young Tod was at least seventy-five, but as Stuart considered Bill much older, he let the remark pass. He'd much more important things to find out.

Weakened, he shuffled until his butt rested on the icy concrete of the dock and he dangled his legs over the edge above the small fishing boat. The gentle rock and nudge of the vessel against the port soothed rather than irritated him. He realized whatever had been in the glass had started to have the desired effect as the acid in his stomach stopped frothing and the spasms died down to an occasional mild clench.

Time passed as he stared out at the ocean, transfixed by the beauty and tranquility of the millpond effect. He breathed in through his nose, a long deep pull of fresh air. There were questions he needed to ask, but the warmth of the sun had relaxed his muscles, and the briny scent of the sea swirled through his senses to freshen them. He patted the breast pocket of his black shirt and drew out the small pad of paper and pencil he'd pushed in there earlier, pleased he'd thought to write his questions down through the dull sludge in his head.

He glanced at the scrawled writing, surprised at how bad it was. He had been walking, and he had been hungover, but it was barely discernable. He tapped the pencil against his teeth while he transcribed his own scrawl, then lifted his hand to scratch his head. Where best to start?

"Was it the whiskey that managed to produce a kaleidoscope of color, or was Disney out playing last night?"

He'd expected Bill to laugh, but the man's expression narrowed at him before he answered. "Och, that would be the Aurora Borealis."

He'd heard of it, of course. He'd even seen the Aurora Borealis when he stayed in Norway a few years previous, but he'd never witnessed such a profusion, variety, and depth of colors. It couldn't be a natural phenomenon. It had to have been paranormal.

He licked his dry lips and tried again. "But it lit the sea a brilliant, emerald green which glowed." He didn't want to admit to the eeriness of it.

"Aye, that would be the phosphorescence." Bill's face creased as he turned to face the sea, the edges of his eyes crinkled as he narrowed them against the glare of the sun on the water. "Sailors used to think—

sometimes still do –on nights like last night, the mermaid come out to play."

Stuart shuffled closer. "And do they?"

Bill barked out a rusty chuckle. "Nay, laddie. There's no such thing as mermaids." He leaned over and swiped a fish out of the giant ice bin at his feet, weighed the huge thing in his hands before he focused on Stuart. "The dolphins frolic in the surf." He glided his hand along the spine of the fish. "See, the phosphorescence in simple terms is plankton, most often seen offshore in the summer." He smoothed an affectionate hand along the huge fish again to demonstrate. "It clings to the scales to produce glow-in-the-dark dolphins." He balanced the fish on the palms of his work-roughened hands and undulated the body to bring it to life as though it were swimming. "They romp in the water, leap over the waves, disturb the plankton even more by their movements, all resulting in weird and wonderful sights which play on the imagination. It's where all your folklore comes from. People's inability to explain nature's wonders."

Stuart watched as Bill placed the fish with a certain respect, back in the ice bin. "So, you don't believe in selkies?"

The old man's head whipped up, and his roaming eye spun before it's sharp gaze settled on Stuart. "I never said any such thing. All fisherman believe." A contradiction of his own words. Bill squinted at Stuart before he turned his back to take up the fishnets in the bottom of his boat. "I've been blathering too long, laddie. It's time for me to get on wi' me work. Now, bugger off."

His stomach more settled, Stuart smiled as he came to his feet and peered down at Bill. "I saw you old man. I saw the selkie in you last night, and not for one moment do I believe you can attribute that to the power of the whiskey."

He turned to make his way along the dock, but the old man's words carried to him. "Aye, laddie, and it's a person's narrow-minded belief which gets them into trouble. If you came to look for magic to disprove and tales to trash, you need to open your eyes and heart before you open your mouth."

Stuart turned back, but the old boy had disappeared into the cabin of the boat.

·•·

Ruth wasn't sure she could wipe the image of his naked body from her mind. Och, he was beautiful. Then again, she didn't really want to. If the windowsill had been a little lower, she would have seen more than just his wide, tanned chest and long, slim waistline. Heat flowed over her bosom and up her neck while the image fought with the memory of the dream for precedence in her mind. The flavor of him still rode on her tongue, and his masculine scent still swirled through her senses. She pressed her hand to her heart. It wasn't simple lust. There was so much more about the man that drew her.

Flustered, she flung open the door to the gift shop. Nana was already there with a cup of hot water and lemon juice for both of them.

Ruth accepted hers and took a delicate sip as she slipped onto one of the chairs, still undecided whether she should tell Nana about the dream. She cast a glance at the open door of the empty shop and decided the time would be better before the ferry arrived and they were over-run with customers eager for her grandmother's skills.

She glanced at Nana from under her lashes, a turmoil of heated embarrassment formed a ball of tension in her stomach. She couldn't divulge the details of her dream to her grandmother. She couldn't imagine discussing such erotic affairs with her, but there were questions she needed to ask because, despite her heritage, there were gaps in her knowledge.

While she took another sip, she composed the question in her mind, and then before she took the coward's way out, she blurted it in the quiet of the little shop. "Nana, have you ever had a dream so vivid when you woke up you believed it to be real?"

Clarisse raised her head to peer at Ruth across the small shop from where she attached price tags to the crystals she'd brought out of the stock room. Her wise gaze narrowed in contemplation, but before she could reply, Stuart sauntered in through the doorway, his dark eyebrows raised as he met Ruth's gaze.

The saliva dried in her mouth as she hoped like hell neither one of them could read minds while a hot flush rose up her neck to burn all the way through to her scorched cheeks. She ducked her head to avoid his inquisitive stare while the persistent throb of desire shot another flood of heat over her skin.

She'd not yet recovered from the imaginary encounter, and his silent approach had taken her unaware.

She managed to lift her gaze, as Nana placed the ink pen down with careful precision. Nerves trembled through Ruth as she hoped Nana would ignore the question and change the subject.

"I've never had a dream that wasn't a reality." Clarisse glanced at Stuart before she cruised her gaze over Ruth, her gray eyebrows lifted in inquiry. Ruth swallowed, reluctant to agree. She'd never experienced such an intense dream. One likely to remain with her throughout the day to haunt her waking hours as well as her sleep. Perhaps if she'd had more sleep, the power of it wouldn't affect her as much. She'd be able to push back the memory, but her mind was weak and hazy.

Reluctant to acknowledge Stuart again in case Nana's faded yet astute gaze picked up on her discomfort, Ruth jerked a small shrug. "I just wondered."

She dipped her head to concentrate on stringing small pearls onto a bracelet.

"I wanted to thank you for the coffee this morning, and the cure-all you sent, Clarisse. I appreciate it."

Ruth raised her head again as Stuart's rusty voice grabbed her attention. On closer inspection, the man was pale as death beneath his normally healthy tan. Almost gray. The smoke of his eyes was red-rimmed, but the focus was still sharp when his gaze roamed over Ruth with an awareness bright enough to keep the flicker of heat going.

She kept her head bowed, determined to concentrate on her shaky fingers while they attempted to thread yet another pearl onto the fine string.

"Ye nae have to thank me lad for the coffee as Ruth saw to it, and Bill let me know last night they'd allowed you to overindulge in the fiery stuff."

Surprised at Nana's wicked chortle, Ruth glanced up again in time to catch Stuart rubbing the back of his neck, a bashful grin on his face.

"They told me to take water with it. I didn't quite catch what they meant until it was too late."

"What were you drinking?"

His slow blink hinted the alcohol still inhibited his system, despite Nana's fix.

"A single malt. From Skye. Delectable at the time." He slumped into the small chair opposite her, the creak of it made her wonder if it could hold his tall frame. Pity with equal parts amusement stirred in her as he cradled his head in his hands, his silky hair tumbled forward over his fingers. His face may be pale, but the dark stubble gave him a dangerous look, enough to have her heart dance the quickstep. "I hadn't realized how much I'd consumed until my head reeled. The heat of the fire, the company…"

"The old men should have known better." Clarisse placed a small glass by his elbow and poured liquid into it. "I dinna know how bad you were or I would have sent this earlier, instead of the other. Though the bacon piece is the real cure."

With a grateful look, Stuart picked up the glass and downed the contents without pause to check what they were. Despite his pallor, he still had the ability to make her tongue stick to the roof of her mouth. His throat contracted while he took huge gulps of the liquid. Funny how he had the ability to dry up her words and fuddle her brain until she spurted out some inanity just to fill the difficult silence. "I'm surprised you were awake so early."

Her grandmother raised one eyebrow, so her forehead crinkled in a question mark.

"I'm surprised you were out so late." He quipped back. Ruth's gaze, still settled on Nana, watched while her brow, deeply furrowed for one instant, smoothed as though there'd been no confusion ever in her life. She'd seen the look before, Clarisse used it to slick over genuine surprise.

With a benign smile, Ruth turned her attention back to Stuart. "It was a lovely night."

"Did you watch the Aurora Borealis too?"

Confused thoughts raced through her head. There'd been no light show the night before. There'd only been the flames from her circle which had been contained for the most part of the night, right up until...

"Aye, and an impressive show." The blankness on her grandmother's face steadied her, and where Ruth would dearly have loved to have questioned her more, she kept quiet and let Nana continue. "Certainly, a thing of beauty."

"Entrancing." Stuart's attention was still on her, but there was nothing she could add as she hadn't been witness to the display the night before, she could only call on her many previous experiences.

"Stunning."

He peered at her, waited for her to say more. When she didn't, he opened his lips to speak, but color flooded his face, and he blinked rapidly, shot upright in the chair, surprise flashed his eyes to silver. She couldn't help but smile. She'd had Nana's cure for hangovers. She'd taken it to university with her. The absolute best.

He slapped his hand to his chest and gasped like a landed fish. Florid streaks raced over his skin. Yep, the evil brew had taken effect.

"What in hell's name is in that concoction?" Breath rasped from his lungs as he turned to Clarisse.

"Nothing you need worry about, son. It's all natural ingredients I use to heal. It'll cause you no harm." She placed a gentle hand on his shoulder and made Ruth smile.

"The inside of my eyelids are lighting up."

Clarisse chuckled. "It's a good sign. You'll be as right as rain in a minute."

"Excellent." His chest expanded as he bellowed out wheezy breath after breath. "I have some questions for you."

The little bell on the door jangled, high and sharp as several elderly ladies walked through, their excited chatter heralded the end of the quiet.

"They'll have to keep, I'm afraid. Ruth and I have the tourists to see to. I'm sure it's going to be a busy day.

Stuart looked as though he wanted to say more, but as the women filled the shop, he vacated his chair and wandered over to the door, his last glance over his shoulder at Ruth gave her a small kernel of trepidation. "We'll speak later."

Desire skimmed dark and dangerous over her, more threat than promise. He swept out of the door, leaving the little bell to rattle its protest while her heart thrummed in primal beat at the shadowed suggestion of lust chasing across his face.

Distracted by the women, Ruth placed her delicate bracelet to one side and gave her attention to the little lady who tugged at her sleeve. There would be time enough for Stuart later, and by then she'd have had time to question Nana about the Aurora Borealis she knew had not filled the skies the previous night.

>>>•<<<

Ruth wasn't an easy woman to pin down, especially as the little gift shop bustled from early morning when the ferry came in until it left in the twilight. There always seemed to be one person left in the shop, too interested to worry whether they missed the last ride back to the mainland.

Each time Stuart poked his head around the door or peered in through the windows, Ruth was engulfed in customers.

It wasn't so much he had to see her, but he needed to. She'd become his darkest fantasy, a desire he'd been unable to rid himself of. He hadn't yet found a moment to apologize for his bad manners a few nights earlier, but she'd made herself scarce in the evenings too. Whether she'd intended to, she'd made him suffer.

The more he wanted to see her, the less available she seemed to make herself. It may be a deliberate avoidance. Even the cats had become scarce.

"She's on the beach."

"Huh?" He hadn't even noticed Clarisse slip in through the kitchen door, her movements silent and wraithlike.

"Ruth. I assume she's who you're watching for."

"I…" There was no point denying it. "I was rude to her the other night." He needed to watch what he said. The older lady seemed to make words inadvertently pour from his mouth. He gave a jerky shrug. "I'd like to apologize and clear the air."

"I'll get supper started, you go and make your apology. I'd appreciate it if I don't have to leave it to keep warm tonight… for either of you."

She knew what he was talking about. It appeared that Clarisse knew far more than she let on. Maybe the old lady had more witch in her than he gave her credit for.

>»»•«««

The sun dipped golden and low on the horizon and skimmed across the water to create a pathway of light leading straight to heaven.

He smiled at his own romanticism. Perhaps he should become a fictional writer instead of journalistic.

As he approached, her silhouette became more distinct until the wild bubbles framing her face found their definition and the shadows which deepened her eyes receded, so her feline gaze stroked his features as he approached.

"Hey."

Her full mouth tilted up at the edges, and she raised her hand in the direction of the sinking sun. "It's a lovely evening."

"It is." He lowered himself onto the rock beside her, wriggled his butt until she shuffled over to allow him more room and decided if he didn't engage her in conversation, he'd reach out and take an armful of her. "I've never seen a sky vary in such a drastic fashion from one moment to the next."

Her light chuckle had him glancing sideways at her. Loose-limbed and relaxed, she held a seashell, stroked the perfect smoothness of it between her fingers and made him wish those fingers were on his skin.

In an instant, lust curled deep in his belly, so he held his breath while he tried to analyze what had turned him on with such ease. No matter how many times he came across her, he would never get used to the perfection of her smile. The cool, clear scent of her took him by surprise every time he caught a waft of her. But her fingers. Those long, elegant fingers he had trouble taking his gaze off were fine and nimble, but at the same time seemed to bear strength enough to set his imagination on fire.

Stuart blew out a slow breath and turned to stare out across the water. He'd come to apologize, not accost the woman while her defenses were down. He cast her a quick sideways glance. "I'm sorry."

Confusion flitted through her misty gaze. "I beg your pardon?"

If he kissed her, would her eyes become bright and sharp, or did he have the ability to make them even cloudier? Right now, the haze had started to clear.

"I wanted to apologize." There was no obvious comprehension in her expression. "For upsetting you the other night, when you told me your tale." Her face cleared, but in the silence, she waited for him to continue. He slid the shell from her fingers to hold it in his and gave a gentle rub at the hard ridges of the outer shell in an imitation of her own actions. "I wanted the story to have a different end."

"You're an author—the story can end whatever way you want it to. You can change it."

"That's just the point. I can't. It's not my tale to change—it's yours. It's more than a story, it's history, whether it's folklore, or accurate isn't the point. It's not mine to mess with." He flipped the shell over to stroke the smooth, shiny inner surface, its delicate pink hues quite different from the rough white outer side. He studied Ruth's alabaster skin, the temptation to stroke it strong, but he remained where he was, and waited for her to make the move if she wanted to. He always seemed to, but this time he wasn't prepared to frighten her off. "And the point was, I insulted you and then walked away without explanation. There is no explanation. Still, I think justice was served with the hallucinations I suffered from all the whiskey I consumed."

Pleased to see he'd made her smile, he forgot his promise to himself to allow her to make the next move. He reached out to place a hand on her thigh and missed just as she slipped from the rock to wander barefoot across the short stretch of white sand to the slow wash of seawater. His heart stirred as she curled delicate toes in the mixture of sand and water and left behind indentations when she moved on. The soft shush of the surf accompanied the slow dip of the sun into the horizon and he half-imagined it sizzle and pop.

With a toss of her head, Ruth flicked her hair over her shoulder and glanced back at him. "There's no need for an apology, but I suggest you're a little more careful with your alcohol, retribution or not if that's the way it affects you."

It had never before caused him a problem. He suspected it may be more to do with the power of suggestion and the natural phenomenon of the Aurora Borealis.

He wandered over to join her at the shoreline but kept short of the water inflow in order to save his boots from a sure death by salt water on leather.

Tempted to skim his fingers down the elegant length of her spine, he concentrated his attention instead on the horizon. "I don't normally drink."

"That would explain it. The stuff is pretty potent."

"Do you drink whiskey?"

She barked out a laugh while she spun on her toes to face him. "I'm a Scot, of course, I partake of a dram now and again." Her accent had thickened while she spoke of Scots as though she'd become aware she was one herself.

He stepped closer and risked the change in direction of the tide. "How come your accent comes and goes?"

The smile still stayed in place, but her expression became wary. "We're all educated on the mainland when we reach the age of eleven. The island isn't big enough to accommodate a senior school, so we board for a few years in Oban. After, I went to Edinburgh University."

"But it's still Scottish, surely?"

"Yes." On fast, naked feet, she tiptoed forward as the flow of water threatened her. In a natural move, she took his outstretched hand so he could pull her away from the surf. Breathless, she shook back her hair, just to have the breeze dance with it again. "But it's quite different. Ours is a heavy brogue. You'll have heard it from the oldies." They sauntered to the rock, and he adjusted his grip on her to tangle his fingers with hers, pleased when she made no move to pull back. "Many of them never got to go to the mainland, the educational needs of the island were only recognized in the 1970s."

She released his hand and sat back on the rock, swiped up her socks to cover her blue hued toes, but he got there before she could slip them on. He cradled one foot in his hands appreciating her quick flash of surprise. Icy toes curled into his hands while he gave a vigorous rub, aware of her darkened eyes while she watched him. A small sigh indicated her pleasure. "Edinburgh University has a huge mix of backgrounds. I found I needed to lose my accent pretty quick to be understood."

He didn't want to frighten her away again, so he kept his moves leisurely as he slipped on one sock, followed by her boot before he took her other foot in his hands to warm it through.

"What did you study?"

"Music." The top of her nose gave a delicate wrinkle as though she thought little of what she'd studied. "How about you?"

"English." He stretched the sock over her foot, resisted the temptation to slide his fingers up the back of her calf, and pushed her boot on.

"Ah."

There wasn't much else to say about the course, except it had been combined with journalism, but he wasn't yet ready to divulge it to her. In a way, he'd also learned how to avoid disclosing matters about himself to learn the truth. Many a secret had been revealed in the face of his friendly, yet non-committal communication techniques. He'd prided himself on it in the past, but he felt no desire to practice it on Ruth.

When she held her hand out for him to take again, the warmth in his chest bloomed.

Her eyes glowed with a dash of golden light as the sun threw its last rays across the land, and filtered buttery tones to warm her skin and highlight the attractive smattering of freckles over her nose and cheeks.

She brushed her wanton hair back from her face as she glanced up at him, her voice turned to a mellow whisper. "I consider myself very lucky I went to Edinburgh."

As they approached the house, he tugged on her hand and compelled her to spin around and face him. Her mouth dipped at the edges, a small line marred the perfect skin between her eyebrows, but the breathless sound she drew in through her lips encouraged him to move in closer.

"I consider myself very lucky I came here." His throat tightened as he tilted his head, savored her sweet breath as it mingled with his and sampled the satin touch of her lips while they feathered against his. Eyes wide open, he watched as hers fluttered closed before he allowed himself to indulge in the aromatic taste of her.

"Supper's ready."

With a guilty jolt, Ruth wrenched out of his arms, the sweet tinkle of laughter followed her to the kitchen door. "Nana's calling."

He followed her through to meet the astute stare of Clarisse. He imagined she'd watched every move from the kitchen window, and had decided to call time just when it had started to get interesting.

He met her bland stare with a regretful smile. There was no reason for the old lady to have any objection to his pursuit of her granddaughter. Ruth was more than past the age of consent with a bright enough brain to make her own decisions, and neither one of them had any romantic attachment.

Clarisse placed their plates on the table with sharp clicks, without a word, but her disapproval spoke volumes.

With a sharp jolt of suspicion, Stuart eyed Clarisse. Perhaps she knew more about him than she'd let on.

Chapter Five

Sweet haunting strains of music filled his mind and drew him from the depths of his manuscript. Surprised at the interruption, Stuart glanced at his watch. Six hours had flown since he'd booted his computer up. Even through the poor computer connection, he'd managed to spend an hour responding to emails, and a live chat with his publisher, which crashed in and out of reception. He'd set up timed tweets, and a couple of Facebook posts. Too impatient with the work at hand, he refused to spend long on social media. When he'd turned it all off, he fell into his latest manuscript, *Feeding the Pain*.

Absorbed in his own world, he wasn't aware of the return of anyone to the house.

He snicked closed the lid on his laptop and pushed back from the dainty desk, mindful it didn't topple over. His stomach gurgled as pangs of hunger griped to give him a sharp reminder that he hadn't eaten in hours. He dipped his hands in his pockets and glanced out of the window as the music soared. He needed to go in search of sustenance and music.

It lifted his heart as he swung open the door to his bedroom and stepped into the cool dimness of the hallway. Enchanted, he turned, not to the stairs, in search of food, but toward the beauty of the sound. He followed its melodious enticement along the hallway until he came to a halt outside Ruth's bedroom.

A small nugget of doubt curled in his stomach at the thought of intruding on her privacy, but he nudged it aside. He had no choice. The music had deprived him of it the moment he'd heard its enticing invitation.

Hypnosis was one of his most bitter contentions, one he'd wrangled with over the years. He'd tried without solid evidence to prove it was all just another load of rubbish. But he watched his own hand with fascination as he raised it and with one finger, gave the door a gentle push, aware he had no choice in the matter.

His heart swelled at the sight of her. Tenderness and desire wrapped together to weave gentle ribbons through his veins. His pulse thickened and slowed while his blood responded to the ethereal pace of her tune.

His body tightened with the gentle sway of hers.

Lost in her own world, silhouetted against the window, her willowy body swayed to the hushed strains which bled from the silver flute she held to her softened lips. With gentle breaths, she coaxed the tune to life until it floated around him and wrenched at his heart with its plaintive invitation.

Weak from the attack on his senses, he leaned boneless against the doorframe, every molecule of him absorbed by the magic of her.

She'd tethered her hair with a loose tie high on her head, so it cascaded in a wild profusion of black curls around her face to leave her long, elegant neck exposed to his hungry gaze.

The sweet swell of music heralded the end of the piece. Aware he'd encroached on her privacy, Stuart hadn't the strength to persuade his liquid muscles to push away from the doorway and leave before she noticed him.

If the devastation of his emotions by her magical composition hadn't beckoned to him, the gentle sway of her delicate body did.

Thick, sooty black lashes fluttered, the hazy dream of the musical romance still heavy in her gaze. She gave a slow, languorous blink, no surprise in the dreamy jade shadows of her eyes.

He should walk away, but the heavy weight of his limbs and the pull of his heart convinced him otherwise. If he didn't have her now, he might just die.

Celtic green eyes glowed with the knowledge of what was to be between them.

With a slow stretch of her arm, Ruth placed the flute on her antique dresser. She never took her gaze from his as she stepped forward. The silken swirl of her long skirts whispered across her bare legs, her naked toes peeped out from beneath the hem to make his blood thicken as she swayed toward him.

Awareness swirled in the depths of her emerald stare.

She'd bewitched him. He couldn't move a single muscle. The drum of his blood thundered loud in his ears to drown out the silence. Her smile melted his heart, and as she reached her hand out to cup his chin in her palm and smooth her nimble fingers along his jawline toward his ear, he was powerless to resist.

When she'd told him she studied music, he had no concept of the power she could wield with the stroke of her fingers over the smooth keys of the flute as she breathed life into the instrument.

He raised his hand to cradle hers and stop the onward move of it through his hair. He brought it to his lips, placed a gentle kiss on her palm, and then touched his mouth to the tip of each one of her delicate fingers, appreciating the brief moment of pleasure at the satin fragility of them. Freesias floated on his palette as he absorbed her scent deep into his lungs. The memory of his dream encounter with her still heavy in his mind.

Spellbound, he dipped his head as she raised hers in perfect symmetry to meet his mouth with her own.

Velvet softness flowered beneath his lips and the warmth of her open mouth invited his tongue to slip inside and investigate the perfumed taste of her.

He took his time to skim his fingers over the curve of her cheek.

His heart bumped up at the touch of her hand on his chest. Light circular motions soothed him into taking his time as he slipped his lips from hers to cruise them with little nibbles across her cheek to her ear. Her soft sighs of pleasure heated his blood, so it flowed thick and sluggish through his veins.

His fingers trembled as he nudged aside the straps of her fine, floaty top to nuzzle at the satin smoothness of her shoulder. He touched the tip of his tongue to her warm skin, tasted it, felt it vibrate beneath him, and then grazed his teeth over her softness, delighting in the delicate shudder she gave as she melted against him.

He took her weight, wrapped his arm around her slight frame and pulled her in tight. Her body bowed under his to expose the top of her breast for his lips to worship. With Ruth's quiet sighs of encouragement, he edged the scrap of material lower until her dark nipple was revealed. The hitch of his heart never worried him as he realized she wore no bra, her delicate breasts firm and pert offered her rosy areola in a blatant invitation for him to test the flavor of her.

Cocooned in a blanket of silence since the music stilled, her gentle hitches of breath stirred him. He glanced up. Arched over his arm, Ruth tilted her head back, her parted lips plump from their recent kiss, pleasure smoothed over her face while she gazed at him from behind the veil of her lashes, invitation heavy.

He dipped his head to take her flushed nipple into his mouth with a delicate suction. Almost blinded by her beauty, he thrilled at the tremulous moan that shuddered from her soft lips. Her pale skin flushed a pretty pink as she trembled in his arms. She raised her hand, skimmed her fingers through his hair until she coaxed it from the leather thong.

Caught up in his emotions, he had no resistance. He raised his head, bent his knees and scooped her slight body off her feet, appreciating the quiet gasp she gave as he strode over to her lacy white linen bed and lowered her, with all the tenderness he could muster, on top of the covers.

The tie in her hair broke loose to scatter her black curls across the pillow in a silken rush. His breath caught in his throat at the sheer magnificence of the woman while she lay in wanton abandon on the white background, framed for his appreciation.

Scared to break the spell, he paused for a long moment before he grabbed the hem of his black T-shirt with fingers that shook in his haste to divest himself of his clothes before the woman on the bed came to her senses and changed her mind.

Six buttons on his jeans seemed just too much, especially with the strain of his obvious erection making it more difficult to unfasten them. Her dreamy jade gaze widened fractionally, in fear, he thought, as he slipped his fingers into his back pocket and flicked a condom packet onto the bed. He pushed at the waistline of his jeans and underwear to glide them both down his thighs together, shaking his oversized feet to flick the clothing onto the floor.

Once more he hesitated, but the smooth undulation of her body invited him to join her on the bed. An invitation he never dreamed of declining. He braced one knee on the edge of the bed, felt the dip of the mattress give beneath his weight and reached for Ruth. He pulled her into his arms as her hair cascaded down her back.

His fingers grazed her skin and made her breath hitch as he smoothed the strappy top from her body and dropped it to the floor to join his clothes in an untidy heap. Her long golden skirt took no effort at all to ease down her hips and off her legs, but the little scrap of lacy black material that barely covered her looked so sexy, he found no desire to remove her panties yet. Instead, he leaned in, placed the palm of his hand over them. He spanned his fingers across her crotch and delighted in the sound of her gentle sighs. He skimmed his fingers under the elastic, fascinated as the pink tone of her skin deepened to rose.

His own breath ragged, he skated his hands back up her hips, followed the indent of her waistline all the way up to cup her breasts while he eased his body on top of hers. The coolness of her skin against his heated flesh drove him insane, with a dark desire to take, but he lashed down the ferocity of his appetite for her and touched his lips with tender assault to her perfect nipple once more.

"Stuart." She sighed his name, and her glazed expression met his while he edged higher up her body. His solid erection pressed into the flesh of her thigh before it slipped into the juncture between her legs as though instinct guided it. He swallowed her tiny mewl with his kiss. His lips seduced hers, his tongue dipped into her mouth, her taste a heady delight.

He slipped his fingers beneath her panties to persuade them off her backside and down her thighs. When they stuck and restricted her movement, his patience ran out, and he gave a quick yank to snap the elastic so it could no longer inhibit her sensual movement.

He supposed he should have asked consent, but permission seemed a long way behind them. The inviting wetness of her proved that as he slipped his fingers between her legs, his own desperate groan a low vibration in his chest.

The heady perfume of her need flooded his senses as he spread her nectar on his fingers and gently circled her swollen flesh until her hips rose in desperation. Her fingers, stronger than he'd expected, grasped his shoulders, kneaded them while she flung her head back in wild abandon and exposed the delicate arch of her throat to him.

Surprised at the quick rise of her desire, Stuart stroked a rough finger over her and drew a shocked gasp from her as he plunged two fingers deep inside her warm velvetiness. Determined to think only of her, he pushed aside the insistent wisps of familiarity which threaded through his memory.

He held himself under control, kept his fingers deep inside her, aware of her every response as they flickered across her perfect features. A deep rose flushed across her skin to slash magenta over her cheekbones and tell him without words she was more than ready.

Torrid heat chased the languidness from his system and sent his pulse racing while the tight reign he'd had on himself strained. The tiny flutters as her body grasped his fingertips snapped the tethers, and all attempt at restraint fell by the wayside.

He withdrew from her, grabbed the condom from the bed, and fumbled it in his haste to rip it open. The moment her hand touched his, he froze, allowing her to swipe the small packet from him.

Without moving a muscle, every thought drained from his head as she slid the condom up his rigid shaft with nimble fingers. Those fingers which had coaxed magic from her flute. If she stroked him, it would all be over. He was so close to losing control. But with a lack of haste, she eased herself back onto the bed, raised her arms in sultry invitation as she parted her legs to make room for him. Her full lips curved, a knowing smile tipped the edges while her narrow-eyed observation glowed with feline attentiveness.

Without hesitation, he slipped his body over hers, wrapped himself around her and gave her no time to draw breath before he pushed inside her already primed body.

The quick flickers of her inner muscles started again. Blood thrummed through his head and filled his ears with the sound of his own heartbeat, interspersed by the strangled little sounds Ruth made in the back of her throat. Low and appreciative, they drove him crazy enough for all thought to blur, more than happy to follow her lead until he was a mindless pool of sensation drowning in a sea of desire.

»»»•«««

With the tip of his finger, he traced lazy circles around her areola for the sheer pleasure of watching her tiny pink nipple pucker.

He propped himself up on one elbow and rested his chin on the palm of his hand so he could gaze at her relaxed features.

Her fresh beauty overwhelmed him. The women he tended to mix with wore make-up, but she needed nothing to enhance her looks. Thick, sooty lashes feathered onto her high cheekbones, still rosy from their love-making. Jade eyes hidden behind closed lids, her face supine, mouth moist and swollen from his kisses. He thought he'd been gentle, but the evidence of his passion was written all over her body, he'd marked her porcelain skin with his roughened fingers. It wasn't deliberate, but the proof of his possession of her was clear.

Her lips parted while gentle breaths puffed through them.

Unable to resist the sweet temptation of them, Stuart leaned in and brushed his mouth against hers. As he retracted, her eyes fluttered open, a glint of emerald visible through her lashes. A half smile touched her lips, and his sluggish pulse became stronger.

A smile tugged at his own lips in response, and he raised a hand to smooth a finger over the perfection of one arched eyebrow.

"I thought you were asleep."

Nothing more than a gentle sigh indicated she wasn't.

"You've enchanted me." His voice, roughened with satisfaction, grazed the air but he wasn't convinced it was the huskiness of it so much as his words that had her muscles tighten while her bright gaze widened before it skittered away from his.

Gone almost as quick as it came, a less observant person may have missed her response. But not him, he'd been born astute, raised to notice, trained to observe.

Her dreamy gaze returned to his as though the brief flicker of fear had never happened. Her smile softened his heart as it spread to dimple her cheeks in quiet apology.

"There was no witchcraft involved."

Her narrowed eyes, together with an edge of defensiveness trickled a train of thought worth parking for later.

"Your music was magical." He grazed his knuckles over the silken skin of her jaw, enjoyed every moment of contact as her flesh heated under the stroke of his fingers. "It enthralled and charmed me. A temptation I couldn't resist."

She jerked upright and all but crashed her head into his as she propped herself up on her elbows, so she was eye to eye with him, her nose almost touching his.

"Are you saying you don't think you're here of your own free will? That I somehow lured you in?"

Her dark concentration, the way her brows twitched downward should have made him debate the question with serious consideration, but he deliberately barked out a laugh. "Oh Christ, no."

He ducked his head to plant a hungry kiss at the rise of her plump breast and chuckled harder at her surprised blink as he gazed into her face. "If I'd had my way and with my own free will, I'd have been in your bed ten minutes after you first bumped into me."

Her surprised gasp confused him. Did she not realize how perfect she was? How lush and gorgeous? What a temptation she was?

With a gusty bump, Ruth lay flat again. She raised her hand to stroke his hair back from his face. The light crease between her eyebrows deepened. "I didn't realize." She turned her head to look away. "I thought it was only me."

Puzzled, he took hold of her chin between his thumb and forefinger and turned her face to him again. "You thought what was only you?"

"The instant attraction. I never realized until you kissed me the other week you felt anything for me. Since then, you made no further advances. I thought you'd perhaps have made more of an effort."

Her sexy bottom lip plumped out in a pout to make him smile and tempted him to kiss her again. When he came up for air, his blood was already heated, and he wondered how to explain to her he'd had to be sure. Sure she wasn't the witch he searched for. How could he make love to her, feel for her so deeply then plunge a knife into her heart?

His suspicion of the old lady was bad enough, but he'd started to think neither was capable of true witchcraft and he'd have to move on. That in itself was a problem. He needed to move on, continue his search and leave Ruth behind.

He traced his gaze over her features while she waited for him to answer. It wasn't so simple. "I wanted to give you a little more time. I knew what *I* wanted, but I didn't want to rush you."

Her little gasp hitched out. "And what do you want Stuart?"

He wondered how fast she would run if he told her the whole truth. That he wanted her, all of her, for all time.

Jesus!

He flung himself onto his back, squeezed his eyes shut.

Jesus.

Where did that come from?

The power of his emotions surged through him. He raised his hand to his forehead to rub away the unexpected pain in his head. Sick nausea churned his stomach so sudden he became lightheaded.

"Stuart?"

He cracked open his eyelids, then slammed them shut again to block out the sight of her. Her desperate concern only made him feel worse.

Christ.

"Stuart? Are you okay?" The cool touch of her fingers over his heated skin did nothing to soothe the wild panic lacing through his veins.

Oh God, what was he to do?

"I'm fine." He grated the words out past gritted teeth while his mind, which two minutes ago dripped in post-coital bliss, charged in blind oblivion through his head like a panic-stricken two-year-old.

He was in love with her.

He'd managed to avoid the stupid, soul-destroying state of affairs all his adult life, but now it had sneaked up on him and slammed him good and hard right in the head. The head, the heart, and if he wasn't supremely mistaken his testicles throbbed too.

"Oh God."

He rolled away from her to sit on the edge of the bed and hang his head low while he stared at his hands as they dangled between his knees. Adrenaline surged through his stomach cramping it in painful clenches.

Thick silence surrounded him, broken only by the graze of his own panicked breaths. The gentle reassurance of her touch was no longer present, but he couldn't bring himself to look at her. He was overwhelmed, his senses had revved into overdrive, and he needed to get his own mind around what had happened before he blurted it out to her.

When he heard the quiet rustle of bedclothes, he raised his head in time to watch her slip from the room, the cotton sheet draped over her as she clutched it to her breast.

He scraped the hair back from his face, searched for the little leather tie he used to tether it back while he wrote. It had to be there somewhere. He came to his feet, scanned the floor for something to do, the frantic flutter of his pulse still not abating. He spotted the tie, swiped it from the end of the bed and looped it around the short tail he'd made of his hair.

When he glanced up, she stood in the doorway dressed in a pale green robe. One hand gripped the neck of it closed, while she held a glass of water in her other hand. Dark eyebrows dipped over turbulent sea eyes.

All he wanted to do was strip her naked again, but he'd made her uncomfortable, which she really didn't need. Except he had no way to explain his stupidity to her.

"I'm sorry, I'm fine." He gave a careless shrug and realized it wasn't the most casual of moves, considering he sported an erection again.

Her gaze dropped down his body, then skittered straight up to his face again while she shoved the glass of water at him. His chest gave an uneasy jitter as his heart flipped over at her perusal. He was done for.

He accepted the glass and slumped down on the end of her bed. An icy slosh of water landed on his naked thigh and almost shot him through the ceiling. He ground his teeth before he sipped.

"This is not easy, Ruth. Why don't you take a seat?"

She edged onto the side of the bed. When she turned to face him, her concern made him wish he'd covered up. It seemed totally inappropriate for him to want her again so soon.

"I'm sorry, I had no idea this would happen and I..." He took another sip of water, this time there was no spillage, but his fingers shook so he dropped his arm down to rest it on his knee and give the glass some stability. When he glanced back up at her, her gaze was so intense that he couldn't look away. "I didn't see this coming, so when I say to you I'm falling in love with you, I don't want you to take this to mean you should run screaming from the room, nor do I expect you to feel the same way."

Her soft lips opened and closed several times. No sound emitted from her mouth, but at least she hadn't made a move to leave. Then again, why would she leave her own bedroom? Perhaps she should throw him out on his ass.

He'd hoped she'd join in the conversation, but it appeared she waited for him to give her more. What more could he say? I love you. End of conversation. End of relationship before it had even begun.

He raised the glass to his lips again, chinked his teeth on the rim of it and gave a quick grimace. "I didn't expect this. I've never made love to another woman the way I made love to you today. My heart, my soul, were wrenched from my body and handed to you on a plate."

The loud gulp she gave twanged down her throat, but still, she never said a word, and his awkwardness grew.

"I guess I'm a little overdramatic, but what the hell, I'm a writer. Writers are prone to over-exaggeration, and romanticism." He searched for excuses, tried to backtrack on his declaration as the discomfort in his stomach expanded to make him feel like a fool. He rubbed his fingers over his dry lips before he tried again. "I don't expect you to feel the same way. This must come as a shock to you." Her sharp nod made him smile but never dissipated the burn inside. "Perhaps I should go and leave you alone because quite honestly I don't know what the hell I'm talking about. I can't fall in love with you. I have to leave in a few weeks' time. I have a job to do and no option but to go and I certainly can't expect you to leave your island to traipse around the world after me."

Wide eyes stared at him, and he imagined the horror of what ran through her mind. He'd experienced it himself when women had been a little too enthused about their emotions. Ruth looked like a rabbit in the headlights, while he couldn't stop his mouth from running away with him. What the hell was he thinking to suggest she come with him? He needed to shut the hell up. Right now.

He jerked his arm out, offered her the half-full glass of water which she accepted automatically, lifted to her lips and took a sip. Her silence was about to kill him.

"I'm going to go. Put my head under a pillow and my mind into my manuscript and try and forget this ever happened. I'm sorry to have upset you in any way." He couldn't bring himself to apologize for making love to her. "The other thing, the sex. It was good. I enjoyed it. Thank you."

He lurched to his feet, cast his gaze over the floor until he located his clothes, grabbed them, and bundled them into his arms. Three times he had to pick up his underpants after he fumbled around and dropped them back on the floor. When he whirled for the door, Ruth had disposed of the glass and stood in front of him. A half-smile played over her lips, and her emerald eyes twinkled in invitation.

"I don't think we should be too hasty about you leaving. After all, it may only be a small aberration this thing you claim to feel." Her elegant shrug almost had him on his knees before her. "You're an author. Who knows, you might change your mind in the short time you have left here." Calm and direct, she placed her hand on his chest and shot fire through his veins. "Perhaps you're mistaken about being in love with me, as you claim never to have been in love before." She raised her eyebrows, the long sweep of her lashes fluttered for a brief moment while she held his gaze with a bold one of her own. "Or maybe I'll fall in love with you too, and it'll all be happily ever after."

He sincerely doubted it, but as she shrugged the robe from her shoulders and it slithered to the floor in a hasty rush to pool at her feet in a silken heap, his tongue stuck to the roof of his mouth and his brain emptied of any lucid thought other than to take the woman to bed as fast as he could.

From a technical point of view, he shouldn't be prepared for her yet, but his hormones were already revved and ready to rock.

This time she met him half way as he crushed his mouth down on hers, almost piercing his lip with her teeth. Her startled yip made him laugh for the sheer hell of it as he swept her off her feet and dumped her on the bed, following her down before her body could bounce off.

At least she hadn't sent him packing. Not yet.

»»»•«««

Did he really think she'd cast a spell to make him fall in love with her?

True witches would never consider it. They never messed with free will. There were always consequences to any spell and to interfere with a person's decisions was not something she'd ever considered. Never mind she didn't have the ability or talent to invoke a love spell.

Or perhaps she did.

Pensive, Ruth stared out over the rough seas while the fresh wind lashed her hair around her face and obscured her view of the white crested waves as they crashed to the shore. She raised her hand and pushed her hair back from her face, and squinted against the sharp whip of spray-filled wind.

Had she used her powers to call to him? Was it her fault?

She took in a breath of salty air. The honest truth was she hadn't known he was in the house. She'd paused outside his door for several beats of her heart to listen for any movement. Normally she could hear the steady tap of his fingers on the computer keyboard, but there'd been nothing. No movement, no shuffle of papers, no footsteps. If he'd been there, she would have given a polite knock, asked him if he wanted a cup of coffee. The same beverage she'd sneaked since she'd bought it and the coffeemaker.

Would the end result have been the same?

The wind tugged at her clothes, warm and balmy, and where she'd normally wrap her arms about her waist to keep out the cold, she spread them wide and let the gusts buffet her.

He'd said she'd enchanted him. It hadn't been an accusation, but she'd been accused before. It may have been a long time ago, but her memory still served her well. The islanders knew she was a poor excuse for a witch. They never came to her, only ever to her grandmother for help.

Yet, since she'd started to practice again, her powers had gained strength, and a private ball of pride had started to grow.

Ruth grabbed her hair and tried to tame it into a ponytail, but the wind had none of it and whipped it back out of her hands to lash it around her face. She closed her eyes to enjoy the bracing gusts of wind better as it pummeled her sensitized body while she gave a secretive smile.

He'd slipped from her room when her grandmother had returned, as both of them sniggered like teenagers. It had felt so naughty to have him in her room in the middle of the day. Yet at the same time, so right. So wonderful.

If she acknowledged the truth, she was already half in love with him too. She just wasn't ready to confess it yet. She wanted to bask in the secrecy of it, hold it to her heart while she considered with care what she should do about it. Especially as he'd blurted it out first and then seemed to want to retract it.

With a sigh, she turned her back on the sea and made her way to the house. She'd always been too cautious, too careful not to put a step wrong. Which was why she'd avoided practicing magic. And why she'd not accepted the position of principal flute with the Scottish Orchestra.

She blew out a breath and laughed as the wind tugged at her dress to pull her back toward the sea while she pressed against it to get home. She should take a stance, stand up for what she really wanted, what she was capable of. All this time she'd believed she was being thoughtful, but her grandmother was right. She needed to be herself.

>>»•«<<

"So, what made you change your mind, young man? When I offered, you were so adamant about not having a reading."

The faded green of the old lady's gaze still glowed with a bright intelligence and wisdom he'd come to admire, which made the deception he was forced to maintain lean heavy on his heart.

"It's research for my latest book." There was no lie there, he'd write about it. Whether this episode of his life would ever be published was another matter.

Her gray eyebrows dipped low for a moment, the crease in the middle of them deepened, and he wondered if she doubted him. Her piercing gaze made him want to squirm in his seat, while she riddled him with guilt. But she settled herself down in the high-back gilded chair opposite, the small card table between them.

"I assume you're cynical of the art of tarot?"

He gave a careless shrug in response to her question. He was used to being challenged and adept at hiding his real opinion. But the thought of any deception with this woman wound thorny ribbons through his heart. "It's nothing I've considered too deeply, but I'm more interested in the technicalities of how it works as opposed to what it may mean to my own future."

His future was bleak, he already knew. He believed no card could tell him what he wanted to hear, nor change what he knew was to come.

In her hands, Clarisse held a plain wooden box which she placed in the center of the small table. She rested her fingers lightly on the lid. There was nothing ornate about it, yet curiosity swirled, so he leaned forward to study it, interested to note that where she stroked the box with her thumb, a smooth rut had formed to indicate her constant habit and many years of use.

Although not a young woman, her hands were unencumbered by arthritis. Still long and slender, her fingers continued their hypnotic caress of the wooden box. Her affection for it, or its contents, struck him as right. Calm and serene, it suited her to sit in the parlor of her tiny shop, with the aged box between them.

A smile tugged the corners of his lips. He'd met so many fakes and charlatans, most of them effused false charm, which was how they managed to sucker people into believing them. But this woman made no overt attempt to persuade him to believe her. Her perfect serenity was the charm which drew him in. An unruffled wisdom which certain women gained with age.

He raised his gaze from her hands to meet her tranquil contemplation.

"Tarot cannot tell you your future, nor direct you. We are on a continual journey, all of us, and I'm sure, although your cynicism rules you, you must be aware we strive to push beyond the limitations of what we believe to be our five senses." She gave one last stroke of the wooden box before she opened the lid and placed it with reverence next to the box. "Some of us would refer to it as psychic vision." The swift shrug of her brows showed she knew he was a cynic.

"Others believe it is allegorical. It's linked to our consciousness and our ancestry. I've found in this life it doesn't matter what your expectations are, there will always be something to surprise you, something unplanned." Her smile, genuine and unaffected creased the paper-thin skin of her cheeks. "You have an enquiring mind and questions you would love the answers to." The bright glitter of her gaze met his. "Believe what you may, but when I lay the cards, have your question in mind and ask it of yourself time and again while we go through them. Judge for yourself whether or not they answer the question. But hold the question you want answered here." She laid her hand on her breast. "And here." She touched her temple with her fingers, then returned them to the open box to remove a black satin pouch from within.

She slipped the tarot cards out of the pouch and returned it to the box which she moved to the counter beside her before she laid the pack of cards on the table between them.

Doubt tangled with curiosity to make difficult bedmates, but as his interest piqued to overwhelm any reservations, Stuart reached out for the cards ready to shuffle them as he'd been instructed time and again by different clairvoyants.

In a lightning move, Clarisse's hand whipped out to cover the cards. "Oh no. You should never touch someone else's tarot cards. These belong to me."

He'd not seen her rattled before, and it gave him a moment's pause. "I'm sorry, I never realized. They're quite tantalizing, and I felt the need to touch them. They're beautiful." He shuffled forward in his chair, leaned over the table to get a better look, but kept his hands palm down on the tablecloth. He told the truth; the cards were the oldest he'd seen. Medieval at a guess from the romantic depictions on the back, but he'd yet to see the artistry on the face of them.

With a quick recovery, Clarisse relaxed and picked the pack up. She turned them over so he could verify his initial observation. Fascinated, he slid his gaze over them, to absorb their ancient perfection.

"How old are they?"

"This pack, or Tarot cards in general?"

"Both."

"I believe these were hand produced many, many years ago. I don't have an exact date."

"Not a Rider Waite set, I presume." He quirked his lips at her as he asked the question. He'd seen many of the more commercial sets, but never one like this.

"No, Rider Waite came in at the turn of the 20th Century. These have been handed down through my family since ancient times. No one quite knows where they originated, but theories about the initiation of tarot cards varies dependent on who you speak with. I like the idea they'd come from Buddhism, but another theory is they existed in Egypt long before. I've always liked to think this set was created in Scotland, along with my ancestors who I believe at one time hid this pack in the Church walls on this very island to avoid being accused of heresy."

Her warm chuckle reminded him of her granddaughter, and he studied the line of her jaw, the curve of her cheek. Still a lovely lady, her skin was carved into laughter lines.

"Not so long ago you'd have had to deny being a witch, rather than celebrate it."

"Aye." She sniffed, lost in her own thoughts for a moment before she shuffled the pack. "Seven times I'll shuffle the pack for you."

Surprised by her abrupt change of subject, he paused for a long moment before he chose his next question. "Does it vary? The amount of times you need to shuffle?"

"It can. But seven is your number, I feel."

As she made the final shuffle, Clarisse took a deep breath in, let it out in a slow exhale. He'd seen it before but never questioned it. He'd been too intent on disproving people's abilities rather than observing the small habits they displayed when they prepared themselves. He'd sneered at their ways before, but with this woman, something had changed.

His axis had tilted, so it had become more important to him. "Why do you do that?"

She gave a slight smile, and the wrinkles deepened to slash across her cheeks. "I need to bathe the deck to rid it of the energies from my last reading."

"Ah." He had no reply. She believed but he didn't, although the stumble in his heart gave him cause to wonder. He believed in dark evil, but this was game-play.

Her smile deepened as though she'd read his mind. "You'll take what you need from this. Be assured. No one expects you to become an overnight convert."

Quite often they did. He had to admire the fact that she remained unruffled by his obvious cynicism. A cynicism he rarely showed to others as he used a friendly façade to cover his distrust. Distrust he felt at ease for her to see.

She was about to show him something she knew he didn't believe in, not he suspected, in an attempt to convince him, but she would walk him through the technique of it and let him decide for himself.

The need to control the situation slipped away and his muscles relaxed as he leaned his forearms on the small table, so they framed the space where the cards were to be placed.

She held them in her left hand, placed them on the table, cut the pack with the same hand and nudged both halves side by side. A spark of power spiraled through him as she met his gaze as though her mind locked with his. "Ask your question, Stuart. Not out loud. I don't need to know it. Hold it in your mind so only you know what you ask."

Will I succeed in saving my brother?

He hadn't meant to take it seriously, hadn't wanted to participate in the game, no question had posed in his mind until the moment she asked. He'd intended to keep it blank, see what she could make up about his past, present, and future with nil cooperation from him, but his subconscious whispered to him, maybe, just maybe he'd get the answers he sought, and the question circled uninvited.

Fingers still lithe and delicate, she dealt the first card with her right hand, turned it face up on the small black velvet covered table.

A quick gasp escaped her, but enough for Stuart to concentrate on the old lady instead of the card. Her features were blank. Almost too controlled. He glanced down at the card. Surprise quickened his pulse.

"The Lovers reversed."

He gazed down at the card, familiar from many hours of study. Although the depiction was different, all the elements were there. As he watched, the flames in the background became stronger, and pulsed in their intensity. The snake writhed its way up the trunk of the tree as the card took on a life of its own.

Did the old lady know about him and Ruth? It wasn't possible she'd found out about their afternoon of lovemaking, but she may be aware of the undercurrents between them.

Stuart raised his hand to chase away the thick cobwebs weaving through his mind. He rubbed his fingers across his forehead for a moment, and when his vision cleared, he gazed into the ancient jade of Clarisse's eyes.

He mustered a smile, but his tongue had dried enough to stick to the roof of his mouth. "Interesting," was all he could manage as he wondered, not for the first time, how much the old lady already knew.

"Indeed." Clarisse looked down, studied the card. "The Lovers aren't necessarily representative of love, or in this case, you may believe it shows the end of love. In actual fact, this card can mean a disharmony, a misalignment of values." She waved the back of her hand over the card. "Perhaps you need to reassess your path."

The smile she gave him was kind, but as she dealt the second card, there was no mistake in the quick rise of her eyebrows.

"Death." His quiet expulsion hung heavy in the small shop.

She paused before she spoke. "Again this card is not a portent of death, so don't fear it."

All right for her to say, and in all fairness, he knew already. It hardly had him shaking in his boots, but the coincidence of the two cards so close together came as a surprise. He'd given no hint of his life, his family. As far as anyone on the island was concerned he should appear as a footloose author who traveled the world in pursuit of tales and folklore. Nothing of his bleak future or his shadowy past had ever been revealed. He kept it close.

The character on the card pulsed, the thick black cloak slithered around him, then stilled as Clarisse gave it a light touch of her fingers. "This can mean the end of a major phase of your life, or that you're caught up in changes which you feel you have no control over."

He knew he had no control, never had. But she dragged him back. "Apply it to your question, Stuart. Only you can tell if it holds any truth."

She touched the back of his hand with the fingertips she'd rested on the card, and fire blazed across his skin, to scorch his arm. He puffed out a breath, but Clarisse had turned back to her cards and laid another three in quick succession on the table. He recognized them all; The Devil, The Tower, The Three of Swords, but the hard jolt to his chest as she dealt the last five cards almost had him praying for mercy, despite his suspension of belief. The Sun, Judgment, Seven of Swords, King of Swords, and the Knight of Cups.

If his cynical mind didn't know better, he'd think he was doomed, but the desire to laugh had long since left him while the trickle of apprehension turned into a raging gush.

She hovered her hand over them, then glanced up at him, her eyes darkened to midnight, the air thickened and the breath he drew in was heavy with water, clogging his lungs to make his chest burn for the want of fresh air.

The voice never came from her lips as she held him powerless with her dark, insistent gaze. Instead, it echoed through the empty corridors of his mind.

"There are great changes about to happen in your life, Stuart, and there will be decisions you must take that will cause you deep pain. You must be prepared for adversity, be ready to take on the challenges you will face and ensure you are equipped to deal with the hardships coming your way." She made no further move to touch him, nor come any closer, but her aged face filled his vision, the steel gray of her hair framed it while the room behind her faded into a pulsating blackness.

Stuart blinked in an attempt to clear his vision, tried to swallow, but the thick throb of the pulse in the base of his throat prevented him from doing so as Clarisse's voice resonated through his head. Her thick brogue smoothed out, so he heard her with clarity. "Think long and hard at what you hold in your heart and soul and decide whether the path you travel is the right one. The lie you live is a deception which will come to light, and the hurt you inflict is yours to determine. Let go of the dark and embrace instead the light offered to you."

Bright white light exploded behind his eyelids to fill his vision and cleanse his mind of all thought.

Confusion swirled as he stared up at the dark purple of the ceiling, tiny silver stars and planets spun in his vision.

Disorientated and sick, the deep ache in his ribcage competed with the thickness in his head.

"Stuart, are you all right?"

He meant to speak, but only a grunt came from his lips.

"Stuart? Nana said you fainted. Were you too hot?"

Red hot pokers stabbed the back of his eyes as he tried to focus on Ruth, concerned more about where she'd come from rather than how he'd come to be lying flat on his back staring up at the stars.

"Hot?" The thought had never occurred to him that he'd never been more than tepid since he'd arrived on the island and he'd never fainted in his life. Her cool fingers stroked the hair back from his face, while she kneeled by his side, but his tongue felt too thick and swollen to enable him to thank her.

He focused his vision while the old woman stood above them, fingers pressed to her lips, worry etched in every line on her face.

"It's okay." He struggled upright from his prone position on the floor. Pain shot through his head, his right shoulder throbbed and his ass ached where he'd hit the floor when he'd fallen from his chair. He had no memory of it. All thought had been seared from his brain. The last thing he remembered was Clarisse's face. He had no idea why he should feel the need to reassure her, but he hated to see the concern wreathed over her aged features.

"What were you doing?" Ruth studied him intently as he brought her into focus.

"I, ah…" He rubbed his head, glanced at the card table to note it was empty. The cards were nowhere in sight, and the black velvet cloth had been replaced by crisp, white lace.

He whipped his gaze up and took in Clarisse's far too innocent expression while suspicion rushed in a fast flood through his mind. She'd cleared the cards away. What had possessed her to? Unless she didn't want her granddaughter to see them. Or him to remember the spread, which was hardly an issue, he had the picture of it emblazoned in his mind forevermore. How could he ever forget what she'd dealt him?

As he studied the old lady's features, a cold fist seized his heart while the knowledge unfolded that Clarisse had not dealt him those cards, but fate had.

Chapter Six

Sunshine bathed the room in liquid honey, warm and golden. Ruth hummed a soft tune to herself as she stripped the linen from Stuart's bed and dumped it on the floor ready to take downstairs to wash. They'd used their best white linen, and with such a beautiful day, she should be able to get it washed, dried, ironed and back on the bed by lunch time. She picked up one of the pillowcases, buried her face in the cool material, and inhaled in the warm elusive scent of him.

Evocative memories from the night before stirred her senses and shimmered through to warm her blood again, just as he'd warmed it during the night.

She conjured the taste of him, the smoothness of his skin so much warmer than her own. Muscles far harder than she'd imagined were carved into his long, sleek limbs. When she'd kissed every ridge, every dip along his ribcage, followed them with her tongue and her lips to discover the delights of his stomach, she'd never realized how much pleasure a woman could take investigating the map of a man's body. She'd never taken the time, nor found such interest before.

She'd no idea where he'd gone, but she'd snuck out of his bedroom in the early hours just so Nana wouldn't know they slept together.

Ruth suspected she already knew, and it wasn't as though she was a child, she was a grown woman, but it seemed more respectful not to flaunt the fact under Nana's roof.

She gave herself a mental shake. The man may be back at any time, and she could indulge in him then, but right now she needed to get on with her chores so she could take over the gift shop for a few hours. She picked up the sheets, ran them downstairs to stuff them into the washing machine. She added the powder and fabric softener before she switched the machine on and headed back to Stuart's room, dragging the old vacuum cleaner up the stairs to plug it in.

She leaned over the ancient desk and flung open the bedroom window. She breathed in the rare warmth of the day and the fresh taste of salt from the sea. Pleased she could air the room while Stuart was gone, she moved back, her hip caught the mouse by the side of the keyboard, and the laptop whirred to life. Strange, she thought he would've powered it down while he was away, but the noise of the fan filled the silence in the room, and the screen glowed bright white, the writing stark against its background.

Not wanting to intrude on his privacy, Ruth lowered the lid of the laptop, so the screen was obscured from her view. Tempted to take a peek at his work, she turned away with determination, flipped on the vacuum, and whirred it through the room.

She ducked under the small desk, yanked the waste paper basket toward her, and sighed. The man could never be accused of being a neat freak. Bits of paper littered the floor behind where the basket had been. He'd obviously thrown his rubbish in the general direction in the hope it would by some miracle end up in the bin.

Ruth switched off the vacuum, dropped to her knees, and crawled into the small space under the rickety desk to retrieve the rubbish.

She raised her head and gave it a sharp rap on the underside of the ancient desk. Tears sprang to her eyes and starlight sparkled through her vision. The quiet whimper she let out, turned into a squeak of horror as the desk groaned and the bottom of the small drawer gave way at the back. The base hung suspended for one heart-stopping moment before the back slipped off, and the contents pounded onto the carpet.

"Oh, nae, ye canna do that."

Ruth gave her head a brisk rub, and the pain subsided to a dull throb. "Aye, ye clumsy oaf." She backed out from under the desk aware it may collapse at any moment. With a steady hand, she picked up the laptop and transferred it to the safety of the bed, and then turned to deal with the drawer.

The bottom had fallen out of the drawer before. Nothing she couldn't deal with. She could just slide the walnut base back into the grooves and hammer on the back panel. Ruth leaned in, grabbed the front and pulled, almost snapping her nails off in the process. Surprised, she bent down to inspect the unit. He'd locked the drawer. Not that he needed to lock his valuable possessions away, but she understood his need for a little security, even on an island with no crime.

A slight ache weaved its way through her stomach at the thought that he might believe Nana and she would snoop through his possessions. She'd never consider it, her own privacy being paramount. She sniffed and rubbed her nose with the back of her hand while the whip of insult died down. He was, after all, American, far less trusting than the islanders, and didn't all American's carry guns?

With a sigh, she dropped to her knees again and reached for the small pile of stuff sprawled on the carpet. She gathered together the papers she'd spilled and shuffled them into a neat pile back into the file they'd come from. She placed it by her side while she swept up a wad of money, flight tickets, and his passport. She paused for a moment. She wouldn't snoop, but a little peek never harmed anyone. A quick glance at his photograph and she smiled. Yep, he looked like a criminal. Just like every other passport photograph. She ran her thumb across his image, and a warm thrill chased through her veins. It didn't really matter how serious he appeared in his photograph, nothing could disguise his unmistakably handsome features. The high slash of his cheekbones, the dark intensity of his storm-filled eyes.

Ruth sank back onto her haunches while she studied the document. She flicked the pages over. Surprised at its age. Dated just four years earlier. But he'd managed to travel to so many places. Curious, she flicked over another few pages, squinted at the stamps of countries he'd collected along the way. She turned another page, and an inexplicable sadness washed over her as she studied one stamp after another. Norway, Iceland, Sweden, through Europe. Germany, France, Spain. Into Africa; Morocco, Tunisia, Namibia. For some reason, she'd assumed he'd come straight from the U.S., but it appeared he'd not been there for some time.

She tilted her head to one side to study his travels. The man had never stayed in one place for very long at all. Sorrow spun its web, not for her sake, but for the man who lead such a lonely, nomadic life.

It didn't seem fair somehow. She knew he wouldn't stay. He'd never made any kind of commitment to her. There'd been no repetition of the declaration of love he'd made, but her heart had held out hope there was more than just a passing passion between them. He'd probably left behind more than one or two women; oblivious he'd broken their hearts. It appeared he didn't know how to stay in one place for any more than a few weeks. She scratched the side of her nose. How had he found enough time to write novels? If indeed he was that kind of writer. She'd never pursued the line of questioning with him, despite her promise to herself she would.

With a quiet sigh, she closed the passport, rubbed her thumb over the dark blue cover of the United States. She traced the insignia on the front with her fingertips. She'd never even had a passport—there'd been no need. She'd only ever traveled over to the mainland for her education. Edinburgh University hardly required a passport.

Saddened, she placed it on top of the other items, and then picked them up, placed them with care on the bed next to Stuart's laptop so he could put them away again once he handed over the key and she'd fixed the drawer.

Pale white light glowed from underneath the partially closed lid of the laptop and curiosity got the better of her. With a quick glance at the bedroom door, she took hold of the lid and raised it to sneak a look at the page.

No wonder he'd locked his drawer, he must have known she couldn't resist.

Guilt swamped her, and she clicked the lid closed as fast as she could, but not quick enough for her not to have processed the copyright date and name on the header of the Word document.

Disturbed, she chewed her lip as she contemplated what she'd seen and tried to shrug off the growing sense of unease. He wasn't obliged to tell her who he was and most authors wrote under a nom de plume, but it would have been nice if he'd mentioned it. Vague recognition tickled the back of her mind, but not enough to persuade her to open the laptop again.

Uncomfortable with the invasion of his privacy, she rubbed her hands on the thighs of her jeans, then wrapped her arms around herself and tucked her fingers neatly out of the way so she could resist temptation. If he'd not divulged the name he wrote under, well, it was his business.

Determined to push all doubt aside, she crawled back under the desk, careful not to catch her head this time, and picked up the last item, a small notebook. The base of the drawer hung down above her head, and she glanced up, craned her neck so she could see better in the darkened little cavern she'd created. How much had he managed to stuff into the drawer? No wonder it had collapsed. She reached up to coax out another pile of paper.

A small wooden box slipped out along with the rest of the papers. She made a grab for it. For such a dainty box, it weighed a lot, and before she could save it, it bounced from the tips of her fingers and slammed into the floor with a heavy clunk.

"Ah, ya daft cow. Do ye have to be so clumsy?" Ruth scrambled to pick up the box, taking a hold of the smooth wooden frame as gently as she could.

She squirmed out from under the desk and sat cross-legged, placing the slim box on the carpet in front of her. Beautifully inlaid with a jade top, Ruth took a moment to study it before she gave in to the temptation to stroke the smooth wood and trace her fingers over the carved surface. It should have been cool to her touch, but the warmth generated by the jade sent a little ripple of surprise over her skin. Magic gave off a strong pulse-wave, drawing her fingers back time and again to touch the polished stone surface.

Uneasy, she glanced at the door, then back down at the box. It would be rude to look inside. An invasion of Stuart's privacy. But how could she resist? It beckoned to her, she went with her instincts and conjured the white light from her core to travel through her body and out through her fingertips.

The zap of lightning struck with such unexpected savageness, electricity flung her backward across the bedroom, and a scream broke free from her throat. The all-pervading taste of ozone filled her nostrils and coated her tongue with acrid bitterness making her head spin.

She scrambled to her knees, her pulse throbbed at the base of her neck, the sound of her own heart skittered in her ears to drown out the white noise which fizzed through her mind.

On her hands and knees, she crawled back across the room, this time she approached the box with caution. Broken, the singed lid lay next to the upside-down container.

Mortified, she stared at the destruction she'd caused. "Och, what have I done? What have I done?" She drew in a calming breath. "I knew it was dangerous to dabble with magic. I knew I shouldn't mess when it always goes wrong." Her fingers trembled as she reached for the box

The angry hiss and sizzle threatened her and stopped her mid-stretch. She fought the sharp wave of nausea which convulsed her stomach, blew out a soft breath, and withdrew her hand as she rolled to her feet. A soft echoing breath came from behind her. The hairs on the back of her neck prickled with awareness as another presence entered the room. With a slow turn of her head, Ruth met the emerald stares of her three cats. The collective growl they sent up washed ice-water through her veins. Evil permeated the room as black magic met white and throbbed in a snarling challenge

Through her adrenaline rush, Ruth cast a quick glance at the mess she'd made. She needed a clear space. She needed protection. The cloying atmosphere closed in to warn her of danger and clenched at her chest, so her breath came in fast, erratic hitches.

In her panic, she dropped to her knees, scooped up the remaining paperwork, careful to keep her distance from the hateful object, and dumped it all on the bed. The small area she'd cleared would have to do. Instinct ruled where ignorance once reigned and Ruth brushed aside everything she'd always believed about herself and her poor abilities and listened instead to the desperate pull of self-preservation.

She flicked her hand over the carpet to clear the last remains of paper from the space she'd created, noting the way her cats drew into her side. The hard punch of evil crawled through her already clammy skin. Whatever lay beneath the box pulsed pure black magic into the room to flood it with darkness. There was no option to leave. The darkness would only follow.

>»»•«««

"Hey, Stuart."

"Ian."

"How're things?"

Stuart narrowed his eyes against the glare of sun on water as he gazed out to sea, his cellphone pressed close to his ear so he could hear his brother's voice through the soft, fuzzy reception. "Not good."

Static crackled, but there was no mistaking the sigh. "In what way?"

Stuart scrunched his face up. His heart beat too fast. "Something's wrong. I can't be in the right place."

"But, what about all the work we did? We've checked and re-checked your location. She has to be there."

The note of desperation in his brother's voice broke his heart. Stuart gripped his hair with his free hand and drew in a long breath. "There's no witch here, Ian. The old lady's nothing more than that. Sweet, old, wise. She gives tarot readings and hope; she administers homeopathic remedies. She's gentle, with no apparent ego. She advises people to get a medical opinion when she thinks it necessary. I've spent hours with her, and there's nothing. Nothing to indicate she has any phenomenal power." His conscience nudged him to mention. "She read tarot cards for me."

"Find out anything interesting?"

He wasn't about to go into detail. "Nothing more than I've heard in the past."

"So, she's a fraud."

"No. Not a fraud. She does nothing deceptive. She's not misleading. She's just...a white witch."

"I didn't think you believed in them."

He tipped back his head, letting out a groan. "I don't, not really. But she seems to bring comfort to people. She's certainly not the all-powerful witch I'd expected to find." He opened his eyes, watched the bloom of dark clouds race in from the horizon, and turned to beat a hasty retreat before he got caught in the rain. "I thought I would come across a monster, one I wouldn't hesitate to kill if I couldn't find another solution. I didn't expect to find a community of old-fashioned, gentle folk.

Ian's reply, when it came was barely audible. "I don't want you to kill anyone on my behalf."

"I'm not going to. I can't. Look, Ian, we have to find another way."

Without warning, the bright freshness of the afternoon crashed into a furious storm.

"What in hell's name…?"

The phone went dead and zapped a loud crack into the atmosphere.

Stuart raced the last few paces into the house before the heavens opened to spit out a deluge of rain and fury and turned the sky from day to midnight within the strike of three flashes of lightning.

Breathless, he paused in the kitchen to listen to the sounds of the old house while he shook droplets of water from his hair.

No haunting music beckoned to him. No hint of another human's presence, just the thrash of rain and roll of thunder accompanied him as he made his way up the darkened stairs, surprised the three sentinels didn't lurk in the shadowed corners.

The walk he'd taken was supposed to have cleared his head of her so he could think straight when he spoke to his brother, but the moment the phone died, all he could think about was her.

Stuart flashed a quick glance up at the violent heavens through the little stairwell window before he shook off the unease.

He sighed as he reached the top of the staircase, his legs a leaden weight. How could he be so wrong?

He'd spoken to so many of the locals, but there was no hint of another source of magic. The only tales he heard were of Clarisse and her abilities to heal.

He couldn't kill her. He hadn't the strength.

Green neon seeped from the cracks around his closed bedroom door and flickered through the darkened hallway to cast an eerie glow over the shadows.

Confused by the strange light, Stuart raised his hand, automatically checking if the door was warm, and sniffed to make sure there was no smell of fire. Nothing. Yet the green hue continued to waver from behind his door. He'd left his laptop on, but unless it had undergone a considerable energy boost, he doubted his laptop was responsible for such a bright source of light.

With a cautious hand, he turned the old-fashioned doorknob and pushed open the door.

Not quite sure what he witnessed, Stuart froze in the doorway.

Cross-legged on the floor, Ruth sat with a cat either side and one posted in front of her. All of them stared at him. Their obsidian eyes glowed in the strange light from the low circle of fire that surrounded them. Shadows sharpened Ruth's features, to emphasize the cut of her cheekbones, the darkened pits of her eyes, and the straight line of her mouth.

The only acknowledgment she knew he was there was the quick downward slash of her black eyebrows.

He'd witnessed many paranormal events before, so-called demonic possessions, séances, and mediums who channeled spirits through themselves. Most of them fraudulent, but he'd come across a few he'd been unable to explain. He wasn't prepared to make a call on this situation yet.

He took a long moment to study the scene while fury spewed at him from the jet black of her expression.

Together with the circle of fire and the three sentinels, she took up most of his room. The bed was stripped. It didn't look like it had been done in a wild frenzy, but perhaps she'd been unhappy with him for some inexplicable reason.

Curious, he brought his attention back to her face, tilted his head to one side. This wasn't a snit she was going through. It appeared to be a full-on display of black-magic. He'd watched Buffy the Vampire Slayer when he was a kid. What hormone filled teenager hadn't? The black eyes had been a specialty of the little red-headed witch. Great contact lenses, but instinct warned him Ruth didn't wear lenses.

The rapid-fire rhythm of his pulse hinted there was far more than just atmosphere and a weak attempt at parlor room tricks going on. The question was, *why*? What had triggered the furious pulse from the flame circle?

"Ruth, honey. Did something happen while I was gone?"

As he stepped forward, the small blue flames gushed bright orange to spurt their wrath skyward, with nothing but the ceiling to stop them.

"Whoa, baby. Take it easy." He forced himself to stay calm, slipped back to the doorway, with his hands held out beseeching her to keep still. "It's okay, Ruth. Everything's cool. Don't singe your nana's carpet." From her deep fury, she was more inclined to raze the place to the ground with the intense heat her flames had thrown out. The clever little trick he'd thought her capable of was nothing less than a miracle. Her blue pilot lights had thrashed up in an instant with no warning from her, no outward gesture to indicate what was about to happen.

As the flames lowered, he met her black gaze with his own.

"Did I do something to upset you?" After all, she was in his room. Last time he'd seen her, she'd sneaked out his doorway, coils of black hair bouncing around her naked shoulders as she'd cast him a final sultry glance and a wicked smile before she disappeared from view.

He kept his distance while he took his time to study her. Tension stiffened her body.

She pulled her lips back from her teeth. The three cats hissed in unison with her and exposed their bright white fangs.

Possession. Maybe. But he'd never heard of it affecting a whole group of animals as though they were one entity, the connection between them so strong their eyes glowed the same preternatural color. Their expressions contained the same feline ferocity. Like the first night he'd arrived, they gathered for protection, their bodies expanded in the dark confines of the room.

He leaned against the doorframe, not entirely confident the exit behind him was a guaranteed escape route. He crossed his arms over his chest in an attempt to show her he wouldn't run scared when in fact, that very fear held him fast in its grip.

The woman in front of him wasn't his lover, his love. The midnight eyes weren't the only hint. The drab brown dress from a bygone age consumed her slender body in a mantel of material giving off a distinct stench of swamp water. The evidence couldn't have been more obvious...

"Okay, so I guess there's something..."

As the flames lowered, his gaze roamed the room until he could see past her. His laptop was on the stripped bed, paperwork littered around it. He spared Ruth a quick glance, tempted to move, but her lips pulled back to expose her teeth while her breath soughed in and out in quick succession, her bosom heaved under the low neckline of the sack-cloth she wore.

"Hey honey, I think you might want to slow down on the fast breathing, you might start to feel a little woozy in a minute or two. Too much oxygen." He pushed away from the door, took two cautious steps into the room, the sneaking suspicion she'd read his computer curdled in his stomach. He should have closed it down, then even if she'd tried to look, it would have been password protected. Instead, he'd left it mid-document when he'd spotted the seals in the bay and decided he needed to get a closer look while he attempted to get a better signal to ring his brother, the tales of selkie far too much of a temptation.

He hadn't been gone long, but evidently long enough for Ruth to tear through his private papers and read his computer.

Undeterred by the low, feral growl which spewed from all four of the creatures within the circle, Stuart stepped deeper into the room. At least she hadn't repeated the flame throwing act. Yet. There was always time, but perhaps the thought of razing her nana's home to the ground had made some impact.

He reached out a hand, tested the heat of the small blue flames. There was none. Not even a hint of warmth.

Puzzled, he hunkered down as close as he dared to the edge of the circle while he scanned the room. He squinted to get a better look past the flickering flames.

The painful jab in his chest accompanied the roll of his stomach as his view beyond the bed pinpointed the one item he hadn't expected to see. He rose to his feet again, raised his chin so he could better examine the evidence. The bottom of the drawer in the small desk hung down at a forty-five-degree angle. Underneath it appeared to be the seared remains of the wooden box that had contained his jade handled knife.

As cautious as he could, Stuart edged around the perimeter of the circle until he was within reach of the upended box. He cast a wary glance at the witch, shocked to find instead of having a side view of her, she still faced him head on, a snarl wreathed her face while her three cats sat in exactly the same formation.

Engrossed, he gazed at her, the sick suspicion he'd inadvertently discovered the all-powerful witch right under his nose congealed in a heavy lump of cold disappointment. It appeared she'd managed to hide in plain sight. His desire for her had become her shield.

He dropped to his knees and reached out for the box, aware of the escalation of distress from the cat community. The pitiful wails grew louder and more piercing as he took hold of the wooden box and flipped it over to expose the jade handled knife. His gaze never left hers. The mournful and desolate noise she emitted filled his heart and tore it in two. What the hell had he done? He'd damaged her.

Aware of the distress the knife caused her, he rolled to his feet and clutched it down by his side to avoid her seeing it as a threat. As he watched her beautiful, pale face, the black eyes wept tears of blood, streaking her cheeks with bright crimson trickles which dripped in slow, thick droplets from her chin.

Her lips never moved, but the sound of her voice echoed his name in his mind. A brief memory of his dream feathered through him. "Moya?"

"What in the name of Satan is going on here?"

Terror crashed through the silence and Stuart whipped his chin up to meet the boiling anger of Clarisse's gaze from across the room. Furious she may be, but at least her eyes weren't obsidian black. He flicked his attention back to Ruth who still faced him, her attention never wavered from the knife at his side. Blood still coursed down her face and dripped onto the back of her hands where they rested on her knees.

He raised the knife to show Clarisse, aware of the sharp hiss Ruth and her companions emitted.

"It's okay—it's okay. I mean you no harm Moya. I won't hurt you. I'm going to put it away now, where it can't hurt you."

Shame constricted his chest until his heart threatened to explode from it. He'd already hurt her. The dull burn spread, while he reached for the broken box. He placed the knife inside, fixed the lid on top to seal the case the best way he could, aware his every move was being followed by Clarisse, Ruth, and the three cats.

He jerked his shoulders unsure exactly what to say. "I don't know what happened. I came in to find my room wrecked. Ruth was just there, but it's not Ruth, Clarisse. It's Moya."

The emptiness in the witch's black expression proved him right. Ruth wasn't there, she was beyond reach, beyond his help.

When the knife was no longer in sight, he tugged at the small drawer so he could slip the box in, forgetting he'd locked it. He gave a second, harder pull and the front of the drawer came away in his hand, and the rest of it clattered apart, its sound muffled by the thick carpet as it thudded onto it.

A quick glance in Ruth's direction confirmed she'd never once taken her attention away from him, her obsidian eyes still spit loathing at him from across the room. Clarisse had kept her place at the doorway, although her expression was a cool glimmering sage, the twist of her lips was almost a snarl not unlike her granddaughter's had been earlier.

With a heavy sigh, Stuart turned away and pushed the box under the bed.

He had no idea what the hell had happened for the box to have been damaged and the knife exposed, but it hadn't brought Ruth to any harm before when it had been hidden away, surely it wouldn't cause any more problems once he'd put it out of sight again.

Except she now knew about it.

When he returned his attention to Ruth, the blood had disappeared from her face, and her eyes had lost the ebony glaze and returned to emerald green, but her cheeks remained the same chalky white.

On his knees, he reached out to her with no idea how to make the situation right. He stretched his arm out above the low flickering flames and into the circle. If she wanted to toast him, now was her opportunity.

As she ignored him, he raised his gaze higher to take in the old lady whose frailness he'd never noticed until that minute. She'd shrunk, wilted against the doorframe. He imagined the weakness in her limbs prevented her from moving, much like the leaden weight in his.

The blue flames gave one last flare before they guttered and died.

Insistent, Stuart shuffled forward on his knees and continued to hold out his hand until Ruth reached for him and accepted his help to her feet. He barely had the energy to pull his own body up, but as soon as her hand touched his, he hauled her out of her circle and into his arms. He cradled her, rocked her body to give her comfort as she crumpled against him, her long limbs wrapped around him.

Relief flooded heat through his body while he stroked her hair. Words of reassurance refused to break past the lump in his throat, but he couldn't let her go.

He'd never witnessed anything like it.

The magic hadn't frightened him, he'd seen enough to last him a lifetime, but the desperate pouring out of her pain shattered his spirit.

He'd deceived her.

He rested his chin on the top of her head, tangled his fingers into her dark curls. Grating out a husky whisper, he met the troubled gaze of her grandmother. "I think we need to talk."

·•·

The cup of tea cradled in her hands threatened to spill its contents, but Ruth gritted her teeth and invoked sheer willpower to overcome the shakes.

Adrenaline caused through fear and fury had crashed to leave her body a jellified mass of weakness. Ashamed she'd actually let Stuart take her weight and lead her downstairs to the kitchen, she couldn't meet his piercing stare as they sat opposite each other. Nana sat at the head of the table.

He was the enemy. One half of her soul knew it. The half he'd shredded.

All three waited in silence while they sipped the hot liquid.

Ruth glanced at the kitchen clock to find time had whisked away. Hours disappeared while she'd been in Stuart's room. She screwed up her face while she tried to assimilate what had happened in the vacuum of time.

The shuddering breath he hauled in drew her attention so when he started to speak, she could do nothing but stare at his lips.

"You need to know the truth."

The sarcastic retort bounced wildly in her head but failed to make it beyond her lips as storm gray eyes met hers with a seriousness that halted her mid-word.

"My brother is about to die."

Confusion stopped all thought as Ruth blinked in rapid succession while her mind tried to grasp the relevance of his brother's life to what had just occurred.

White knuckled fingers curled around the cup he grasped while he stared at the pattern he traced with his thumbs. He raised his head and pinned her with a gaze of such intensity, the pulse in her temples threatened a vicious headache.

He chewed his lip for a long moment before he released the mug and spread his hands palm down on the table. Nana's silence drew her attention. Strain deepened the wrinkles around the old lady's mouth, but her expression was bright and questioning.

Stuart's small cough dragged her back.

"He has a heart condition. Each day he becomes weaker."

His brother meant nothing to her, but she considered what he may mean to Stuart. "What about a heart transplant?"

His rough spurt of laughter accompanied the shake of his head. "It's a possibility, if they find a match—if someone dies in order for him to live, but it won't happen. He will die on his son's tenth birthday because that's the way it's always been."

"I don't understand."

Pure agony wreathed his face. "No. How could I expect you to when I don't either, not fully, but I know it will happen."

He took another sip of the black coffee, sighed, and placed the cup back on the saucer.

"I need to start at the beginning, and I'm sorry if this seems unbelievable or doesn't make sense, but I think you need to know I've lived with this the whole of my life. I know it to be true and I've spent so long…" He grazed his hand through his hair, a gesture so weary, despite her fear and her anger, it tugged at Ruth's heart. "So long investigating this." He leaned his elbows on the table and linked his fingers, touched them to his mouth before he continued. "According to the research I have, a relative of mine, another Stuart Caldwell, fled from Kilchoan in Scotland to South Carolina in 1673. We can only assume he feared for his life, and rightly so, it appears. For generations, there have only been males born to the Caldwell family. At first, I'm sure it went relatively unnoticed, but after some time the Caldwell's realized each time the first-born of the next generation reached the age of ten, his father would die. Of course, Stuart Caldwell never knew it at the time, but he knew something bad was about to happen."

Pain-filled eyes met hers. "My nephew will be ten in less than three weeks. In direct relation to that, there's been a rapid deterioration in my brother's condition."

Doubt mixed with curiosity to help her find her voice again. "How do you know this for certain? It can't be true."

"It is true, and I know for certain because my own father died on my tenth birthday. He was forty-four. Since the death of his father on his tenth birthday, he'd taken up the research himself. My father's investigations probably reached deeper than anyone before."

When he reached a hand out, unsure whether he was about to place it on hers, she leaned back in her seat not certain she could bear his touch. Only the slight narrowing of his eyes gave any indication he'd noticed, but his voice was stronger as he continued. "Probably because technology was starting to develop at a rapid rate, it opened up a whole world of research opportunities. He had a breakthrough in our ancestry when he managed to trace it back to Scotland. It had always been assumed Stuart Caldwell had committed some kind of crime which made him flee Scotland, but my father traveled there and discovered his diary. Caldwell fled his very wealthy estate along with just his wife and three young children for no apparent reason. The youngest, a newborn, died on the crossing. According to Caldwell's diary, the journey was arduous and took its toll on the health of all of them. An experience he never recovered from and which he attributed to a curse."

"A curse?"

Clarisse leaned forward, and her own teacup rattled in the saucer as she clipped it down. "What made him believe there was a curse?"

"We don't know. He wrote about it with such tentativeness, we weren't sure, but his son, Robert, traveled back to Scotland, and we've discovered his name carried great significance in the witch trials there throughout the seventeenth century. He was responsible for the death of hundreds of women and young children. From what we can gather, he was single-minded in his pursuit of what he referred to as demonic possession."

"He was a witch finder."

"Yes." Stuart bowed his head as though the shame of it still affected him.

The fast burn of acid turned Ruth's stomach as she thought of all the needless deaths the man had been responsible for. Innocents as she already knew, accused of witchcraft because they had a mole, a birthmark, a scar which may indicate the devil's mark. All borne of ignorance of the day, but ignorance had ruled for centuries and still did. She'd had a taste of it herself.

She raised her cup to her lips and took a sip of tea to wet her parched tongue. "Did he also die when his eldest son reached the age of ten?"

"No. He had no children. He refused to marry. He was the eldest of the two surviving children and lived until he was quite elderly. His accounts of witch-hunting are extensive. His brother Henry died at an early age of ague." Stuart dipped his head. "I believe he was thirty-two and it was on his son's tenth birthday."

A chill seeped through her, so she wrapped her fingers about the teacup to pull in the warmth. "So, every male descendant who has a child dies when the child reaches the age of ten?"

Stuart nodded.

"But, if you don't have children, you live on."

"Yes."

"Is that why you've never married?"

His crooked smile was full of regret. "I never met anyone I loved enough to marry."

She stared at him in silence until Stuart pushed his chair back, rose to walk over to the kitchen window, and stared blind out at the dull, grayness of the day. After the fury of the storm, the heaven's wept their grief over the island.

He stood silent for a long moment, as though a war raged inside him before he continued. "Every generation has researched. Each step slow and painful put to an end by each death. You can't imagine how difficult it is each time to realize that the progress made is put on hold until the next one is ready to take up the gauntlet. We are, all of us, ten when our father's die. There's so much backtracking to be done." He turned and leaned against the counter so he could look at both Ruth and her grandmother, his eyes as bleak as the sky. "Every ten-year-old's childhood is cut short by the demise of their father and the weight of the next generation on their shoulders."

The ten-year-old's pain and suffering pulsed from him, to overwhelm her with the sheer pointlessness of it all, but the questions she had still needed to be answered.

"What has this got to do with us, with me?"

He drew in a breath, his steady gaze fixed on her. "You know who I am?"

Puzzled by the question, she squinted at him. "Stuart Caldwell."

He nodded. "Yes. Better known as Stuart Harper." He paused, and the small tug of recognition she'd felt when she'd read his name increased.

"I know who you are." Clarisse's voice grazed out, rusty and ill-used. "I knew who you were when you arrived, son. You don't need a pseudonym when you're so famous your photograph is over the back cover of your books. Books I have read and returned to the library. We may be antiquated here on Breggar, but we do have access to books."

Ruth had no idea what Nana spoke about. Who was Stuart Harper? She turned her blank gaze on her grandmother. "I don't understand. Who is he, and why haven't you mentioned it?"

"He's famous, Ruth. I'm surprised you didn't recognize him. He's also a witch-finder."

Stuart opened his mouth, shook his head in denial, but at Clarisse's cool stare he kept quiet.

"You may not use the ducking stool and burn us at the stake, young man, but you still hunt us down and ruin lives."

"I don't…"

"Yes, I'm afraid that's exactly what you do."

"I expose cheats and liars to stop them from harming normal, everyday folk who grieve for people they've lost and seek help in the afterworld instead of living in this one."

"It's not your decision to make. What path a person takes is their choice."

Surprised at Nana's passion, Ruth leaned back in her chair to watch them both.

"I agree, but not when there's a deliberate deception in exchange for money. Some of these practitioners take hundreds, thousands of dollars or pounds, or Euros." He flung out his hands, as passionate in his belief as Nana was in hers. "I only expose the ones I know are false. If there's any doubt, I leave them alone."

Silence hung heavy in the air until Stuart glanced at Clarisse. "Why did you let me stay?"

Expression sharp, she folded her arms across her boney chest. "Because I wondered what you sought from us. There was no exposure needed because neither of us…" she flicked her fingers to include Ruth, "… exerted the powers you're so familiar with disparaging." With a small nod, Clarisse tightened her lips. "I felt your pain the moment you arrived. I've seen your agony and your future in your cards. I may not have known what your story was, but my own tarot indicated I was to help."

Stuart stalked to the table and slapped himself back into the wooden chair, making the table shake as he thumped his arms on it. "You should have thrown me out. Made me leave."

With a regretful smile, Clarisse's composure never wavered. "Perhaps I should have, but I believe it's too late now for us to have a choice."

"Those cards you dealt me should have warned you, Clarisse. You should have kicked my ass out there and then."

Her grandmother's lips relaxed, quirked up at the edges with natural amusement while Ruth's heart gave a nasty hitch. She'd no idea Stuart had had a reading. Neither of them had told her. While she squinted from one to the other, their buzz of mutual admiration filled the air as her ire rose.

"What reading?"

Stuart reached across the table and laid his hand on Clarisse's blue-veined one making Ruth splutter with indignation.

"What damned reading?"

"There's no need for bad language, dear." Her grandmother's eyes twinkled, and Ruth gave over to the desire to grind her own teeth.

"Nana! When did you read Stuart's tarot?"

Nana raised her free hand to pat her hair. She left her other one under Stuart's while she fluttered at him. "Oh, now, I'm not quite sure. Was it last Wednesday, Stuart, or the Wednesday before?"

"Almost a week ago? Possibly two?" Ruth's head was about to explode. "Neither of you thought to tell me?" The quick guilty glances at each other settled the matter.

Ruth surged to her feet, paced to the window, paused a moment before she whirled to face them. A whole host of emotions rolled confused and free through her. "You kept it hidden from me." A thought occurred to her, and she waggled her finger at him. "It was when you fainted."

"Blacked out."

"Same thing." Slower, she wandered to the table, her mind a whirl. She sank back down. This time when she spoke, she kept her voice cool and calm, with a whip of danger under the surface. "What the hell happened to make you...*black out*?"

Her grandmother wriggled, but Stuart met her gaze head-on. "Probably lack of breakfast that morning. I was out early." He rolled his shoulders in a negligent shrug, but she knew there was far more to it. The pair of them were too casual.

"And...?"

"Clarisse dealt the cards."

Ruth cast her mind back, squinted at Nana while she tried to visualize the scene. She'd been concerned about Stuart, but she was pretty sure... "There were no cards out when I got there."

"No dear. I thought if you saw them, you'd want answers, ones neither Stuart nor I had at the time."

"Answers."

This time she just sighed and waited.

Her grandmother turned her hand over and held Stuart's for a moment before she let go. "The spread was a bad one."

"Really? What was it?" She leaned in to hold Nana's gaze with her own. "Don't tell me you can't remember Nana, you always remember." It seemed Ruth had somehow become the parent while the two recalcitrant children continued to procrastinate.

"The Devil, The Tower, The Three of Swords, The Sun, Judgment, Seven of Swords, King of Swords and the Knight of Cups." Nana's lips tightened before she glanced at Stuart from under her lashes for confirmation before she continued. "Death. The Lover's reversed."

Mouth open, Ruth stared at the pair of them. "Whoa."

"Yeah." Stuart hunched his shoulders.

"Aye." Nana linked her fingers together.

"That's a very dark spread. Whatever Stuart's question, the cards are stacked against him." Concerned by the waxiness of Nana's skin, Ruth took a closer look. "What happened when you dealt your own?"

The idea Nana was about to deny it made Ruth frown, but Clarisse shook her head and gained a little of her matriarchal dominance back. "That's my business young lady." Her gray eyebrows lifted in a superior fashion, but Ruth could see Nana was shaken, so she continued to hold her stare until Clarisse conceded. "Suffice to say—the deck had changed considerably from my previous reading." She patted the back of Stuart's hand as though she needed to lend him support while he was the one who'd brought all the evil down on them. "Mine wasn't as dark as Stuart's, but there were elements which overlapped."

As a thought occurred to her, Ruth reached out to touch Nana's hand. "Did you do an *other reading* based on me?" She knew she would have done, but she needed Nana to confirm it.

"What's an *other reading*?" Stuart's chair creaked as he leaned forward.

"It's when you do a reading based on someone else. In this case, Nana read *my* cards without me there."

Stuart nodded. "I've heard of it. Never seen it in practice though."

Fear burned hot while Ruth turned her attention back to Nana. "What did you find, Nana?"

"That they were all linked." Nana's eyes sparkled with unshed tears as she glanced from one to the other. "That's why I couldn't turn you away, son. The threads of our lives are interwoven, and if you leave before the matter is dealt with, then it may never be resolved. There is a reason you are here, and we can no longer ignore it."

In the silence, they all raised their cups and sipped.

Clarisse was the first to place hers back on its saucer. "You say your family have suffered for generations because of some kind of curse which dates back hundreds of years. I assume the reason you're here is because you believe this curse was placed by a distant relation of ours." At Stuart's brief nod, Clarisse continued. "Do you know more about the curse? How it came about? The reason behind it?"

"Not much." He shook his head, and his straight hair moved in a sleek black velvet curtain around his chiseled features.

"Moya." The name exploded from her lips before Ruth's mind processed it.

Stuart's dark eyebrows slammed down in a deep frown of recognition. "Where have you heard that name?"

"I…" The rush of heated blood filled her face at the remembered passion of her dream. "She…" Flustered, Ruth pushed her hair back from her hot face. "When I cast my circle…"

"Moya was there, not you in the circle when I went upstairs."

Reluctant to correct him, Ruth gave a weak smile. She couldn't see the harm in not divulging her dream to him. Except when he stared at her, his eyes pierced her mind. "Was that the first occasion you've channeled her?"

Caught out, she stared at him for a long moment before she shook her head. "No, I came across her a few weeks ago. Not long after you'd arrived." She cast Nana an apologetic look. "After you told me to acknowledge my heritage."

"What happened?" Stuart drew her attention back to him as wildfire raced over her cheeks.

"I was her. Moya." A vicious shiver ran through her.

"Are we talking reincarnation?"

"No. No. I don't believe so." More at ease now they'd steered away from the actual contents of the dream, Ruth conjured up the memory of her two encounters with Moya. "Nor is she a ghost. I've never had any dealings with her before, but I think her spirit has been invoked by you, Stuart."

"She looks just like you."

Surprise fluttered through her stomach.

"She doesn't smell as good, though." His straight lips curved in a wry smile "Eau de swamp water."

Clarisse's strained voice broke through their contemplation. "Is that the only time you've witnessed her? When you've been in your protective circle?"

"Yes." Ruth never hesitated in her response.

"No." Stuart's sharp reply was just as confident. He shrugged before he continued. "I've seen her three times."

"Three?"

"Yeah. Just after I first arrived. The day I…" He glanced at Clarisse and gave an apologetic jiggle of his shoulders before he smiled at Ruth. "…first kissed you."

Surprise lit Nana's face and wrinkled her forehead as she stared at her. "Well, you worked faster than I thought."

The same surprise snaked through Ruth's mind, but for another reason. "When? I don't understand."

"When you walked toward me across the garden."

"You nearly fainted."

He shot her an irritated look. "It was jetlag."

Ruth fluttered a hand for him to continue. "In any case..."

Stuart huffed. "She looked like you, but she wasn't. I researched the clothes you wore." Ruth frowned as she cast her mind back to that day. She remembered the faceless sketch he'd made. He hadn't needed the face as it would have been hers, but the ancient clothes had been depicted clearly.

"It was difficult to place the exact era as styles in Scotland didn't change drastically for several centuries, but with the other information I've already gathered, I guess we're talking late sixteen-hundreds. She wore an arisad, I'm pretty sure, under the mud brown covering of swamp water. That's what it smelled like to me."

"Attractive."

"Aye." Nana agreed with a wry twist of her lips. "But I've heard of no such relative of ours living near swamp water. There's no swamp water on the island, only fine sea water. Our history only began wi' a wee bairn when she was brought by the selkie."

"So, I believe." Stuart agreed. "But the woman I saw definitely had Ruth's face." He concentrated for a brief moment as though he could picture her. "Perhaps a little coarser, but the eyes were the same. She wore a small brass buckle here." He indicated the middle of his breastbone. "It helped to narrow the timeline down. Which also could possibly mean she was more peasantry than gentry. Silver brooches or buckles were worn by the more affluent."

Yet again, Ruth was taken aback by how much research Stuart had already conducted. She shouldn't be. That was his job, his forte. Uncomfortable with the thought that she had no idea who he was, she turned her face away to stare out of the window, but the stench of swamp-water swirled in her memory. He was right. The second time she'd channeled Moya, she'd been aware of the fetid smell which had remained in her nostrils long after Moya had gone. The memory of the first time had been a passion drugged haze, and she was certain there'd been no linger of the distasteful aroma. A fine shiver rolled off her before she built up the courage to cast him a furtive sideways look. The storm gray of his eyes reflected the memory of their passion too. It took a full minute before she composed herself enough to continue. "So what you're saying is our lives are entwined because of something which happened centuries ago."

"Correct."

"But it doesn't make sense. I have no idea who this Moya is. Do you, Nana?"

"I dunna know. What I can tell you with absolute conviction is every child born since the first bairn was delivered here by the selkie has been a female, and every one of them has had their name entered in the book of births up at the church. There's nae a single one of them called Moya."

Frustration boiled just below the surface, but one look at Stuart's blank face and Ruth knew. "You already checked the register."

He never tried to deny it.

"So where does Moya come into it?"

Stuart shook his head, and his eyebrows pulled low. "I've been back through my ancestors, traced them all the way to the thirteenth century. When Moya called out my name in the dream, I thought it might just be wishful thinking."

Heat raced over Ruth's skin at the mention of the dream. He must have experienced the same whip of passion as she had. "Was it?"

"No. There were a number of my relatives called Stuart. The name was popular in Scotland for a long time as you know. It still is. I've made a list of them, on my computer," he flicked a hand to indicate upstairs, "but where I've tried to cross reference their deaths in comparison to their children's birthdays, it's less clear the further back I go, especially as records weren't so well kept. They often went astray. Also, child mortality was much higher, so often I've traced a relative, just to find the lead fizzled out as their children died well before their tenth birthdays."

"But Stuart Caldwell fled Scotland, only a year after the child was brought to these shores by the selkie."

He nodded. "Yeah. And with the discovery of Moya's name I've managed to research deeper in the last couple of weeks, although Internet speed here isn't the most reliable." He gave a rueful quirk of his lips before he continued. "Records can be quite sketchy of the time, but my search threw up Moya's name in connection with the witch trials in Kilchoan. In the testimonies, the witch trials go into some depth." He scraped his chair closer and laid his forearms on the table top. "There was one Moya Gillies in the archives. Accused of witchcraft in 1672 by...Ellen Campbell."

Ruth held her breath as her heartbeat pounded through her head, but Nana placed her cup down on her saucer. "Wife of Stuart Campbell?"

Stuart nodded. "According to Ellen, Moya was an unwed midwife who had delivered her of two healthy baby boys." He blew out a breath. "She claimed her third baby perished at birth and that Moya must have had a pact with the devil as she had become impregnated at the same time as the death of Ellen's baby and managed to conceal her pregnancy until full term."

Ruth picked up the teapot and poured more of the brew into Nana's empty cup. "It wouldn't be difficult to do back then. The women's clothes were bulky, and most of them would have tartan shawls to keep them warm."

"Aye," Nana agreed, "and many a woman was accused of witchcraft if they became pregnant out of wedlock. It was a handy way to dispose of unwanted mistresses by jealous spouses or husbands who didn't want their reputations tarnished with bastard children."

"Or women you believe have effectively stolen your baby from you." Ruth agreed. "The end of the sixteenth century was probably the most prevalent time for witch-hunts in Scottish history. So many innocent women, burned at the stake for little, or no reason."

Stuart shook his head. "Moya wasn't burned at the stake. According to the testimony, she was tied to the ducking stool to extract a confession. When the confession wasn't forthcoming by the time evening arrived, the villagers became frenetic, and Moya drowned."

A deep shudder wracked her, and she covered her mouth with her hand. "Oh, dear God. The poor woman."

Nana's forehead creased. "But, if Moya and the baby died, how could we be descendants?"

Stuart sat back and drew in a long breath. "The parish priest documented that when the body of the witch was retrieved from the ducking stool the next morning, there was no evidence of Moya being pregnant. The baby had gone."

Weak with revulsion, Ruth closed her eyes. "What a tragic story."

"Horrific." With a weary sigh, Stuart cradled his face in his hands, making her long to reach out and touch him, but Ruth mustered her courage. She wasn't ready to forgive yet.

"What has the weapon upstairs got to do with all of this?"

He dragged his hands down his face and peered from between his fingers at her. "I don't know." Voice muffled he shook his head. "All I know," he dropped his hands from his face so she could see the agony there. "...is I'm meant to kill the witch to break the spell."

Head woozy, Ruth drew in a shaky breath as her mind struggled to hold onto what he'd told her. "You were going to kill me?"

"No, I..." The rapid glance at Nana wrenched Ruth's heart, and she shot to her feet with a swiftness that knocked the delicate kitchen chair onto the tiled floor.

"Nana? You were going to kill Nana?"

"No, Ruth, no." Stuart leaped up, reached across the table to her, but she whipped her arm away and hid it protectively behind her back. "It wasn't like that."

"Well, what was it like?" Ruth reached over to Nana to place a supportive hand on the old lady's frail shoulder, worried at the pallor of her skin. "We brought you into our house. Welcomed you. Made you feel at home. Please. Feel free to explain."

"I don't know. I'm sorry Clarisse, but I don't know." He raised his hand and rubbed the back of his neck. "I've carried the knife with me for as long as I can ever remember, my father came across it when he was alive. Only recently my brother managed to track down some paperwork, which seemed to tie into the whole history of the curse. He managed to obtain them from the old Caldwell Estates. He had them shipped to meet me as I traveled here from Zambia. With the documents was an old piece of parchment. There's instructions on how to break the spell, but much of it is damaged and illegible" His voice slowed and faded as he stuttered to the end of his explanation.

"What exactly are the words on these instructions?" Nana's voice crackled out.

Stuart scratched his chin, his mouth twisting with regret. "From what we can make out, it says: *Have the strength to bare thy breast. With one strike, straight and true. Take the heart of the witch and be sure to never let it from your keep.*"

Ruth drew her hair back from her face, wove her fingers through it, until the curls pinged free, all the time conscious of Stuart's attention on her. "And you believe these instructions mean you're to kill the witch?"

He jerked a nod. "I never came here with the intention of killing anyone. It's only since the documents arrived that I've had to consider what the instructions meant with relation to the knife. What other interpretation could it have?"

"I think the instructions could be open to interpretation."

"Then what has the blade got to do with it? Why else would I have the knife?"

She curled her lip in disgust. "So, you considered killing Nana?" Ruth gave Clarisse's shoulder a gentle squeeze to reassure her.

Clarisse raised her hand and placed it on top of Ruth's, her fingers icy. "Only, I was not the witch he sought out, but you, my dear." Her fingers tightened on Ruth's. "I'm sorry, he may never have realized if I hadn't taunted you into using your powers."

"I would have got there." He narrowed his gaze as he studied them both. "All the indicators were there. I simply chose to ignore them for as long as possible."

"So, when did you intend to kill us?"

Harsh laughter snorted out as he made his way around the table to put her chair upright. "I never intended to kill you. I couldn't kill another living creature, let alone two beautiful women, both of whom I've come to love."

Weak with relief, Ruth sank into the chair he'd righted for her. Tiredness battered her in dark waves until she let her mind float free. Reluctant pity tugged her heart. The poor man. Torn between saving his brother and crucifying his own soul. "But if you're supposed to kill me to save your brother and the future generations of your family, surely it's not a hard decision to make." She cracked open her eyelids to peer at his ashen face as he took his own seat once again.

"If I'd arrived to some dark evilness, perhaps it would have been different." His lips turned down at the edges. "Even so, I don't think I could have done it. I'm not cut out to kill, Ruth. My skill is in wielding a pen, not a knife. All the time I've been here, I've researched to find another resolution, but there's nothing I can pin down, apart from the connection to Moya. There's a link, but what could it possibly be? Would such fury and evilness last generations because of Ellen Caldwell's accusation of witchcraft? And why would the curse affect all the fathers and sons of the line?"

She gave him a moment, a beat in time before she spoke. "Perhaps I can cast a circle and see if I can contact Moya?" The brief flicker of fire in his expression was doused by Clarisse's next words.

"No. It's too dangerous."

"Nana."

"No, Ruth. If you invoke this witch again, there's no telling what powers you may release."

"I don't think she has any power anymore."

"Of course she does. She's cast a spell so powerful that it's lasted generations. Blighted the lives of so many."

"Clarisse." Stuart's weary voice drew their attention. "This may be my last, perhaps my only chance, to save my brother. If we can find out more detail about Moya and her reason for the curse, then maybe…" he stretched over the table to place his hand on top of Clarisse's. "Just maybe, we can find another way."

Clarisse's face crinkled into a sad smile. "Aye lad. Perhaps you're right. The cards indicated a battle, so perhaps a battle it is." She finished off her tea and placed the cup back on the saucer. "But I think right now we need food and sleep." Clarisse ran her gaze over Ruth, her aged eyes filled with a deep sadness that dragged at Ruth's heart. "I think my granddaughter needs to gather as much strength as possible before she embarks on another encounter with this lady."

Stuart slipped to his knees and held onto both of Clarisse's hands with his own with such tenderness, Ruth's chest ached with sorrow.

The slow trickle of tears down Nana's face brought a prickle to Ruth's eyes, the rapid blink she gave only served to haze her vision more until she turned away, no longer able to watch. Hurt constricted her chest and left her breathless while she stared out of the window at the setting sun. She narrowed her eyes against its brilliance as fiery hues of orange burned the sky while blackened clouds raced in and boded of another wild, stormy night.

There was no choice. They could only go forward, and if it meant another encounter with Moya, then so be it. She'd just have to ensure they were all protected by the strongest magic she knew.

She swiped the tears from her cheeks and faced Nana and Stuart with a bright smile. "What shall we have for supper?"

»»»•«««

A healthy fire blasted out heat to fill the room with pungent aromas of fragrant whiskey mixed with wood smoke and the musky undertones of fishermen's woolen clothes.

Stuart slipped into the bar and shoved the door shut against the wild weather to avoid the disapproval of the old boys. The wind hadn't subsided and carried with it the icy threat of hailstones which had whipped at his coat and trickled down the back of his neck. Never in his life had he experienced rain quite like it. It had the ability to sneak in through the smallest gap. Its insidious fingers even found their way under the protection of his Stetson. It didn't drive in one direction but swept in from every which way to chill him to the bone.

Relieved that the intense heat of the room evaporated the saturated chill before he even managed to shed his hat and coat, Stuart gave a brisk nod to the inhabitants of the small sitting room bar. Something he'd been quick to realize was part of their acknowledgment etiquette. Men of few words, a nod was the height of politeness.

"Looks as though ye could do wi' a wee dram, lad."

Bill held out a small tumbler. Firelight sparkled from the crystal and sent shards of light to dance around the room. Its amber contents glowed a warm invitation as he gave them a gentle swirl. Eyes crinkled at the edges, Bill's penetrating gaze met his with an astute steadiness Stuart hadn't noticed before. The nomadic eye had stilled and focused on Stuart with uncomfortable intensity. "Come, tell me what's on yer mind."

As Bill lowered himself into a high-backed chair, his old bones creaked and groaned, his mouth straightened into a tight line, but he never let his gaze wander from Stuart's. "What can I do for you lad?"

Stuart leaned forward. His forehead almost touched the old fisherman's while he lowered his voice so only Bill could hear. "I know what you are." Bill never flinched, but the liquid ink of his eyes swirled. "It doesn't matter to me. That's your business. But I need your help, Bill. I'm desperate."

The firm pressure of Bill's hand pressed down onto Stuart's shoulder. "It's my duty to protect those two women you currently reside with. The witches have always had one of us in their lives ever since the first wee bairn arrived on the isle." Stuart should have been surprised, but somehow it all made sense. "Whatever you need, son, if it's for the good of the women. When a man's desperate, it's normally for a good reason."

Stuart opened his mouth, inclined to tell Bill he couldn't discuss it, but the fisherman beat him to it. "I don't need to know what it is, that's your business," his mouth quirked, the gray whiskers twitched, "I just need to know it's for the greater good, and what you want me to do."

Satisfied he could trust the old man, Stuart allowed the slide of warm whiskey to relax his muscles and sooth his stomach, wise enough to know the small amount he'd been poured was measure enough.

Now he had a plan.

»»»•«««

It didn't seem right to sneak along the hallway to her bedroom, but her brave smile had broken his heart more than ever her tears had.

Clarisse had long since gone to bed to leave the house dark and quiet with the heavy cloud of her despair.

His stomach clenched as he approached Ruth's door. There was nothing he could do to make it better for any of them. He'd brought the problem to their door with the single-minded determination to save his brother and nephews. Not once had he considered the consequences of his actions. Never in all the years of his research had he thought beyond finding the witch to break the curse. Until recently, it hadn't occurred to him that he would be required to take another's life to save his family.

In the gloomy silence of the hallway, he paused, surprised Ruth's door had been left ajar.

A soft sigh came from the black velvet silhouette at the window. "I thought you would never come."

His chest eased. "I wasn't sure you would want me to."

Her low voice slid over his senses. "I will always want you, Stuart." The silken rustle of her movement accompanied her slow approach.

Relief flooded him as she wrapped her arms around his neck and raised her face to his for a kiss. Her cool lips gave a fleeting brush before a soft sob broke from her and wrenched his heart in two.

"I was about to ask if I could come in." There was no shame as his voiced thickened. "Just to hold you." Careful not to crush her in his desperation, he folded her in close. Her thick hair clouded around his face as he tucked his nose into the silky curve of her neck and inhaled. The fresh scent of sea and freesias swirled through his senses. "I just want to hold you Ruth, to let you know I would never, could never, harm you or your nana." He gave in to the urge to clasp her closer, got a little jolt of surprise as she tilted her head back and took his mouth with her own. Not the gentle, seeking caress he'd expected, but a hot, fervent kiss which demanded more. Desperate, he wrenched his mouth away from hers to smother her face in fast, insistent kisses. "I'm sorry." He traced the contour of her cheek, followed the line of her eyebrows. "I'm so sorry." With small pecks, he smoothed his way down the length of her nose just to reach her delectable mouth once more. Before he could take it with his, she slipped cool fingers over his lips, but he still managed to mumble through them. "I'm sorry."

"Don't. Please don't apologize again. It's not your fault."

"It is." Her smooth stroke muffled the sound of his voice as it tried to escape him.

"No." With a tender touch, she feathered her fingers along his jaw to cradle his face in her hand. "It's not your fault. This was coming. We've known for some time there was trouble on the horizon. If not now, it would have been soon."

The gentle pressure of her hand against the back of his head drew him closer. "We'll think about it tomorrow. Like Nana says, we need rest."

Rest wasn't the first thing on his mind, but he understood her need to gather strength in preparation for the forthcoming events. If he could just lie with her for a few hours, hold her in his arms, he'd consider it an honor. That's all he'd hoped for, but her explosive response had fired his blood to rush from his brain, so he'd forgotten why he was there. Primarily it had been to comfort, but he couldn't ever imagine being with her without wanting her.

The fresh scent of sea and flowers wound its way through his senses, and with a ghost of a smile, he skimmed his lips against her forehead in a light kiss.

He peered at the reflection of them both in the night-darkened window.

Dawn would soon arrive, and he'd have to deal with the arrangements he'd made with Bill. Until then, his time with Ruth was precious, and she needed him to be with her.

Stuart smoothed his hands over her shoulders, down her arms until his fingers linked with hers so he could tug her toward the bed.

Without hesitation, she followed, trust shimmered in her gaze as it held his while he slipped his hands beneath her thick, woolen sweater. He glided his fingers over her warm flesh, aware of the jolt and quiver while he peeled the sweater over her head. She remained silent and still before him, her eyes glowing a rich sea green.

Desire squeezed his emotions, but he tamped it down while his fingers fumbled for a moment at the clasp of her trousers until success had them slipping down her legs to pool over her naked feet. Left only in her white, lacy underwear, Stuart resisted the temptation to divest her of those too. She needed some protection from him if his intentions weren't to devour her.

He flipped back the covers of the bed, gently scooped her into his arms. The mattress dipped as he placed her on it with a tenderness he had to breathe through just to keep in check.

His own clothes were shucked with as much haste and abandon as possible, and he slipped under the covers, surprised when she scooted closer and plastered herself against his body. The fresh scent he'd become so familiar with clung to her skin, in a heady invitation.

He wanted her with such urgency, but more, he wanted to make her forget for a short while, to wipe away the evil he'd brought to her home, and the only way he could was to give her the comfort she needed.

The light shimmer of a sigh passed through her. "Are you just going to hold me?" She murmured.

He drew back so he could see her in the dim light while he fought the rise of desire which begged him to take what she so sweetly offered. "I think it would be best if I did."

"For whom?"

Warmth washed over him, and he raised his hand to smooth back the curls from her forehead, thrilled when she took his hand in her own and drew it to her lips to kiss his palm.

"You, Ruth. I think you're confused."

The smile was sultry and knowing as she reached her finger out to draw it down his chest in a straight line toward his belly, so his flesh jumped and quivered. "There's no confusion. I want you to make love to me. To take away the pain, just for one night. For you. For me."

If it had only been about his own need, he may have been able to resist, but the demand she made of him broke his restraints, and he gathered her close. His mouth took hers in a hot kiss designed to burn away all thought and memory.

She melted, warm and compliant against him, wringing out every regret he had until she swept them away with one small whimper of animalistic desperation as she wound her fingers in his hair and dragged him closer.

He inhaled her scent, tasted the richness of her mouth, aware he should soothe her, but he couldn't help but devour her. Her clever fingers danced over his rib-cage, slipped around him to scrape at his back and make his muscles ripple under the demanding dig of her nails.

"Closer." Her surprised gasp had his pulse racing and his body keen to oblige. He slipped his fingers under the elastic of her panties and pushed them down while he followed the middle line of her body with light kisses and nips until he managed to pull the panties off her feet. Clumsy in his desperation, he pressed his face against her stomach. Her small shudder stopped him from retreating. Instead, he placed open-mouthed kisses over her flesh to taste the woman while he inched his way back up her body. He flicked the clasp of her bra open and drew it off so he could cup one pert breast in his hand. Her sweetness still hovered on his lips.

He took advantage of her compliance and sucked her nipple into his mouth. He drew on it until her body bowed beneath him. Her nails scraped his back and sent flashes of fire to shimmer over his skin, while electric pulses snapped through his veins.

He roamed his lips freely up her neck until he buried his face in her throat and drew in the scent that drove him wild. He shifted his body, raising his head so he could look at her as he pushed himself inside her. So ready for him, her warmth welcomed him while she pulled him in tight, and cradled him as though he was the most precious thing.

In utter harmony their bodies melded together, fiery and molten, with no control their limbs tangled, and their bodies bucked until the covers slipped from the bed unnoticed. Flesh slick, pulses racing, he gloried in his whispered words of love and her desperate moans of desire.

So much for tenderness and understanding. Not as gentle as he'd intended, he tried to rein in his ravenous hunger for her, but she was more than a match for him. She demanded everything as she drew him deeper until their passion exploded in a torrid flash of heat to leave him weak and mindless.

Chapter Seven

Guilt dogged his naked footsteps as he sneaked from her room, leaving her wrapped in the downy warmth of her quilt which he'd dragged up over them while she lay boneless next to him. His body was drained, but his mind wouldn't let him sleep. The gentle sound of her breath evened out almost immediately to reassure him she slept in the deep aftermath of exhausted satisfaction. He turned his head to look at her, her face highlighted by the thin sliver of moonlight which snuck in through the window.

He left his clothes where he'd dropped them a few hours earlier in case he woke her, but caution reminded him to check the hallway for any sign of the old lady before he tiptoed back to his own room. He didn't need to give anyone a heart attack, although he suspected Clarisse was much tougher than the impression she gave.

His mind wallowed with the thought of Bill and his descendants of selkies sent to protect Clarisse and her lineage.

Dressed in thick woolens, Stuart abandoned his long leather coat in preference for the slickers Bill had lent him. The heavy odor of fish and oil permeated through, but the dash of wind as he opened the kitchen door made him thankful he'd got them.

Warned the sea would be rough, Stuart glanced up at the clouds as they scudded across the dark sky. He tugged the waterproof hat lower to cover his ears. He patted his chest where he'd slipped the box with the jade handled knife under the slicker to keep it dry. Ironic he still felt the need to protect it, but it had been with him most of his life. However he felt about it, he knew the decision he'd made was the right one.

As he stepped off the jetty onto the bobbing fishing vessel, he squinted against the arrow of light which pierced his eyes and threatened to burn holes in his corneas. He raised his hand to shield himself against the pain, but the light was extinguished almost as fast as it appeared and Bill's voice grumbled at him through the darkness. "You're late."

One minute late that was all, but Stuart clenched his jaw so he wouldn't reply, the low rumble of the boat's engine covered his growl. Blinded by the white spots still flashing in front of his eyes through the treacle darkness, he never saw the package Bill shoved into one hand, but instinct made him grab it and hold on as a second item was thrust into his other hand.

The pungent aroma of bacon wafted up as he unwrapped the warm parcel, not able to thank Bill as the old man took to the wheel and guided the boat through choppy seas.

The motion of the boat never bothered him as he crammed the food into his mouth, recognizing the hot, spicy, brown sauce Bill had smothered it in which helped it to slide down with ease. The tin mug of black coffee Bill had handed over was even more welcome. Stuart let out a deep sigh as the rich flavors played over his tongue. He'd never given food or drink a thought as he'd crept out of the house like a thief.

His mind turned to her as they left the shore behind, the motor powered them through the waves and toward the thin dawn light.

Guilt wasn't the only emotion he felt, and nor was it the strongest one. He stared back through the inky blackness. Regret shimmered over him. He had no choice as he could see it. None at all. It was the only way.

There was no longer any question of being torn. This was the sole solution.

He wiped his greasy fingers on the oil-slicked material of his trousers and made his way to Bill's side at the bow to watch with him while the gray light pushed back the night. When Bill cut the engine, he allowed the boat to be tossed on the crest of the waves as he poured his nets over the side and watched them spread before they sank beneath the wallowing sea.

In the silence, the old boy met Stuart's gaze and then held out his square palmed hand for him to place the box in. He stroked his work-worn fingers over the jade inlay, and his quiet sigh carried on the wind like regret. With surprising tenderness, Bill wrapped the box in a piece of oilskin and secured it with a length of rope before he stepped to the edge of the boat and shucked his waterproof like a skin. His old man's body curled down on itself, his pale skin wrinkled and flaccid, but despite the pale illumination of the sky, his shadow turned into a dense blackness before he slipped over the gunwale and into the choppy sea to leave Stuart alone on the boat.

Whether or not he'd truly believed it before, Stuart stared opened mouthed at the spot where the seal had disappeared without so much as a splash. He gave in to the weakness in his legs and sank to his knees onto the wooden deck.

His whole life he'd hovered between the conviction of belief in magic and the continual disappointment with each line of pursuit as he'd managed to disprove the subjects of his investigations.

He dangled his hands over the side as he watched for Bill to return. He'd discovered more paranormal activity and true magic in the last few days than he'd come across in his life. Proof of its existence swam in the waters below him.

It might have been a lifetime, but it was only moments before the glossy outline of a seal's head broke the surface of the water and bobbed for a long moment before the creature reached out a man's square, work-worn hand and hauled himself over the side into the bottom of the boat.

His transformation was slick and effortless, but Stuart pulled back on the urge to go to Bill's help as his human form, bent almost double with pain and cold, struggled to pull his clothes back on.

When he was finished, his ink-jet eyes met Stuart's. "It's done." He blinked, and the first ray of sun struck his sallow skin to give Stuart a deep appreciation of the effort it had cost him.

"Thank you, Bill. I'll never forget what you've done.

"Och, aye lad. But the deal is not done yet. Now it's time to haul in those nets and get this catch back to shore. I hope you're up to it, son."

>»»•«««

Witchcraft didn't guide her, but the magic of love had a strong pull. He'd slipped from her bedroom in the dead of night without a word, and she'd known he needed his time alone. Time to think, time to make decisions. Just as she needed to make hers.

Much of it depended on the outcome of their experiment later in the evening. For it was an experiment. She'd never before conducted anything like it. It wasn't to be a séance, nor did she want to invoke Moya's wrath. They simply needed to know what had possessed her to cast such a powerful and malevolent spell.

The more Ruth thought about it, the more she was convinced her way would be right. She just needed to convince Nana and Stuart. She needed to make sure they were protected too.

Salt-laden wind whipped at her face and tugged her clothes from where she had them wrapped around her. She encircled her body with her arms to keep in the warmth while she braced herself to stay upright against its viciousness. The pale gray light of dawn fractured the clouds to throw insipid rays on the small fishing boat as it made its way back to harbor in its daily fight against the choppy waves.

Ruth squinted through the half-light, but with instincts a tingle, she knew he would be on it. As it approached the dock, Bill's distinctive silhouette stood hunched over at the helm. But the tall, lean cowboy was the one who captured and held her attention. Minus his long, black leather coat and Stetson, it occurred to her he made just as good a fisherman as he did a cowboy.

Butterflies fluttered in the pit of her stomach at the pure beauty of the man who leaped with feline grace to shore, with no hesitation as he wrapped the boat's line around a cleat on the dock. With a sleek whirl, he moved to the stern to take the second line Bill threw to him and secured it too before the boat could scrape against the dock in the choppy waters.

The dim light gave way to a stream of golden sunshine as dawn broke and cast its brilliance over the day.

Ruth's hair danced in wild abandon, but she never attempted to restrain it as the wind tugged it from her face, allowing her to see Stuart clearly. His slow smile spread to dimple sexy lines along his cheeks.

"Hey."

The leisurely trip of her pulse disguised the hammering of her heart. "Hi."

She reached out to take his hands in hers, quite aware of the attention it would draw from Bill, but secure in the knowledge he wouldn't say a word to anyone. Her business was hers as far as the old selkie was concerned.

She sucked in a sharp breath at the iciness of Stuart's fingers as she tangled hers with them while he held on. He stepped over the ropes to circle her around. "Oh my goodness, did you have your hands in the sea the whole time you were out there?"

"Ha," grumbled Bill from behind them. "I've been in seventy mile an hour winds with waves as high as forty foot over the side of the boat, and my hands never turned as blue as the landlubber's there."

Stuart's lips curved into a deeper smile, but stormy seas still filled his eyes as he glanced over her head out at the horizon. "I helped haul in a catch." The voice was steady and calm, but it struck her a flat note ran through it. For a moment, she just stood and allowed the warmth of her hands to soak through to his while a chill ran down her spine, nothing to do with the outside temperature.

"What did you do?" The sharp squeeze of her hands against his grabbed his attention as guilt rippled through his gaze and the tingle in her spine spread to form a fist in her stomach.

As he tried to turn away, she yanked him back. The smile dropped from his lips and his dark eyebrows raised. "I disposed of something I felt I no longer had need of."

With a quick glance behind, Bill's jittery gaze slid away from hers before he ducked his head and tipped the squirming, slippery catch into a huge freezer box on the dock ready for him to gut and fillet what he needed.

Sick suspicion curled in her stomach as she turned her attention back to Stuart. "You took the knife out to sea." It wasn't a question, and she already knew the answer. His indolent shrug didn't fool her. He'd just thrown away the only lifeline his brother had, and in doing so, he'd proved how honorable he truly was. A life for a life just wasn't the way.

The gentle squeeze of his cool fingers on hers never helped to rid her of the sadness that invaded every part of her. Whatever was to come, he'd already made his decision. "We'll find another way. This one wasn't an option, and I don't ever want it to become one once I've gone and another generation pursues the curse."

»»»•«««

She did her best to protect them all as she prepared the stone circle. She took the time to rid the clearing of the branches that had blown into it during the recent storms. With meditation, she pushed any negativity from the area and followed up with witch hazel sprinkled on each of the stones.

The glossy coats of her cats shimmered in the dying embers of the day, and she pleased herself as she skimmed her hand over their heads and along the length of their spines. A small smile curved her lips as each of them arched their backs with pleasure.

Sea salt weighed heavy on the stagnant air, but she drew it in through her nose and breathed it out through her mouth, the tang of salt coating her teeth.

Aware of her sentinels drawing closer, she took comfort in their presence as she settled cross-legged on the ground. Strong enough to heat her skin, energy vibrated through her with a reassuring pull.

She watched Nana's approach and pushed back on the regret which threatened to overwhelm her if she allowed it. Nana was a strong woman. She'd survived the loss of her own love, held the hand of her daughter as she'd died, and witnessed the desertion of her granddaughter's father, and still managed to bring up a child on her own. Nothing so far had managed to break her. Ruth could only hope this wouldn't either, but worry shimmered just beyond the protective circle as Nana stepped inside. Wrinkles Ruth hadn't noticed before feathered the edges of Nana's lips and deepened with the tight smile she gave as she took her seat to the left of Ruth.

The small hesitation Stuart made before he stepped over the stones into the circle stirred a little more remorse, but Ruth appreciated the support of his presence as his knee bumped hers while he settled himself to her right.

A gentle hum rumbled from the three cats as each took up a position between the humans to form a circle of six.

Clarisse nodded her approval, indicating the time was right to begin.

Ruth rested the backs of her hands on her knees, so her palms were turned upward. As she closed her eyes, she drew a slow breath in through her nose.

»»»•«««

Flames licked low across the circle of stones, and if he'd been in cynical journalist mode, he would have searched for the fire-starter. But he knew without a doubt this was no trick, but magic. Magic in its truest form. The thing he'd sought most of his life and discarded with reckless abandon.

Here, though, was the real thing. There were no cheap tricks, nor any attempt to pull the wool over his eyes. What it gave him was hope. With a deliberate decision, he'd kept his thoughts to himself. Clarisse and Ruth had enough on their minds without him applying more pressure. There was no regret for the disposal of the jade-handled knife, but a small kernel of tremulous optimism grew in his heart that Ruth's magic was enough.

"Are you ready?" Her calm green gaze met his, and all he could do was dip his head in acknowledgment of her question. Any words he could have formed would have sounded wrong in the space she had cleared. She'd made it her domain, and his voice would have been an intrusion.

Her flicker of a smile did little to reassure him, but as she curled her fingers into his, the surge of power from her gentle grasp raced through him, igniting his blood until it flowed hot and fast through his veins. The clenched fist in his stomach relaxed while his warmed muscles loosened. He reached out his other hand and completed the circle as he took Clarisse's fingers in his. This time there was no surge, but a gentle vibration of reassurance.

These women, between them, held more power than he'd imagined possible. The protective pull of it bathed him in a bubble of serenity until he raised his head and stared into the obsidian gaze of his lover.

"Moya."

The quick squeeze Clarisse gave his fingers stopped him, but fear for Ruth's safety trembled through him.

Black lashes fluttered to emphasize the delicate purple bruises under her eyes. Lack of sleep and desperation deepened the hollows there as sorrow gazed out at him.

He smothered the temptation to reach out and smooth the hair back from her face. She may have looked like Ruth, but she *was* Moya.

"Stuart." The voice came from another world. Whispered down through the ages, it echoed with a Scottish brogue far stronger than Ruth's. "Did you not declare your love for me?"

She tilted her head as though she listened to another voice. Her lips, a delicate blue, trembled. "Aye, Stuart. I know you have your bairns, but what about this one?" She placed her hand on her own swollen belly. "She belongs to you also. Are you willing to see her die because you will nae claim her as your own?"

A silent tear slipped down her cheek in the cold darkness, and the powerful sensation of a small shadowy cell with moss covered walls persuaded its way into Stuart's consciousness. He drew in a breath and tasted the mold, almost choked on the heavy atmosphere as it clogged his lungs. The desperate desire to glance in Clarisse's direction was overpowered by the need to watch Moya.

Tattered curls dropped forward to cover the gentle curve of her cheek as she dipped her head with slow nods. "Aye, milord. I ken what ye say, but they'll burn me for being a witch. Me and the bairn from your loins." She raised her head, met Stuart's gaze with her own and the slash of pride burned deep. "I've na'er told another being, so they think I carry the spawn of the devil as your wife decreed." Her dark eyebrows raised and her full lips tightened. "There's nae a devil inside of me, just the seed you planted with nary a thought for your wife and sons." She raised her chin, gave her head a small shake, so the tumble of curls waterfalled over the shoulders she squared up. "A witch I may be, but your child is innocent. Are you willing to watch us both die?" Her voice gained in strength, reverberated through her chest, so it resounded around the small clearing. "That's the price of my silence, my Laird. If you can sacrifice us both, then I wish for you to live in the hell you created for the rest of your life. And when your life is over, may hell continue from the grave through those sons you sacrificed me for and their sons beyond."

Silence dropped its velvet curtain to cover the protected circle in a suffocating weight as Moya's chin dropped onto her chest, her body slackened, and her shoulders rolled forward.

For one long moment, Stuart stared, unsure whether he should leap up and grab the woman into his arms, but he'd been warned under no circumstances should he break the circle.

The gentle, rhythmic purrs from the sentinels pushed back the silence until Ruth's head shot up, her green gaze centered on his as she dragged in one breath after the other into her heaving chest.

Clarisse dropped her grip on Stuart, and he surged forward to grab Ruth and haul her without protest into his lap. Fear for her safety shot through him in one fiery lance to the heart, but he had her. He held her in his arms and rocked her, too overcome with emotions to speak. He buried his face in the wildness of her hair and breathed in the scent of freesias instead of swamp water. She was safe. He had her where he needed her the most. In his arms.

Relief flooded him, just to feel her, warm and whole.

His Ruth.

She squirmed in his arms, and he loosened his grasp on her with reluctance but refused to release her entirely. She'd just have to understand he needed to hold her, to touch her, and know she was safe.

"It wasn't me." She feathered her fingers over the brow he never realized had furrowed in his anxiousness. He dropped his head down until he rested it on hers, while she smoothed her fingers down his face to cup his cheek in her hand. "It wasn't me."

He nodded, kissed the tip of her nose, and nodded again. "She was expecting his baby."

"Yes."

"His wife must have been furious to accuse her of being a witch."

"Yes."

"An important man with land and responsibilities by the sounds of it."

"She called him her laird. It *was* Stuart Caldwell."

This time, Stuart just nodded, rubbing his brow against hers. "What a tragedy. She died because she loved him enough to keep quiet about his indiscretion."

"Yet she cursed him in the end."

"Maybe she believed he would change his mind and save her." He withdrew just enough to be able to look into Ruth's face. The dark bruises had disappeared to leave her face fresh and young, much younger than Moya's, although he suspected the woman had been no older than Ruth, but the life she'd lived had been a much harder one.

Ruth nodded in agreement while she untangled herself with a gentle tug from his arms. Reluctant to let her go, he touched her shoulder with just the tips of his fingers to show his support should she need him. She rolled to her feet and stretched up, tipped her head toward the clear black sky sprinkled with masses of bright stars. The glow of the full moon permeated through the thick leaves of the canopy of trees to bathe the circle in a silver light.

"There's supposed to be a blood moon tonight."

"A blood moon?" Stuart glanced up at the night sky with no sign of any aurora, but the clarity of it stunned him.

"It's a total lunar eclipse."

He knew what one was, but he'd been too distracted to realize one was due.

He slanted a look at Clarisse who still hadn't moved from her place on the ground. Aware of her cool, piercing appraisal, it occurred to him if she hadn't known about his relationship with her granddaughter before, there was no doubt about it now.

"I've never seen one." He offered his hand to help her up.

"Nor me, not in this lifetime." Ruth's voice floated from behind him.

The crow's feet deepened as Clarisse scrutinized him, but with a slight inclination of her head, she raised her hand for him to assist her to her feet.

Slim and elegant, age had still allowed her muscles to stiffen as she'd sat cross-legged on the damp ground, but the only hint was the tightening of her jaw, accompanied by a small stagger as she took her first step. Concerned for her, he tightened his hand on hers to steady her.

"Stuart."

He whipped his head up at the sound of the disembodied voice, and Clarisse's fingers gripped his as Ruth faced him from outside the stone circle. Her eyes blazed obsidian while the wind thrashed her dull brown clothes and tore her hair into a frenzied mess.

He lurched forward, but Clarisse grabbed at him with both hands. "Dunna step outside the circle. You're protected here."

But Ruth was not. The stench of swamp water rose, soaked into the thick linen of the peasant dress.

Moya raised her chin, fury blazed from every particle of her as thick, black mud dripped down her face to coat her alabaster skin in an oily residue. "I would far rather have burned than drowned, Stuart. How could you have let them do it?" She pointed a shaky finger at him to make his soul quake. "You had the power to change it, and you did nothing. Nothing." Mud thickened water bubbled from her nose and spilled from her lips.

A furious gust of wind clutched at her dress and flung her off balance. Stuart reached out, wrapped his fingers in the sodden material and gave a desperate jerk. Ruth fell into the circle and Clarisse and Stuart clasped her tight in their arms, forming their own inner circle as flames shot skyward over them, bright crimson and sapphire.

"What happened?" He held both Ruth and Clarisse and gave them a fierce squeeze in his fear. "What the hell happened?"

Clarisse's face had aged in seconds. "She didn't cleanse before she stepped out of the circle. She forgot to cleanse."

He kissed Ruth's forehead relieved he didn't have the same problem as his brother. He would have died on the spot if there'd been any weakness to his heart. A heart which still threatened his life as it thundered out of control. He needed to touch her, soothe her, and reassure himself.

He slipped his hand through her now silky-soft hair and stroked it back from her face. Her own wild bird heartbeat matched his. He brushed a gentle kiss over her open lips and absorbed her violent shudder. "I have you. You're safe now. I have you."

With one arm circling his waist she squeezed him hard, then let go to wrap her arms around her grandmother. "I told you I was rubbish at this witchcraft game."

Clarisse's rusty chuckle came from where she had it pressed against Ruth's thick, fluffy sweater. "I've never known a witch with so much power as you. Or her." Clarisse drew back to look from one to the other. "Cleanse your magic circle now, child, and then we can away home."

Reluctant to let her go, he nevertheless allowed Ruth to step free and witnessed while she withdrew a small candle from the pouch she'd brought with her. He kept his silence while she called upon the elements of earth, air, fire, and water, invoked her god and goddess to consecrate the circle and bless them all. She sprinkled water and salt while the scent of lavender and sage laced the air. Once she'd released the deities and thanked her gods, she waited, until he was steeped in the peace she'd invoked. She blew out a light breath and extinguished the circle of flames, and then invited Clarisse and Stuart to step outside.

The cats followed close on their heels. Their black fur puffed out to make them appear larger than normal, they flicked wary glances around, their straight tails giving sharp twitches to heighten the anxiety of the small group as they headed back to the house.

The warm glow from the kitchen had never been more welcome. Once the door was closed behind them, the heavy coating of fear lifted.

"A cup of tea, I think." Ruth turned her back to fill the kettle.

"I could do with something a wee bit stronger." Clarisse opened a cupboard and took out a full bottle of single malt whiskey. He couldn't agree more and accepted the bottle with a grateful smile while Clarisse searched out miss-matched crystal whiskey tumblers, and placed them with a shaky hand on the scrubbed wooden table.

Stuart splashed the golden liquid into the glasses, all the while aware Ruth hadn't moved a muscle. He reached out to offer her the whiskey as her pain filled expression met his with such poignancy his knees weakened. He'd battened down the fear, but he could no longer ignore her need, and his. He wrapped her in his arms, touched his mouth to hers with all the tenderness he held in his heart. He allowed his lips to linger while the haunting vision of Moya cleared from his mind, so all he saw was Ruth. Alive and vital, the sweet smell of her floated through his senses until relief flowed through his body to replace the fear.

»»»•«««

"Stuart."

The snatch of a sob carried down the line and echoed in his chest as he envisaged his delicate sister-in-law on the other end of the phone. "Where have you been?" Her voice cracked.

What explanation could he possibly give?

"What's happened? Where's Ian?"

Another sniffle broke from his sister-in-law and tore at the essence of him.

"Susie?"

"They have a heart, Stuart. They're running the final tests and dependent on Ian's condition, they say it's viable." A quaver of hope and fear filled her voice. "It's his only chance. If he deteriorates any more, he won't be strong enough for the operation. He can't wait any longer. We need you, Stuart. He needs you."

Stuart glanced at his watch, his mind a whirl of activity. He'd planned to return before his nephew's tenth birthday in any case, which was still almost three weeks away. He hadn't expected just to drop everything and go. He'd have to check the flights, get to the mainland and board a plane. He needed a direct flight.

"Tell him I'll be there when he comes out of recovery."

"Where were you, Stuart?" The quiet whisper of hope reached over the miles between them. "Did you break the curse?"

He pressed the heel of his hand against his forehead to stop the pain in his head. "No." Regret shuddered from him. "No, Susie. There's nothing here. Just another dead-end."

"I thought…" There was nothing but the soft sound of her muffled cries for a long moment before she managed to speak again. "I thought you must have broken the curse when they told us there was a heart. It's still weeks until Ben's birthday."

Stuart sighed, opened eyes he hadn't realized he'd had screwed shut and faced Ruth. Concern wreathed her face, and it twisted his gut to see the regretful smile of understanding.

"I'm sorry, Susie."

With a quiet rustle of clothes, Ruth came to him.

He clutched the cell phone tighter. "Tell Ian I'll be there. Just as soon as I can."

He reached out, encircled Ruth's waist with his free arm and pulled her close to better absorb the warm scent of spring flowers that always accompanied her.

"Travel safely, Stuart. We love you."

"I love you all too."

A final choked sob and then static filled the line.

Without releasing Ruth, Stuart moved to the window and placed his phone on the old table. "I have to go."

"I know."

"I have no choice. I can't ever come back. When Ian dies, I'll have the boys to look out for. It's no childhood to know you live under a curse. I don't want that for Ben. He doesn't need to know yet. I'll continue with my research. There has to be another way." Other than to kill Ruth, or allow his nephews to track her down in the future.

"I understand."

Her quiet acceptance made it all the more difficult.

"I need to book a flight."

She turned her face toward the window just as the silver glow from the moon morphed to golden and bathed her skin with a warm radiance. "You should do it now. If you don't mind, the eclipse has started, I'll stay and watch a while."

Used to booking flights, it took him a matter of minutes to find one. Frustration gathered in his chest. The earliest flights he could get weren't direct and with stopovers would take twenty-two hours, but if he caught a later, direct flight, it would only be eight hours from Edinburgh to JFK.

With a sigh, he pressed the final button to confirm the booking and back-tracked the time in his mind. He had four hours before he needed to leave.

Her back to him, she cast a quick glance over her shoulder, raised her hand, and pointed for him to look out of the window with her at the dark shadow as it inched across the moon and the night sky darkened. An eerie silence danced on the air.

He reached out and opened the window to give them a better view while the moon disappeared behind the black disc and the crimson glow deepened with each minute that passed. Cool air washed in, and the tremble of her slight frame touched him as he pulled her body close against his, her back to his chest. He hugged her tight against him, relieved at the give in her as she leaned into him.

"Before I go, tell me you love me, Ruth."

Her breath staggered in through her throat, but she never hesitated. "With all my heart."

His own almost broke in two. He'd never wept, not since he was ten years old, but the thick swell of tears tightened his throat and pricked his eyes, so he had to blink several times before he was capable of a response.

In the end, it was much simpler, he turned her in his arms and held her for the last time. "I'll never forget you, Ruth."

"I know."

"I'm sorry it had to be this way."

"Aye." She snuffled her face into his neck, and her warm tears coated his skin. He had to concentrate with gritted teeth, so he didn't cry out his agony and frustration.

In his mind, the curse lived on, not just for the men who died but also for the ones who lived. During his research, he'd discovered a few in his family tree who'd never married, nor had there been any evidence that they lived anything but solitary lives. Just what he could see in his future. Whatever the tarot had foreseen, he knew he'd been doomed to live a lonely life.

He tucked a finger under Ruth's chin to raise her face up to his and wondered if Moya had ever considered how her curse was to affect her own lineage, or whether in her fit of jealousy and rage she'd never stopped to consider her baby would live on. From the evidence he'd seen, all the women in her line also lived a solitary existence.

The warm magic of moonlight bathed the room, and in the red haze, he dipped his head, so their faces came closer together to enable him to see the gentle mystery of her. Wet cheeks glimmered in the shifting light until he smudged away the tears with the pad of his thumb.

"I love you."

Barely able to force the murmur past his constricted throat, he traced the path of his thumb with his lips, tasted the saltiness of her damp skin. He found her pliant lips with his own and swallowed her sigh. "Promise me you'll make something of your life. You have too much talent to waste. Take up the offer from Edinburgh."

She slipped her arms around his neck, pressed her body against his. "It feels as though I've waited forever for you. If I'd left the island before now, we'd never have met."

He wasn't so sure. His search had brought him to her island and fate had ensured they'd met. Time and again she'd thrown herself at him. Literally. It felt to him that he'd have found her wherever she was. Or she'd have found him.

Whatever the case, it seemed a cruel fate had also decreed they couldn't remain together.

He smoothed the hair back from her face, captured her lips with his in a long, deep kiss. When he came up for breath, he still felt compelled to push her. "I want you to find someone. Someone to love."

"I love *you*."

"I don't want you to be alone, Ruth. You deserve so much more. I want you to find love."

"I found love." Her voice became stronger. He realized there was no point arguing. It was too close. Maybe the distance of years would change her mind.

With gentle fingers, she cupped his face, her smile only hinted of regret. "Whatever the future may bring, I love you now. Make this moment a memory to last forever."

Defeated, he deepened their kiss, opened her lips with his so he could sample the taste of her mouth and delighted in the fact she didn't so much as yield but met him halfway. She danced her tongue over his while her nimble fingers peeled away the layers of his clothes.

Pleasure, stunning and powerful, surged through him, so his own fingers weren't quite as gentle as he robbed her of her clothes and dropped them with careless abandon at their feet.

The cool night breeze whispered over their naked flesh as though to draw their attention once again to the total lunar eclipse. Bright flames licked the perimeter to set the moon on fire and throw fingers of crimson to dance over their skin and illuminate each dip and curve. He traced the shadows with light flicks of his tongue, gave a gentle suck on the hollow at the base of her neck to taste the floral silk there.

Reality slipped away as he scooped her up and placed her with such tenderness on her bed, and followed her down to cover her lithe body with his own.

With a soft sigh, his name trembled from her lips, while he murmured his own endearments in her ear as he skimmed his hands over her slender body. Satin on silk. He glided over her, into her.

Unrushed, they moved together in harmony as though they had always been. As if they always would be.

Stuart lay in the aftermath, bathed in golden moon dust as the eclipse moved on and the sky once again lightened. He drew her closer so he could place a tender kiss on her ear, smooth her hair back from her face, and stroke the satin skin of her shoulder.

She'd asked him to slip away while she slept. A small request he'd agreed to as they used their time left to make love. A sweet memory he'd hold forever in his heart.

Reluctant to move, he knew it wouldn't be long until he had no option, but he wanted to absorb every last moment, treasure his time with her.

In the darkness, he watched the shadows flit across the ceiling and down the walls. The muted call of owls once again filtered through the night as though they'd never been silent through the passage of the eclipse.

Her body relaxed against his, the rise and fall of her chest slow and even to indicate she'd fallen into a deep sleep as he frowned in the dark of the night. How the hell was he supposed to just walk away and leave this woman behind?

Pain stabbed at him. How was he supposed to turn his back and never see her again?

He stole from the bed and swept up his clothes mindful of his promise not to wake her as he sneaked from her room and left her there in the peace they'd created, while his mind screamed for him to go back. Just for a moment longer in her embrace.

The creak of the stairs broke the silence of the night. Although he knew no-one would come after him, he cast a last, longing glance up the into the dark above him before he pushed the door to the kitchen wide and welcomed the gentle warmth of the Aga

While the cats wound their way between his ankles so he could slick his hands over their silken fur, he shot a quick look at the kitchen clock. It was no use, none of them had the power to turn back time. He straightened, hauled his rucksack onto his shoulder and pulled the door closed behind him with a quiet snick

》》》•《《《

Moya sank beneath the swirl of blood-muddied waters, her pale face ravaged by fear and fury at the loss of her love. Eyes wide, they stared sightless up at the dense black of the night sky, broken only by the crimson reflection which surrounded the blood moon.

Breath whipped into her lungs as Ruth shot up in bed, the image of Moya's pain wracked face filled her vision. Not a dream but an image of the woman's death to be forever impressed on her mind's eye.

Ruth understood as pain surged through her own breast in empathy and rendered her incapable of anything other than small sips of hiccupping breaths to stay alive.

Poor Moya had never had the choice between life and death. Her fate had already been chosen for her.

Ruth reached out to smooth her fingers over the rumpled sheets already cold from the loss of Stuart's warm body. Pity filled her soul for her long-dead ancestor. A woman who'd loved with such depth that her lover's desertion had destroyed her and the lives of generations of young men.

She tucked her knees up to her chest to keep the chill of the early morning away for a little longer as she stared out of the window at the rain filled clouds which obscured the sky. Her vision blurred by the tears that hovered and threatened to spill over.

She loved. Loved more than she'd ever believed possible. Loved enough to let Stuart go. She dropped her chin to her knees and allowed a tremulous smile to touch her lips. She could have railed with anger and frustration when he left, but there was no point. There was a world of difference between the long-ago relationship Moya and Stuart had, and Ruth's own affair. She swiped the tears from her cheeks. She'd allow them to fall a while longer before she pulled herself together and got on with her life. No one would judge her for the occasional spillage of tears. She had a lifetime to live without him. If she couldn't cry now, when could she?

A small sob escaped her, and she wiped at her wet cheeks again.

She'd delayed long enough and the hold on her to stay on the island evaporated with the loss of her love. Time now for her to live another life. He'd already be on the ferry. Off to the mainland to catch his flight home from Edinburgh. Her stomach cramped. She would never have considered holding on to him. He needed time to be with his brother before he died.

She refused to contemplate the bleakness of her own life without him. He was about to suffer a far worse fate, knowing he could have saved his brother and nephews if only he'd been able to break the curse. Instead, he'd sacrificed them all.

No longer able to stay in the same bed she'd shared with him, Ruth tossed back the covers and grabbed her wrap before the damp could chill her bones. She stood for a moment to glance out of the window as the first rays of sunshine broke through the clouds. A new dawn.

She raised her chin and forced a little hope into her heart. She had a life to live.

Chapter Eight

London, England, four months later

The husky sound of her laughter floated up the stairwell.

Stuart pushed himself away from the wall he leaned against, only to halt as a man's voice echoed in response to hers.

Perhaps he'd made a mistake to show up without forewarning her he was on his way. He paced away down the hall, a flutter of doubt in his belly. He should have contacted her before he arrived, but Clarisse had nudged him to go with what he'd assumed was enthusiasm.

Encouraged to hear Ruth had taken up the place offered to her by the Edinburgh Orchestra, he'd also been relieved when Clarisse had admitted she would no longer winter out on Breggar Island, but she'd stay with Ruth in Edinburgh and only return for the summer months. The hardship of the previous three years had taken its toll, and he knew it would be a relief for Ruth to know Nana would not be left alone during the tougher months. He'd had to smile at the old lady's streak of independence when she'd insisted she wasn't about to sell the shop or house as they could close them down in the winter and use the house as their holiday home during the summer. It had warmed his heart to know Bill would keep an eye on the place, just as he'd always watched over his witches.

It had been good to hear Clarisse's Scottish brogue, broadened by the distance and echo of the telephone line. He'd told her his news, his intentions.

He'd grabbed a last-minute ticket to catch up with the Edinburgh Orchestra's tour in London. He'd watched Ruth's performance, amused at the way she'd tethered and tamed her hair into a smooth bun at the back of her neck, only for spirals of it to spring loose in wild abandon and dance to the melody as she played. He'd sat absorbed throughout the evening while her music drew him like the first time he'd heard it to evoke memories of their love-making.

The doubt evaporated while he turned and made his way back to the stairwell. Of course, she hadn't met anyone else. She'd told him she loved him. A smile stretched over his face. She'd given him her heart. He had living, breathing proof of it.

The man she was with reached the top of the stairs first. A quick flash of surprise shot his perfectly waxed blond eyebrows up his forehead, followed by a swift glance of hot admiration as his broad shoulders filled the doorway to block Stuart's view of Ruth.

"Please tell me I've not just dreamed up a cowboy because if I have, I never want to wake up."

A delicate hand appeared, gripped the man's arm and shoved him without ceremony out of the way.

"Stuart?"

His smile widened, to make his cheeks ache.

She was beautiful. She was there, and she was his.

He could have acted cool and leaned against the wall to wait for her to come to him, but he hadn't the patience nor the restraint. He opened his arms and stepped forward. He ignored the excited gasp from the blond god and moved past him to sweep Ruth into his arms.

The soft choking noise she made could have meant he squeezed her too tight, but from the way she hugged him back, and the tremble of her willowy body in his arms, he sensed emotion overload rather than lack of oxygen.

He drew back, cradled her face in his hands and gazed into the depths of her emerald eyes. Her lips trembled until he touched them with his own, determined to melt away the icy chill of them.

Soft and sweet, her lips parted under his and allowed his tongue access to her mouth. Her fingers flexed into his back to encourage him closer while he consumed her mouth with his own. Unable to satisfy himself with the silky feel of her skin, he cruised his fingers along the length of her neck until he touched the erratic beat of her pulse and circled it with his thumb.

A delicate cough drew his attention, and with reluctance, Stuart raised his head to meet the gaze of the other man.

"Whilst I'm devastated at the loss of my *gorgeous* cowboy…" The young man flicked his blond locks back with a toss of his head and quirked his lips into a regretful moue. "I suspect, Ruth, you'd like to be alone." He reached out long, elegant fingers to dangle a set of keys in front of Ruth.

She took a moment to recover before she reached out her hand to accept them. "Are you sure, Jason? Where will you go?"

He flicked his fine fingers and gave a wicked grin, baring perfect, bright white teeth. "I think I'll pay Geoff a visit. He's asked me to call on him a few times. I may just surprise him." He turned to make his way down the stairwell and called over his shoulder. "Have fun kids, I'll see you in the morning."

The light echo of his footsteps lasted no more than a minute, and then the hallway was filled with silence.

Ruth's serious gaze met Stuart's. There were so many questions to answer, but for now, he simply needed her. He dipped down, swept her off her feet and into his arms with an appreciative murmur at her muffled squeak as she threw her arms around his neck and buried her face in his shoulder. Pleasure and anticipation shuddered through him.

"I suggest you get that door open, quick as you can because there's no way I can wait any longer."

She fumbled to insert the key into the lock with fingers that shook. As the key turned, he bumped open the door with his hip, so it rebounded off the wall. With a flick of her hand and a puff of laughter, she indicated the way to her bedroom. Desperate to taste her, he pressed light kisses over her face, her brow, her eyelids, and the curve of her satin cheeks until he reached the tender morsel of her mouth and took pleasure from her sheer perfection. By the side of the bed, he lowered her feet to the floor while he kept his mouth plastered on hers as her small gasps of pleasure warmed his chest and filled his heart with the reassurance she loved him.

He'd never wanted to leave her, but he'd never regret his homecoming knowing she'd missed him as much as he'd missed her. He'd never leave again.

He rubbed his lips against hers, and then raised his head to watch her while he tangled his fingers to release her hair from captivity, taking pleasure as it sprung wild and free around her face.

"Stuart…" she sighed, the cool touch of her fingers grazed the heated skin of his jaw.

He smoothed his hands over her shoulders and caught the dress zipper with his fingers to glide it all the way to the base of her spine and expose the warm silkiness of her back to his touch.

Small murmurs of pleasure vibrated her throat as he cruised his lips along her neck, thrilling at the delicate noises of encouragement.

He slipped the long-sleeved dress from her shoulders. Sleek and sexy, the black material of her orchestra uniform slithered from where it clung to every curve to land in a waterfall of heavy material at her feet. Naked, apart from the tiny black thong, she stood before him unchanged in her tall slenderness, even more beautiful than he'd remembered. Four months away from her had been a lifetime, and he'd never do it again.

He raised his hand, cupped her breast in his palm, and smoothed the roughness of his thumb over her taut nipple while a thrum of appreciation slid through his veins.

Her sea-swept gaze met his. "I missed you so much."

Choked, he managed a gruff response. "Me too."

The slap of leather as his coat hit the floor barely distracted him, but when he ripped off his black T-shirt, he knew he'd run out of time from the flash of turbulent passion which streaked across her face.

Ruth's nimble fingers had the buttons of his jeans undone in a moment and took his breath away as she pushed them over his hips. He toed his boots off, stepped out of his jeans, his hands never still on Ruth's almost naked body. Her panties went the same way as his jeans.

"I thought you were never coming back."

He snaked an arm out and hoisted her up onto the bed. "I was always coming back for you. No matter what. There was no doubt in my mind."

"But…"

"I would have found a way.

"But…"

"Later." Desperate to have her, he stopped her questions with his mouth, smoothed his hands along her rib cage, down her waist, and then slid them under her ass to raise her hips up to meet his. In one smooth glide, he was inside her. Hot velvet surrounded him, and small spasms clutched at him while her silken limbs encouraged him closer, deeper.

Consumed by their hunger for each other, they matched one another's rhythm, the frantic rise and fall of their bodies in perfect harmony. Heat gathered to burn his flesh and brand his soul with her name as it burst from his lips, the agony of being apart from her squeezed his chest.

He gathered her hair in one hand and let it spill over his fingers as he tilted her head back to gaze into her misty eyes. "I will never leave you again." It was a promise, a pledge.

Wet lips, swollen from his kisses, parted in a satisfied smile. "Of course you won't. I'll never let you go again."

She wrapped her legs in a tight circle around his hips so he could plunge deeper into the silken depths of her body as she welcomed him home.

Chapter Nine

She had so many questions she needed to ask, but not one of them came to mind as she lay in the circle of his arms, her head pillowed on his shoulder. Her fingers traced lazy patterns in the smattering of dark hair on his chest while ripples of pleasure still warmed her.

His breathing had evened out some time ago, but she knew he wasn't asleep. His fingers still trailed through her hair from time to time.

She tilted her head so she could take a closer look at him. The smile of satisfaction plastered across his face had creased his cheeks and tempted her to smooth her fingers over his beard-roughened skin.

His lips parted. "Who was the guy who let us use his bed?"

With a half-hearted chuckle, she tugged at the hair on his chest. "It's not his bed, but it is his apartment. He has his own room." He turned to face her, the velvet gray of a storm passed filled his eyes. She knew she needed to give no deeper explanation, but he deserved it. "We went to Uni together. Jason joined the Edinburgh Orchestra two years ago and encouraged me to take up a place with them ever since. He hired this apartment for us to share while we're touring the south of England, then I'll go back to Nana. She's in Edinburgh now so we can be together most of the time."

She let out a small grunt as he heaved himself up to prop his back against the headboard, he almost tipped her off his chest as he hauled her unceremoniously back up. "I know; I spoke with her."

Surprised by his confession, Ruth propped herself up on one elbow so she could peer into his face. "Really? When? I only spoke with her this morning, and she never mentioned you.

His lips twitched. "I asked her not to. I wanted to surprise you."

Surprise her, he certainly had.

She feathered a finger down his chest and traced the hard definition of his muscles. "It was a nice surprise." She knew the lingering pain of it choked her voice, but when he placed a finger under her chin to raise it so he could meet her gaze, tears pricked the back of her eyes and choked the breath in her throat.

"Don't cry, baby. I'm here. I'm not leaving."

"Good." She poked him with a short fingernail and forced her quivering lips into a tentative smile. "But, why? What happened?"

She knew his brother was gone, and the pain of it must resonate through his spirit, to know he was unable to help, but there were still his nephews to consider. His fight would never be over until he found a resolution.

The smile of genuine happiness he gave tripped her heart. "My brother is alive and well, with a new heart which we hope will keep him going for a good many years."

"But…"

Stuart stroked the hair back from her face, but it insisted on springing forward again as soon as he let go. He quirked a smile and smoothed it back again. "I arrived back just in time to see him come out of recovery. The heart they had for him was a good match. The surgery went well."

The strain of the wait showed in his features. He shook his head and pulled her closer to his chest. "I still thought he'd never make it through Ben's tenth birthday. We had three weeks to wait, but he seemed to go from strength to strength. All the tests indicated his body hadn't rejected his heart. From the last time I'd seen him, he was a different color. Instead of a pasty gray, his skin was warm and glowing." A strained gasp shuddered through him and instinct made her stroke her fingers over his warm skin. "Ben's birthday came and went and another three months on, Ian's weak, but getting stronger day by day." He placed a tender kiss on her forehead, then leaned back again, his face full of wonder. "I tried to contact you, but that deserted island was damned impossible to communicate with." He gave her a squeeze, and she dipped her head to place a sympathetic kiss on his shoulder. "I couldn't leave him, so I waited until he was well enough to tell me to go. It didn't take much persuasion, especially once I knew the curse was broken."

She jerked upright, leaned her hand on his shoulder and stared into his face. "How can it be broken? You never killed me. I know your brother's alive at the moment, but so am I. What if you were wrong about the curse?"

He persuaded her back down with a firm hand on her back.

"I was. But not the way you think. I absolutely know each of the deaths occurred on the tenth birthday of the eldest son. This happened for generations, so there's no need to provide further proof of the events. It's documented." He readjusted her, so she was more comfortable, her arm draped over his waist. "We celebrated Ben's tenth birthday in the hospital with my brother. I fully expected him to die. When he survived that day, I can't describe the hope I felt. Then he lived the next day and the next. I stayed in his room with him, had all my notes, our father's notes and his father's before him. I brought them all together and poured over them, trying to find the connection between the curse, the jade knife, and the little piece of paper with the instructions on how to break the curse."

Hope fluttered in her chest. She smoothed her fingers over his waist and gazed at him with fervent anticipation. "What was the connection?"

"There wasn't one. As your nana suggested."

Confusion sent ripples of goose bumps over her flesh. "What do you mean there's no connection? None at all?"

"Well yes, there is a loose connection." He soothed her with circular strokes over her back. "I went back through everything, as far back as I could. Some of the original notes are very difficult to decipher, but I managed to piece together the information on the jade handled knife."

A shudder of revulsion ran through veins which had turned to ice at the mere mention of the item, but the warmth from his body cradled her as he continued.

"There is nothing. No proof to connect the knife. The pure evilness of it seems to be the only factor involved. It was discovered in 1859 by one of my ancestors, Phillip, on his trek across China. His diary seems to confirm he'd been given it by a Chinese medicine man who he'd sought out to try and cure him of some horrendous disease. One which he doesn't actually name as it appears too horrific to put into writing, although from the description it sounded strangely like leprosy. It certainly wasn't a commonplace disease in Scotland by that time, but he was a traveler."

Transfixed, she never took her gaze from his as Stuart continued his story. "Anyway, the Chinese medicine didn't work, and on the day of Phillip's son's tenth birthday, he died. His possessions were returned home, and in there, his son discovered the knife. It's been assumed since that date the knife was to be used in some sort of ritual to kill the last known descendant of the witch who placed the curse on the original Stuart."

"Why would he have assumed that?"

"Because he was a ten-year-old without a mother, who had died while her husband was away, and presumably left the child to his own devices. There's no mention of anyone else who took care of him, but this is where the jade knife came into play."

"So, the jade knife was nothing but an evil weapon."

"It appears so, although none of my ancestors ever found it a threat. You and your nana are the only ones who have ever reacted like that to it."

Her hair shimmered over her shoulder to lie across his chest, while rampant curls still wriggled and settled. "Chinese black magic, or Ku."

He nodded in agreement.

Ruth drew a finger over his taut muscles and thrilled as they contracted. "So how come the spell was broken?"

"I have a theory." His lips quirked as he picked up a handful of her black curls and gave them an affectionate rub between his fingers.

"What's that?"

"The curse and the partially burned piece of paper are the ones connected."

"Okay."

"Can you remember the one sentence we could define?"

"I could hardly forget it, could I? They were the instructions for you to plunge the knife deep into my chest and wrench my heart out."

He tugged at her hair and brought her face closer to his so he could plant a rough kiss on her mouth. "Yeah. Except that's not what it said. The presence of the jade knife totally confused matters, but think back to what was actually said."

She tried to recall the words, but they wouldn't come, the memory of the instructions too painful for her to recall clearly. She prodded him with her finger again in her impatience to learn the truth. "What did it say?"

He closed his eyes to recall the exact wording better. "Have the strength to bare thy breast. Take the heart of the witch and be sure to never let it from your keep." He stared deep into her soul. "The intention was never for me to kill you, but for me to love you—bare my breast, which I did. I told you I loved you. I'll tell you every day for the rest of our lives." He feathered a kiss on her eyebrow, swiped a tender thumb across her cheek. "That in itself wasn't enough. You needed to love me in return, as deeply as I love you."

She could barely swallow, her throat tightened while her heart pounded. She'd told him she loved him. Loved him so deeply she'd had to let him go.

She jerked upright so she could look down at him as comprehension wound through her mind. "You took my heart with you."

He raised his arm to cushion his head on it, all the time giving a gentle nod, while his gaze held hers.

She covered her mouth with her hand while thoughts raced unheeded in her head. "Even if you'd never returned, I would have always loved you."

The smile he gave her creased his cheeks. The knowledge in his expression shone out.

She sank back onto her haunches. "We broke the spell."

"We did."

"Our love for each other broke the spell."

"It did."

As a thought occurred to her, she jerked free again. "It was a full blooded moon."

"The night I left. Yes, I remember. How could I ever forget?"

"No." She poked his shoulder. "When Moya cast the spell. I woke after you'd gone and I remembered the dream, but the significance never occurred to me. I thought it had become entangled with my own despair." She smoothed her fingers over his chest in apology for the hurt. "She stared up at the sky, and blood streaked over it. It was a total lunar eclipse that night too. The night she truly realized he'd rejected her." Power surged through Ruth's body, and a dozen candles leaped to life in the bedroom. With little more than an impressed quirk of his eyebrow, Stuart never flinched. "We broke her spell and never even realized."

The stillness in his face made her think again. "You realized, which is why you came back for me."

As something else edged through her mind, she stroked her fingers over the taut muscles of his stomach and smiled as his skin twitched under her touch. "He never loved her. Stuart, the original one, never loved Moya." A wave of sadness washed over her.

Stuart rolled his shoulders. "I think you're right. At least, not enough." He pushed himself up from the bed, folded her in his arms and rocked her. "How miserable that she loved him so completely, but in the end, it seems he chose his wife and sons and let her perish at the hands of the villagers."

Reassured, she snuggled in his embrace. "They were both at fault. Him, for being unfaithful to his wife. He may have had emotions, certainly lust, for Moya in the beginning, but what he did was wrong. He condemned both Moya and his own child in order to cover up his guilt."

"Hmmm…" Stuart's lips on her neck provided a welcome distraction, but he pulled her back again with his next question. "Why was she at fault?"

"Because she, in turn, condemned an entire lineage for one man's sin."

"True enough." He placed his mouth on hers and warmed lips she hadn't realized had turned cold. His hand glided over her skin to make the goose bumps disappear. "We've righted their wrong." His mouth took hers in a deeper kiss as he rolled her body beneath his. He raised his head, his eyes crinkling at the edges as he smiled. "Now my brother and his sons have a future, thanks to you." She opened her mouth to deny it, but he sneaked in another kiss which stopped her words before he murmured against her lips. "And you've set me free. With your love."

There was no denying that. Instead, she entwined her arms around him and held him tight to her breast with the knowledge that she'd loved him enough to let him go, was lucky enough he'd returned, and their love for each other would never die.

About the Author

Diane Saxon lives in the Shropshire countryside in England with her tall, dark, handsome husband. She has two gorgeous daughters, a Dalmatian, a one-eyed kitty, an old ginger cat, various rare breed chickens, and a gorgeous black Labrador called Beau—a name she's borrowed for her hero in For Heaven's Cakes.

She's an avid rescuer of all creatures damaged or dying.

After working for years in a demanding job, on-call and travelling great distances, Diane gave it all up to write when her husband said, 'Follow that dream.'

Having been hidden all too long, her characters have burst forth demanding plot lines of their own, and she's found the more she lets them, the more they're inclined to run wild.

She subsequently had twelve romances published for the US market for which she has had the rights returned and decided to self-publish.

Diane has turned to the dark side with her new psychological thrillers.

With a four-book deal through Boldwood Books, (see below) she's currently killing someone else in her new upcoming standalone.

More Romance from Diane Saxon

Atlantic Divide Series

Gun Shy
Loving Lydia
Bad Girl Bill
Finding Zoe
Flynn's Kiss
Barbara's Redemption
Along Came Dani
Flight of Her Life

Montgomery's Sin Series

Banshee Seduction
For Heaven's Cakes (short story)

Standalones

Under the Full-Blooded Moon
Short Circuit Time (short story)

Over to the Dark Side - Psychological Thrillers from Diane Saxon

Published By Boldwood Books

DS Jenna Morgan Series

Find Her Alive
Someone's There
What She Saw
The Ex

Printed in Great Britain
by Amazon